AND NOTHING BUT THE TRUTH

AND NOTHING BUT THE TRUTH

KIT PEARSON

HarperCollins*PublishersLtd*

And Nothing but the Truth
Copyright © 2012 by Kathleen Pearson.
All rights reserved.

Published by HarperCollins Publishers Ltd

First edition

HarperCollins books may be purchased for educational, business,
or sales promotional use through our Special Markets Department.

HarperCollins Publishers Ltd
2 Bloor Street East, 20th Floor
Toronto, Ontario, Canada
M4W 1A8

www.harpercollins.ca

Library and Archives Canada Cataloguing in Publication
information is available upon request.

ISBN 978-1-55468-854-8

Printed and bound in Canada
DWF 9 8 7 6 5 4 3 2 1

For Olivia Pryce-Digby, Jane Farris,
and Hannah McDonald

"But wonder on, till truth make all things plain."
—William Shakespeare, *A Midsummer Night's Dream*

PART ONE

"I WON'T LIKE IT"

CHAPTER ONE

THE FIRST DAY

"I won't like it," repeated Polly.

"Oh, hen." Noni looked exasperated. "If you keep saying that, you'll make it true! I know you don't want to go to boarding school. You've made that very clear! However, you have no choice."

Polly put down her fork. The cake had tasted good at first, but now her stomach was churning. "Oh, Noni, why can't I share Biddy and Vivien's governess?"

"Polly, how many times do I have to tell you this? You wouldn't learn enough with a governess. St. Winifred's is an excellent school, and I want you to get the best education possible. And what about your art? I've taught you all I can. Now you're going to have regular *and* extra art classes. You're lucky—not many girls have this opportunity. Please cheer up, hen, and try to be positive." Noni smiled at her. "Think of how much Maud loved St. Winifred's. Who knows? You may like it, too!"

I won't! said Polly, but only to herself.

Noni signed the bill and picked up her gloves. "Come along now, Polly. We're supposed to be at the school by five."

They left the hotel restaurant and fetched Polly's suitcases from Noni's room. The bellhop hailed them a taxi and they began to drive to the outskirts of Victoria.

When the taxi driver learned they were from Kingfisher Island, he told them he had relatives there. All the way, he and Noni chatted about his cousins. Polly stared out the window, clenching her hands. How could Noni do this to her?

The car turned off the road at a stone gate with a sign saying "St. Winifred's School for Girls." It made its way along a winding drive-way through wooded grounds and a playing field. They reached three buildings grouped in a semicircle around a cement space. Two of them were low and modern; Polly knew that one contained the classrooms and one the gymnasium. The third building was the ugly stone resi-dence where the boarders lived. Dark ivy cloaked one of its walls.

The driver helped carry Polly's bags up the wide steps of the residence. The headmistress, Miss Guppy, opened the door. Polly shrank as the tall, grizzled woman advanced towards her greedily. "Why, it's Polly—here at last! Say goodbye to your grandmother, now. She won't want to keep the taxi waiting."

"No tears, hen," Noni warned. "Remember to be brave, and try to enjoy yourself. We'll see you very soon." She pecked Polly's cheek and hurried down the steps.

Polly watched until the taxi was out of sight. She couldn't believe that what she had dreaded for so long was actually happening! *It's only for a year*, she told herself.

"Come inside, Polly," Miss Guppy barked from the door. "Mrs. Blake will take you up to meet your roommates."

The hall was panelled in dark wood, its walls covered with group photographs of uniformed girls. A young woman approached Polly and shook her hand. "I'm Mrs. Blake, your matron," she said in a lilting English voice. She picked up both of Polly's suitcases and led her up some steep stairs. They went down a hall lined with open rooms; excited voices and laughter floated out from them.

Finally, they reached a room with four cots in it. Their white iron frames were blotched with dark patches where the paint had peeled. The floor was bare. Only one picture hung on the dingy blue walls: a sampler that spelled out *Work, For the Night Is Coming* in crooked letters. Polly grimaced; she had always hated that hymn.

"This is the junior dorm," said Mrs. Blake. "Now let me introduce you."

Three pairs of eyes stared curiously at Polly and three voices said hello. She knew she should answer, but her tongue wouldn't work. She forgot the girls' names as soon as Mrs. Blake said them.

"You are all new girls, and I'm new, as well!" said Mrs. Blake. "So let's try to be patient with one another. I hope we'll soon become friends." She had a friendly smile.

"Mrs. Blake, why is this called the 'junior' dorm?" asked one of the girls. "*We* aren't juniors!"

"You're juniors because you're the youngest boarders," Mrs. Blake told her. "Now, finish unpacking. Polly, your bed is the one by the door. I'll take some of these empty suitcases down to the storage room. Dinner is in ten minutes."

Polly's hands trembled as she opened her suitcase. Her back was to the other girls, but she could still feel them staring at her. She slipped her sketchbook and paints into a drawer and covered them up with her underwear. Then she took out the family photograph that Noni had framed for her and placed it carefully on top of the small chest of drawers beside her bed.

A gong sounded loudly. Mrs. Blake came back and led them down to the dining room. Four tables of girls made such a din that a huge chandelier trembled from the ornate plaster ceiling. Polly and her roommates were divided up among the tables. Most of the shrieking, laughing girls at Polly's table were as big as women. "So you're Maud's sister!" several said, reaching over to shake her hand. She couldn't return their smiles.

Miss Guppy was at the head of one of the tables. She stood, and the girls copied her, their chairs all scraping in unison. "'For what we are about to receive, the Lord make us *truly* thankful,'" the headmistress's gruff voice intoned.

Everyone chorused "Amen" and plunked down again. Polly poked at her grey meat and pale vegetables; then she took a few nibbles of some wobbly white junket.

After dinner, they were herded into a sitting room, where they sat cross-legged on the rug, still keeping up their chatter. When Miss Guppy entered, the noise stopped as abruptly as if a gramophone needle had lifted off a record.

"Good evening, girls," she said.

"Good evening, Miss Guppy," the girls answered tonelessly.

Miss Guppy gazed at them down her long nose. She rubbed her hands together with relish as she said, "What a treat to have my girls together again! Will the new boarders please rise."

Polly stumbled to her feet. She looked around: of the twenty-eight boarders, only the girls in her dorm and one other were new.

"Five new boarders—that's more than we've had for years! Welcome to St. Winifred's. We hope that you will soon feel at home." Miss Guppy spoke sternly, as if that were an order.

Everyone clapped and the new girls were allowed to sit down. Miss Guppy sat in an armchair in front of them, her long legs stretched straight out. They were so wide apart you could see the tops of her stockings. Beside Polly, one of her roommates suppressed a giggle.

"I hope this Christmas term of 1935 will be a fresh start for all of you," began Miss Guppy solemnly. She told them that the boarders were a special family within the school, a family who had to encourage each other to do her very best. Then they all stood as Miss Guppy led them in some prayers. Everyone droned "Abide with Me," which one of the girls picked out haltingly on the piano. Finally, they were sent back to their dorms.

At eight-thirty, Mrs. Blake came in and told the junior dorm they were to start getting ready for bed. Polly had never undressed in front of strangers. She made a tent of her nightgown and removed her clothes under it. When she glanced at the others, she noticed they were doing the same.

Clutching their towels and toothbrushes, the four girls went down the hall to a long bathroom full of sinks. Three toilet cubicles were opposite them.

Half an hour later, Mrs. Blake turned out the lights. "Not a word now," she said. "I'm sure you're all tired and will go right to sleep."

Polly's bed creaked as she squirmed on its narrow mattress, trying to find a soft spot between the lumps. Moonlight coming through the window at the end of the dormitory made squares of light on the floor. If only she had the bed by the window! Then she could at least look out at the night sky.

Her roommates breathed around her. To keep from crying, Polly tried to sort them out. Daisy, the tallest, smiled a lot. Sturdy-looking Rhoda had a mop of dark curls and a pouty mouth. She was the one who had complained about being called "juniors." She had also complained when Mrs. Blake told her she had brought too many clothes and had to store some in her suitcase. Eleanor wore glasses with thick lenses. She was quiet, but seemed confident.

The others had asked Polly a few questions, but Polly still couldn't speak, and had only shrugged or nodded. They probably thought she was really stupid.

It's only for a year, she reminded herself again. But a year was *forever!*

Never in her life had she been so alone. Daddy or Maud or Noni had always been near. She didn't even have Tarka. Did he miss her? Did he wonder why Polly wasn't in her own bed?

Feeling more like six than almost thirteen, Polly put her pillow over her head and finally let loose her tears.

"Polly! Hey, Polly . . ." someone was whispering, shaking her shoulder.

Polly lifted her wet face. It was Eleanor, standing over her.

"Shhh! Come with me."

Eleanor pulled Polly by the hand and led her across the room. To Polly's astonishment, she pushed up the window and went onto the fire escape.

"Quick, before the others wake up!"

Polly lifted the hem of her nightgown and stepped over the sill. Eleanor pushed down the window, and they sat on the highest of the wooden stairs leading to the ground.

Polly breathed in the warm September air and her sobs subsided.

"Why are you crying? Are you homesick?" Eleanor asked in a matter-of-fact voice.

Polly nodded, wiping her face with the back of her hand.

"Is that why you aren't talking to us?"

"Yes," said Polly. "I'm sorry to be so rude. I just—I just couldn't."

"Well, you are now," said Eleanor comfortably. She stretched out her legs. "Isn't it swell to be outside? I'm so lucky I was here first. As soon as I saw the fire escape, I knew I wanted that bed."

"But are we allowed to come out here?"

"Probably not. But who will know?"

Eleanor was so calm that Polly felt calmer herself. She gazed up at the bright moon and stars, the same ones she saw from her window at home.

"I'm a bit homesick myself," said Eleanor, as if she were surprised. "I miss my family, but most of all I miss my dog."

"Oh, I miss mine, too!" cried Polly. "I have a border terrier named Tarka. He sleeps on the foot of my bed every night."

"Mine is a collie—Breeze."

Their words tangled as they described their dogs. Tarka and Breeze were both male, and almost the same age. Breeze sounded much better behaved than Tarka, however.

"Where are you from?" Eleanor asked.

"Kingfisher Island. It's one of the gulf islands between Vancouver and Victoria."

"We went there once on a picnic! It's really beautiful."

"It is," said Polly sadly. "Where are *you* from?"

"Nanaimo. It's about seventy miles up island from here."

Eleanor told Polly about the rest of her family besides Breeze: she had two older brothers and a younger sister. Her father was a high-school principal. "Dad was really lucky he could keep his job when the Depression started. Otherwise I wouldn't have been able to come here."

Polly winced as she remembered how Daddy had never been able to find steady work; that had been his downfall. "Did you *want* to come?" she asked Eleanor. "*I* didn't!"

Eleanor nodded. "St. Winifred's has a really good reputation. I'm going to be a science teacher one day, and I'll learn more here than I would have in Nanaimo. What do *you* want to be?"

"An artist," said Polly at once.

"Are you talented enough to be one?"

Eleanor's bluntness was startling, but Polly nodded. "Yes, I think I am."

"Good! Now tell me about *your* family."

Polly swallowed. "Well, I live with my grandmother, and my great-aunt and -uncle are right next door. Their son, Gregor, just got married, and now he and his wife, Sadie, are living in Chilliwack. Gregor's going to be a curate in the Anglican church there. I have an older sister, Maud, who just started university in Vancouver. She graduated from St. Winifred's last year—she was head girl!"

"What about your parents?"

Polly took a deep breath. "My mother died when I was two. And my father . . . well, he lives in Kelowna, but right now he's in Winnipeg for a while."

"Why don't you live with him?"

Eleanor hadn't read about Daddy in the paper, then. "It's a long story," muttered Polly. "I'll tell you sometime, but not tonight, okay?"

Eleanor shrugged. "That's perfectly all right. I didn't mean to pry."

There was an awkward silence, then Eleanor asked, "I hope you don't think this is nosy, as well, but why did you come here if you didn't want to?"

"Because the Kingfisher Island school only goes up to grade seven. I'm only here for a year, though."

"You are?"

Polly nodded. "After I wrote the entrance exam, Miss Guppy and I made a bargain—but my grandmother doesn't know about it. I promised to try St. Winifred's for a year, and if I don't like it, I don't have to come back. If I can get Noni—my grandmother—to agree, of course, but the Guppy said she'd support me. Then I'll share my friends' governess on the island."

"Miss Guppy seems quite fierce. I can't believe you got *her* to agree. And do you really call her 'the Guppy'?"

"Maud says that everyone calls her that, but never to her face," said Polly. "She *is* fierce, but that's our bargain—we shook hands on it. Don't tell anyone, okay?"

"I won't. But I hope you'll stay until you graduate, like me, Polly. Maybe you *will* like it."

That was nice of her, but Polly said firmly, "I know I won't. At least I'm not a full-time boarder. I'll be going home every weekend."

"Then you'll see Tarka! You're so lucky—I won't see Breeze until Thanksgiving."

They sat in silence. Polly gazed at the inviting lawn below. The trees swayed in the light breeze and the grass looked so soft. Eleanor noticed her longing glance.

"We *could* go down and run around," she said. Then she yawned. "I'm getting pretty sleepy, though. Should we go back to bed?"

She carefully opened the window and they slipped inside. "Good night," whispered Eleanor.

Polly whispered good night back and got into her cot. It was just as uncomfortable as before, but she pulled the covers around her and finally slept.

Chapter Two

IF ONLY SHE COULD RUN AWAY

CLANG CLANG CLANG CLANG CLANG CLANG CLANG!

"Omigosh, what's happened?"

"It's the morning bell. It means we have to get up."

"Make it stop—I can't bear it!"

Polly had been wakened so violently that she almost fell out of bed. She sat up, rubbing her stinging ears.

"Is that awful noise going to happen *every* morning?" asked Rhoda.

"You'll get used to it, love," said Mrs. Blake. She was standing at the door. "Rise and shine, girls! You have half an hour to get washed and dressed and make your beds. Don't forget to turn over your mattresses first. It's such a lovely hot day you don't need to wear your blazers, and you can put on short socks instead of stockings. I'll be back soon for inspection."

"This place is like an army," complained Rhoda. "Who invented this *ghastly* uniform?" she went on. "I've never seen anything so ugly!"

Polly agreed as she assembled her clothes. Each item was labelled "P. Brown," even her underwear. She and Noni and Aunt Jean had spent many evenings last week sewing on name tapes.

St. Winifred's uniform was intensely uncomfortable as well as ugly. The stiff white blouse chafed Polly's neck. Over it was an itchy woollen grey tunic. After she tied a maroon belt around her waist, her top half sweltered. At least her legs were bare; but she had to wear sateen bloomers over her regular underwear and heavy black oxfords over her short white socks.

They all struggled with their mustard-coloured ties until Eleanor fastened each girl's with a neat knot. "I tie my father's every Sunday," she explained. When she came to Polly, they exchanged a glance. The other two didn't know they'd been outside last night.

"Your beds are perfect, girls," said Mrs. Blake when she returned, "and you all look very nice."

"Mrs. Blake, do we *have* to wear these horrible bloomers?" Rhoda asked. "They're so hot!"

What a whiny voice she has, thought Polly.

"I'm afraid so, Rhoda."

"But who will know if we don't?"

"It wouldn't be proper, especially in gym. And I'm sorry, but you and Polly will have to take off your jewellery."

"But this ring was my grandmother's!" protested Rhoda.

"All the same, you'll have to put it away for now." Mrs. Blake put out her hand. "Give it to me and I'll find a box for you. Then you can keep it in your drawer so you can wear it on the weekends. Polly, what would you like to do with your necklace?"

Polly undid her necklace and slipped it into her pocket. Daddy had given it to her: a small silver heart on a chain. Her neck felt vulnerable without its comforting presence.

Rhoda handed over her ring to Mrs. Blake. She looked around the room angrily and found a target. "Mrs. Blake, shouldn't Polly do something with her hair? It's so messy!"

Mrs. Blake smiled. "Rhoda's right, Polly. Your long hair may get in your way—I'll braid it for you."

Polly scowled. As usual, she was the only girl who didn't have bobbed hair; but that was none of Rhoda's business! Mrs. Blake quickly braided it and fastened the end with an elastic. When she finished, all the girls looked the same: tidy and tight, like four grey parcels.

Now Mrs. Blake seemed embarrassed. "It's time for Devotions. You are each to kneel at your beds and pray for five minutes."

Polly buried her face in the rough grey blanket. "Please, *please* make this year go fast," she begged.

Breakfast was runny oatmeal and as much toast and marmalade as you wanted, but Polly still couldn't eat much. At least it was quieter this morning as the roomful of girls bent over their meals, yawned, or murmured to one another.

"Where are you from, Polly?" Daisy asked, as she had yesterday. This morning Polly told her, but she didn't say she lived with her grandmother, not her parents.

"*I'm* from Bellingham. That's in the United States," said Rhoda importantly.

Polly ignored her. She found out that Daisy was from a small town on northern Vancouver Island, and that they had both gone to one-room schools at home.

"I'm sorry you had to put your hair in a braid," said Daisy. "I like it long. It's so lovely and wavy."

"Long hair is so old-fashioned," said Rhoda. "Why don't you get a bob, Polly?"

Polly just shrugged. She wasn't going to tell this nosy girl that Daddy liked her hair long.

"I get *my* hair cut at a real salon," said Rhoda, primping her curls.

"It's so thick," said Daisy enviously. "I wish mine wasn't so thin and flat."

"I could put pin curls in it for you if you like," said Rhoda.

"Thanks, Rhoda! I've tried, but the bobby pins keep slipping."

Daisy kept talking to Rhoda, while Eleanor and Polly munched their toast in silence.

After breakfast, they had fifteen minutes to go back to their dorms and get ready for school. Out the window, they could see the day girls arriving, some on bikes, some walking, and a few being dropped off by cars. The junior dorm gazed at one another nervously.

"I know," said Daisy, "let's call ourselves 'the Fearless Four'! Come on, troops!"

She led them over to the school, a long, low building opposite the boarders' residence. It was a gloriously bright day. Again, Polly looked yearningly at the woods and lawn she had seen from the fire escape. The sun lit up a patch of emerald moss behind an enormous sequoia. It would be so soft to sit on . . . but she had to follow the others.

They asked a prefect—she wore a mustard-coloured belt instead of a maroon one—the way to the Form IVB classroom. "It's so weird that you don't have *grades* in Canada!" declared Rhoda in a superior-sounding voice.

Polly was glad to correct her. "We do in public school, but St. Winnie's has forms the way they do in England," she explained. "Four B is also called the 'upper fourth.' It's the same as grade eight."

"I still think it's weird," said Rhoda. "And why do you call it 'St. Winnie's'? I've never heard anyone else say that."

"*All* the girls call it that," said Polly coldly. "I know, because my sister went here."

"No talking in the hall!" admonished another prefect.

That rule didn't seem to apply in the classroom. The girls who were already there screeched and giggled and banged their desk tops. As other girls entered, they were greeted with dramatic hugs.

The Fearless Four huddled in a corner. "They all seem to know one another," said Daisy.

"They must have been together last year," said Eleanor.

"Look, there's someone else who's new," said Rhoda, pointing out a quiet girl by the door.

"Silence, please, young ladies!" A short, sour-looking woman strode into the classroom and rapped a pointer. She told them she was Mrs. Horner, their homeroom teacher.

"Not the Hornet!" Polly heard a girl beside her whisper.

Mrs. Horner read out a seating plan and directed the sixteen girls to their places. The five new girls were put near the front.

"Polly Brown . . ." said Mrs. Horner with a frown.

Polly flushed. Had she done something wrong?

"I hope you will follow your sister's excellent example," continued Mrs. Horner. "Maud was the best pupil I have ever had." She frowned even more, as if she already knew that Polly wouldn't be the same.

As soon as they were seated, they had to stand up again and walk in single file to the gymnasium building for assembly. Polly squatted on the hard floor in a line with the rest of her form. Behind her sat the youngest students: the lower fourth form, and the upper and lower third. Prefects handed out hymn books, and one hundred voices boomed out "Onward Christian Soldiers." Then the girls were ordered to sit again.

Miss Guppy stood at the front. Her gruff voice preached to them about living up to the high standards of the school; Polly stopped listening after the first few words.

They sang another hymn, chanted the Lord's Prayer, and droned "God Save the King." Then they filed back to their classrooms.

Mrs. Horner passed out notebooks, pencils, pens, nibs, and textbooks. She announced that Pauline Abbott and Ivy Moore would be this term's class president and vice-president. More tasks were assigned, but none to the new girls.

The ink monitor, Phyllis, was told to fill each inkwell. Then they had to copy out the schedule that Mrs. Horner had written on the board.

Polly couldn't believe all the periods that were crammed into each day: four in the morning and three in the afternoon. She tried to keep her hand steady as she copied the subjects she would be taking this term: Scripture, British history, geography, literature, composition and grammar, chemistry, botany, mathematics, French, and drawing. Some days ended with gymnastics or folk dancing, and Noni had told Polly she would also be taking piano lessons.

This was why Noni had wanted her to come here: to get a good education. But when would Polly have time to relax? She thought of her tiny school on Kingfisher Island, where she had shared a desk with Biddy, her best friend. Mrs. Oliver had been so busy coping with the little ones that she had let the older pupils learn on their own. No one had to sit still for long; there was always an excuse to get up, whether to fill the woodbox or help pass out books or take a younger child to the privy. Except for arithmetic, Polly had always done well in school, but how would she cope with all these new subjects?

She examined her schedule again and calmed down when she saw "drawing" every Wednesday afternoon. At least she would shine there! And Noni had told her she was to take extra art classes, as well. Polly wondered when they would happen.

Mrs. Horner explained the house system to the new girls. There were four houses that competed for points during the year: Kent, York, Sussex, and Cornwall. "You can gain points for your house through sports or other activities, which you will learn about later. But if you do *anything* against the rules, such as talking in the hall, or being rude or slovenly or late, you will receive an order mark, which will be deducted from your house points. If you get five order marks, you will get a conduct mark, with serious consequences. Do you understand?" She glared at them as if they had already received conduct marks.

The other new girls murmured, "Yes, Mrs. Horner," but they looked confused. Polly, however, knew all about the house system from Maud. She also knew, before Mrs. Horner told her, that she would be in Sussex, because sisters were always in the same house. Polly was glad Rhoda wasn't assigned to Sussex, but she was disappointed when Eleanor wasn't. She was in Kent, and Daisy and Rhoda were in Cornwall.

"I will be teaching you British history, girls," Mrs. Horner informed the class. "Our first lesson will be after lunch. Now, put away your things and fold your hands on your desk until the bell goes for morning break."

This clanging bell was just as imperious as the one that had woken them up earlier. "Stand," ordered Mrs. Horner. All the girls rose, then they filed quietly out of the building.

The boarders dashed into the dining room and grabbed apples, then stood around outside on the concrete square. Polly felt as if she'd been released from jail. For the first time since she'd arrived, she was free to do as she pleased. She stood on the edge of the chattering crowd and nibbled her apple, fingering Daddy's necklace in her pocket.

Then she noticed a group of older girls staring at her and whispering. Did they know about Daddy? She glanced at the woods again, and the patch of moss that looked so inviting. If only she could escape into there with her sketchbook and stay there all day! She could try drawing the sequoia's furrowed trunk . . .

Two of the staring girls came over. "You must be Polly!" one said. "I'm Amy, and this is Becky. Maud asked us to look out for you. Are you enjoying your first day of school?"

Polly tried to smile. Amy and Becky went on to tell her how much they missed Maud.

A teacher came out and swung another hand bell to signal the end of break. When they got back to the classroom, Mrs. Horner had disappeared. "Stand for Miss Draper!" shouted Pauline, who was watching by the door.

Miss Draper entered and said, "Good morning, girls."

"Good morning, Miss Draper," droned the class. Then they had their first geography lesson. Polly relaxed a bit; she knew she could easily do their homework of sketching meandering rivers.

Miss Draper left and another teacher—Mrs. Partridge—arrived to teach them mathematics. Polly's ease disappeared. Mrs. Partridge began explaining the elements of algebra, and already Polly didn't understand. "You certainly don't take after your sister, do you?" said Mrs. Partridge, when she came around to check their work.

Polly squirmed. Why did they all expect her to be as good as Maud?

At lunch, the dining room was even noisier than it had been last night, because many of the day students were eating there, as well. At least they were allowed to sit where they wanted. Again, some older girls came up to Polly and told her they'd known Maud. "How's she doing at varsity?" they kept asking. Polly didn't know—she hadn't had a letter yet.

If only Maud were still here! She could protect Polly, as she had always done. Polly could sit beside her at meals, and Maud would explain the confusing rules and sympathize with her about staying inside and never being able to be alone for one minute.

Or maybe not . . . Maud had loved St. Winifred's from the start, so she'd probably just be impatient. Polly could *hear* her: "Buck up, Doodle! Don't just sit there like a lump. Eat your lunch and talk to your new friends."

Polly took a few bites of her sandwich, but the bread was so dry she could barely swallow it. She turned to the other members of the Fearless Four. "What do you think of Mrs. Horner?" she asked.

Daisy grinned. "She's a terror! I can see why they call her 'the Hornet.' But I'm sure she'll be nicer when she teaches us history."

Eleanor examined Daisy curiously. "You're a very optimistic person, aren't you? I'm afraid I don't agree with you. Mrs. Horner isn't going to change."

"It's such rotten luck!" said Rhoda. "I heard one of the girls say she was the crabbiest teacher in the whole school! All the teachers are much stricter than in my old school. And why do so many of them have English accents?"

"That's just what Victoria's like," Eleanor explained. "Dad says people here are more English than the English."

"Well, I think it's weird," said Rhoda. "Where I live we have our *own* accent, not one from another country."

Polly glared at her; why did she have to keep criticizing Canada?

Miss Poirier, the other matron, came up to them with a note-book. "What are you doing after classes today, girls? Games, walk, or free?"

"What do those mean?" asked Eleanor.

"'Games' means you're playing on a team or watching one. 'Walk' means a walk in the neighbourhood. 'Free' means spending time in your dormitory or on the grounds."

"Why do we need to say?" asked Rhoda. "Can't we just do what we want after school?"

"Certainly not! We need to know what each of you is doing and where you are every minute of the day."

"But why?" persisted Rhoda.

"Because the school is responsible for you. You're very close to being impertinent, young lady! Do you want to go and talk to Miss Guppy?"

"No, Miss Poirier," muttered Rhoda.

"Let's start again," said Miss Poirier. "What are you each doing after class?"

"Free, I guess," said Eleanor.

"Free," agreed Polly. "Are we allowed to just wander around the grounds?"

"Yes, but you mustn't go into the woods—that's strictly forbidden."

"A walk around the neighbourhood, then," said Polly. That would be better. She and Eleanor could explore.

Daisy and Rhoda decided on games. "Finally!" sighed Miss Poirier, writing in her notebook. "Tomorrow I expect you all to tell me right away."

"What a grouch!" said Rhoda as the matron walked away.

"I'm glad our dorm usually has Mrs. Blake and not her," said Daisy. She jumped up when a prefect clanged a bell. "Come on, Fearless Four. Back to the fray!"

———

Mrs. Horner spent the whole of British history telling them facts about early royalty. "I expect you to have all the names and dates up to 1066 memorized by next week," she said. "There will be a test."

Next was chemistry, which was in a room full of long tables and high stools in the gymnasium building. Eleanor beamed as Mrs. Diamond explained that later in the term they would be doing experiments. "You're very privileged," she told them. "St. Winifred's is one of the few girls schools in Canada with a science laboratory."

The last period of the day was gymnastics. They were allowed to take off their ties. Then they tucked their tunics into their bloomers and marched in a line with wooden batons. "I told you it was like an army!" puffed Rhoda.

"No talking, please!" called Miss Gower, the gym teacher. "I know you find this difficult right now, but by the end of the year you'll be in perfect precision. In June, St. Winifred's is participating in a province-wide drill competition. Last year we won third place. This time we're going to receive the cup!"

"We have to do that awful marching for a whole *year*?" complained Rhoda as they walked back to the classroom. Polly wiped away the perspiration that coated her face. Her armpits dripped, as well, and she felt trapped inside her sweltering tunic.

After the Hornet dismissed them, they ran up to the dorm, stripped off their tunics, and collapsed on their beds. "Pe-uu!"

laughed Mrs. Blake as she came in. "Go and wash, all of you. Then you can go to tea."

Polly felt better after she'd soaped her armpits and splashed her face with cool water. But then she had to put on the heavy tunic again.

"Don't forget your hats for your walk, Eleanor and Polly," said Mrs. Blake. "Since it's so hot, you can wear your summer ones."

Polly frowned at the brown straw hat. If only it weren't so dull! She followed Eleanor to the dining room and sipped hot tea, which made her even hotter. She wished there were cookies, but there was only a plate of brown bread and butter. At least she and Eleanor were going for a walk on their own.

Miss Poirier appeared in the dining room. "Everyone who signed up for walk, meet outside the front door in five minutes," she announced.

Polly and Eleanor joined six other hatted boarders. "Excuse me, Miss Poirier," said Polly, "but can you tell us how far we can go and what time we have to be back?"

"We'll probably just walk around the block today, since it's so hot, and we'll be back in plenty of time for prep," the matron answered.

We? Was Miss Poirier coming with them?

It was even worse. The matron lined them up two by two; Polly and Eleanor had to go first because they were the youngest. Then Miss Poirier led them in a line down the driveway.

"I think this is what's called a 'crocodile,'" whispered Eleanor. They were allowed to talk, but because she and Eleanor were right behind Miss Poirier, they couldn't speak freely.

Polly was furious. This was a *walk*? A real walk was ambling along, stopping to look at things and chatting to your friend. She stomped along the wooden sidewalk, barely noticing the houses and trees they passed. She didn't even feel glad when they paused to pat a wandering terrier—it just made her miss Tarka.

"Tomorrow we'll say free," she muttered to Eleanor. But there would probably be a catch to that, as well. Nothing at this school so far was at all *free*! She fingered Daddy's necklace again. What would he think if he knew his daughter was being treated like a prisoner having supervised exercise?

Before dinner, there was an hour of prep. All the boarders sat in the school library and did their homework, supervised by Gwen Pritchard, the head boarder. Polly stabbed her pencil over her history assignment. Egbert, Ethelwulf, Ethelbald, Ethelbert . . . how was she supposed to remember such similar names? And memorizing the years the kings reigned was more like arithmetic than history.

Dinner was disgusting: horrible dry liver and greasy onions. "Get used to it," an older girl told them. "It's the same every Tuesday." Polly messed it around on her plate; no one seemed to notice. At least dessert was good: a hot steamed pudding with lemon sauce. Polly had eaten so little all day that she had two helpings.

After dinner, there were prayers in the sitting room, just like last evening. Then they went back to the school building for another hour's prep. Finally, they were allowed to go to their dorms and get ready for bed.

Tonight the other three whispered to one another after lights out, but Polly ignored them. What a horrible day it had been! St. Winifred's was even worse than she had expected. The rules were ridiculous, the food was appalling, and she couldn't bear to be inside so much. Eleanor and Daisy were all right, but every word Rhoda uttered grated on Polly. If only she could run away . . .

But she was so exhausted that she fell asleep.

Chapter Three

AN ORDER MARK

"Please see me in my study after breakfast, Polly," said Miss Guppy.

Polly flinched as the other girls at the table looked at her pityingly. What had she done?

Miss Guppy ushered Polly in and closed the door. Polly sank into one of the chairs and waited.

"I want to talk to you about your father," Miss Guppy said.

So she knew.

"I was shocked to read in the paper that your father is alive." Miss Guppy frowned at Polly as if this were her fault.

"It must have been a shock for you—and Maud, as well—after thinking he was dead all this time."

"We knew he was alive," said Polly, "but we kept it a secret."

"You knew? You had to pretend all this time that your father was dead, aware that that was a falsehood? I'm surprised he asked you to live such a terrible lie. I wish Maud had told me that. While she was here, she sometimes seemed unhappy, but I assumed that was because she was grieving. It's too bad she didn't confide in me. I could have helped her cope."

Now she was blaming Maud *and* Daddy! Polly tried to keep her voice calm. "It's my father's business what he chose to do." Then she quaked. Had she gone too far?

Miss Guppy frowned. "That is an impertinent comment, young lady." She sighed. "Well, it's all water under the bridge. It turns out that your father *is* alive, and of course I'm very glad for you and Maud that he is. Even though . . ."

He's a thief, finished Polly in her mind.

"Let's forget what happened and think of the future. Your father confessed, and by January he'll be cleared. What will happen to you then, do you know?"

"What do you mean?" whispered Polly.

"Will you continue to live with your grandmother?"

It had never occurred to Polly that she wouldn't. Daddy had to stay in Winnipeg until the end of December. Then he would come to see them on the island, and then he'd return to Kelowna, where he had been working as a bricklayer. Polly would be overjoyed to see him again, but she could never leave the island.

"Of *course* I'll keep living with my grandmother!" she said firmly. "She's my official guardian now."

"I'm very pleased to hear that. I was worried that you'd have to leave St. Winifred's."

"I'm only here for a year, though," Polly reminded her.

The Guppy waved her hand impatiently. "Yes, yes . . . I remember our bargain. But Polly, can't I persuade you to become a full-time boarder? You'll miss so much if you go home every weekend."

"I don't care. I *have* to go home every weekend. You said I could!"

Miss Guppy stared at her coldly down her long nose. "There is no need to speak to me in that tone of voice. I know I agreed to that arrangement, but I want you to at least consider changing your mind. Will you?"

Polly nodded because she had to . . . but she never would.

"Thank you. Now, Polly, I don't imagine many of the girls know about your father, but if anyone tries to talk to you about him, you don't have to reply. Just send them to me."

Polly nodded again.

Miss Guppy smiled for the first time. "Now, tell me, have you heard from our Maud?"

Polly shook her head.

"I'm surprised I haven't had a letter myself. I asked her to write to me—you might remind her of that. I want to know if she's attending the church I recommended. It's so easy for girls to stray from the narrow path when they go to university. Maud is such a stalwart Christian, however, that I'm sure she'll keep up her high standards. You're a lucky child, Polly, to have such a sterling example as a sister."

"Yes, Miss Guppy," mumbled Polly. *I'm not a child!* she wanted to add.

"Off you go to your classroom now," Miss Guppy instructed.

Polly paused at the door. "Miss Guppy, when will the extra art classes begin?"

"Probably next week. I've had to look for a new teacher, but I think I've found one."

———

The morning chugged along in its allotted slots just as tediously as yesterday. At break, Polly again noticed some girls staring curiously,

then whispering to one another. At lunchtime, she was nibbling another dry sandwich when she heard her name called.

Alice! The red-haired girl rushed over to Polly's table and pulled
up a chair. "Welcome to St. Winnie's, Goldilocks! I'm sorry I wasn't
here before. I had a toothache, so I had to go to Sidney to have it out."

Polly was so relieved to see someone from home she wanted to
weep. "Noni told me," she said. "Are you better?"

"I'm fine. See?" Alice opened her mouth and pointed to a raw-
looking cavity. "Now, tell me who's in your dorm," she ordered.

Polly introduced the Fearless Four. Alice quizzed each girl so
boisterously that they were all intimidated, even Rhoda.

"Has anyone at school asked you about your father?" said Alice
as they walked back to the school building together.

Polly shook her head. "Some of them stare at me, but no one's
said anything."

"You come and tell me if anyone bothers you," said Alice. "I'll
take care of them!"

Polly smiled, remembering how fierce Alice could be.

The last period of the day was drawing. Polly lifted her head as Pauline announced, "Stand for Miss Netherwood!"

Miss Netherwood, a tired-looking woman with a sallow face,
handed out pencils, rulers, erasers, and drawing paper. Polly's hand
itched to make the first lines on its crisp white surface. She gazed out
the window and decided that she would draw the majestic beech tree
that stood against the blue sky.

First she had to listen as Miss Netherwood explained what they
would be doing this year. "St. Winifred's follows the curriculum of

the Royal Drawing Society in England," she said. "At the end of the Easter term you will complete a prescribed set of drawings, which will be sent to England to be evaluated. At the end of the year, those of you who were successful will receive a certificate saying you have passed the first level."

A certificate from England! thought Polly. Noni would be so proud.

"For the whole of this term we will be studying perspective," said Miss Netherwood. "No one can draw properly until she knows the rules of depth and distance. We will begin by drawing a cube in one-point perspective. Please copy what I draw on the blackboard." She instructed them to pick up their rulers and draw a horizontal line.

After Miss Netherwood had drawn a cube, she came around to inspect their progress. "Your lines are crooked," she informed Daisy. "Erase it all and start again."

Rhoda was next. "Excellent work!" said Miss Netherwood. "Have you done this before?"

Rhoda looked proud. "I took art lessons in Bellingham."

Polly sat back and waited for Miss Netherwood to praise her, as well.

But when the teacher reached Polly, she drew in her breath. "No, no, child—what is your name?"

"Polly."

"You can't draw it freehand! You have to do it as I've shown you, with lines to a vanishing point."

"But I don't have to. Watch!" Polly quickly sketched another perfect cube.

Miss Netherwood's pale cheeks turned pink. "Of course you have to! I won't tolerate insubordination, do you understand? I'm giving you an order mark."

"I *don't* understand," whispered Polly. "What have I done?"

"You are disobedient and a show-off. Now, draw it again properly."

Polly's cheeks blazed. She picked up her ruler and tried to draw the cube the way it was on the board, but her hand wouldn't obey her brain. Making sure Miss Netherwood's back was turned, she drew a cube freehand first, *then* filled in the required lines.

"That's better, Polly," said Miss Netherwood coldly when she came around again. "This one is much more accurate than the ones you did freehand. You see? You're not as good as you think you are!" She gazed around the room with a triumphant smirk.

Yes, I am! thought Polly. But that didn't help. She had been so excited about drawing, and it had turned out to be so disappointing. And she'd received an order mark!

At least she had the extra art classes to look forward to. But what if that teacher was as hopeless as this one?

After school, Polly glanced at the weekly charts posted outside the staff room. There was one for posture, with stars by the names of the girls whose straight backs had been noticed. Beside the weekly charts were the house charts. Sure enough, a numeral one was written by her name on Sussex's chart. Hers was the only order mark there. Polly fled to tea.

"I'm sorry you got an order mark," Daisy told Polly. "I don't think Miss Netherwood was fair."

"Of course she wasn't," said Eleanor. "I saw Polly's cube and it was just like the one on the board."

"It's not how it looks—it's how you do it," said Rhoda. "Polly, I could help you, if you like."

How dare she? Polly tried to control her voice. "I don't need any help, thank you. I already know how to draw—I've been doing it for years."

"Polly's going to be an artist one day," Eleanor told them.

"A real artist?" Daisy gazed at Polly with awe. "Golly!"

"*I'm* going to be one, too!" said Rhoda quickly. Polly knew she'd just thought of it. "I won first prize in our school contest," Rhoda added.

"You did? That's swell, Rhoda!" Daisy went on to ask her about her art, but Polly pushed back her chair. "Let's get out of here," she said to Eleanor.

She and Eleanor had chosen free for their after-school activity. They ran out the door and kept running across the lawn to the woods.

Polly looked around; no one was watching. "In here!" she said, leading Eleanor through the trees to the patch of moss she had seen behind the sequoia. They leaned against its wide trunk, the sun making dappled shadows on their faces. They couldn't see out, and no one could see in.

"I've wanted to come in here since yesterday," said Polly. She wished she'd brought her sketchbook; but she would feel self-conscious drawing in front of Eleanor.

"Good choice!" said Eleanor. She looked around. "This could be our secret hideaway. Let's not even tell Daisy and Rhoda about it." She took off her steamed-up glasses and rubbed them on her tunic. Her large hazel eyes were so pretty it was too bad she had to hide them behind her glasses, thought Polly.

"Miss Netherwood is almost as mean as the Hornet," said Eleanor. "I like Mrs. Diamond, though, and Mrs. Partridge is quite nice, as well."

They listed the teachers they liked and the ones they didn't. "At least we don't have the Guppy for anything," said Polly.

"We will next year, for Latin, but I guess you won't be here then."
Eleanor looked mournful, then she said, "Tell me more about Alice.
She's very confident, isn't she?"

"Alice lives on the island. She's nice to me here, but when she
went to my school, she was a terrible bully—we were all afraid of her.
But that's because her *mother* is a bully. Sometimes she whipped her!"

"That's wrong," said Eleanor firmly. "My parents have never hit
me, have yours?"

"Daddy never did, and I'm sure my mother didn't. I guess we're
lucky." Polly swallowed. "Would you—would you like me to tell you
about my father?"

"If you want to," said Eleanor.

Polly told her an abbreviated version: how Daddy had stolen
some money because they were so poor, how he had been caught, but
had run away and pretended he'd drowned . . . how she and Maud
had had to leave Winnipeg to live on the island, and how hard it was
to keep the secret that Daddy was still alive. How he had turned up
on the island on Polly's twelfth birthday, and how she'd hidden him
for a week.

"I haven't seen him since," she said sadly, "but now he's confessed and everyone knows he's alive."

"Did he have to go to jail?" asked Eleanor.

"No. The judge gave him a suspended sentence. That means he
has to stay in Winnipeg until the end of this year. If he hasn't committed a crime during that time, he'll be free to go back to Kelowna."

"Gee . . . what a story! It's like something in a book. You've been
through so much, Polly."

Polly shrugged. She hadn't told Eleanor how Daddy had let them
believe he was innocent, and how betrayed she felt when she found
out he'd lied.

But now she'd forgiven him and had written him a letter telling him so. Just before she came here, she'd had a long, loving letter back. Polly blinked away her tears.

"When will you see your father again?" Eleanor asked.

"He's coming to the island for New Year's—I can hardly wait! Then he'll go back to Kelowna, but he wants Maud and me to spend Easter there with him."

"Thank you for telling me," said Eleanor.

Polly smiled. "It's a relief to talk about it. But don't tell the other two, all right? It was in the papers when Daddy turned up alive. I think some of the older girls must have read them, the way they keep staring at me. And Miss Guppy and Alice know. But I'd rather keep it a secret from Daisy and Rhoda."

"I won't tell," said Eleanor. She looked thoughtful. "*I* don't have any secrets. Our family is happy, but my life is boring compared with yours."

It sounds more peaceful than boring, thought Polly. Peaceful, like sitting in here on the soft, warm moss almost falling asleep . . . Then she noticed something move.

"Eleanor," she breathed. A small flock of quail scratched at the moss close to them, their plumes bobbing.

The commanding bell sounded. The quail flew up in a startled bunch, and Polly and Eleanor hurried away for prep.

———

"I can't sleep," complained Rhoda that night. "I never go to bed this early at home!"

"Don't talk so loud!" whispered Daisy. "Mrs. Blake might come back and check on us!"

"She won't," said Eleanor. "I heard her tell Miss Poirier how much she enjoyed going to her own room with her book after lights out."

Polly lay silently. Part of her mind was going over the injustices of the day, and part listened as the other three chattered freely.

Daisy told them what a struggle it was for her family to send her away to school. "My father is a carpenter. He did a lot of repairs to St. Winifred's the week before school started. Miss Guppy accepted that as part of my fees."

Rhoda's family, on the other hand, was well off. She lived in a large house and her family had a cook.

So does my grandmother, Polly almost said, but she didn't want to sound as boastful as Rhoda.

"I'll tell you something really interesting about me," said Rhoda. "I'm adopted!"

Now all of Polly was listening.

"You *are*?" said Eleanor. "I've never known anyone who was adopted."

"That *is* interesting!" said Daisy.

"How old were you?" Eleanor asked. "I hope you don't think I'm being too nosy," she added.

"I was just a baby," said Rhoda. "I don't mind talking about it. I was *chosen*," she added proudly. "So was my older brother. That makes us special."

As usual, Rhoda managed to sound superior.

Every day after lunch, Polly checked her mail slot in the sitting room. On Thursday, she got two letters. Polly snatched them out of the slot and curled up on one of the soft chairs to read them. One was from Maud and the other from Noni.

Maud was adoring her first week of university. "U.B.C. is huge—about two thousand students," she wrote. "I'm meeting so many interesting people. And I feel so free! I only have a few classes every day, and in between I can do what I like. One of my new friends actually has a car. We pool our money for gas and all pile into it and go downtown."

Maud shared a room with Ann, a friend from St. Winifred's. She and Ann had been to a "frosh" dance and had had a wonderful time. "I noticed a handsome boy standing on the side, looking shy. So I asked him for a dance! We had almost every dance together, and this weekend we're going to a movie. His name is Robert. He's my very first date."

Polly smiled. Robert had better watch himself!

Maud liked all her courses and was working hard. She didn't say a word about going to church. "Please let me know how you're enjoying school so far, Doodle," she ended. "I'm really looking forward to seeing you at Thanksgiving."

Polly put down the letter and sighed. She was glad that her sister was so happy, but she was also envious. University sounded like a lot more fun than boarding school.

She opened Noni's letter. It was brief, just saying how much she and Aunt Jean and Uncle Rand missed Polly, and how eager they were to see her on the weekend. "Your wee dog has tried hard to behave and sometimes he succeeds," Noni wrote. "He sends his love, as we all do."

At the bottom of the letter was Tarka's dirty paw print. Polly kissed it, and suddenly felt lighter. Tomorrow evening she would be home.

CHAPTER FOUR

฿ACK ON THE ISLAND

POLLY HAD NEVER TRAVELLED TO THE ISLAND BY HERSELF. MRS. Blake drove her down to the harbour in Miss Guppy's little grey car. She waited with Polly until it was time to board the steamer. "Now, don't talk to strangers, and be sure you get off at the right island," she said.

"Don't worry, I've done this trip *zillions* of times," said Polly happily.

She ran up the gangplank, almost forgetting to turn and wave goodbye to Mrs. Blake. Right away, some women from Kingfisher Island recognized her and asked her about school. To avoid their questions, Polly spent the whole time on the deck.

How wonderful to smell the salt air again! She pulled off her hat, released her hair from its braid, and let it stream in the breeze. She was wearing her own clothes and Daddy's necklace.

Polly drank in the familiar landscape greedily: big and small islands, the rounded shapes of distant hills, and the ever-changing, rippling water below her. She spotted many sleek seals, a few otters, and, in the distance, a school of leaping dolphins. By the time the steamer docked at Valencia Island the sun was starting to set, and the air became chilly. Polly pulled her hat over her ears and put on her gloves. Her feet and nose were still freezing, but she didn't want to go inside.

Finally, the fir-covered cliffs of her own island came into view. Now the sky was pink. The boat rounded a point, and Polly could see the long wharf and the familiar buildings on either side of it: the hotel, the store, the church and rectory, and, best of all, the white house with the blue roof—the house that had sheltered her for the past three years. She was *home*.

Noni waved from the end of the wharf; Tarka was prancing at her feet. In a few minutes, Polly was in her grandmother's arms. "Oh, Noni—oh, Noni . . ." she sobbed. "I've missed you so much! And Tarka, my little Tarka-dog!"

Tarka scratched at her legs, squealing hysterically. Polly picked him up and buried her face in his fur, sobbing even harder.

"Whisht, Polly!" Behind her glasses, Noni's grey eyes looked worried. "I've missed you, too, but you've only been away for a week! It can't be as bad as all that. Cheer up now, hen. You have two whole days ahead of you to enjoy."

Walking home felt like waking up from a bad dream. Polly's legs trembled she was so relieved to be scuffing her feet in the dirt road. At least Noni didn't ask her about school. Instead, she told Polly how Tarka had stolen a whole loaf of bread out of the larder.

"That's why his tummy is so fat!" giggled Polly.

Aunt Jean and Uncle Rand came for dinner as usual. *They* asked about school, but Polly tried to divert their questions by quizzing them about what had been happening on the island.

"Well!" said Aunt Jean. "You won't believe this, but Mildred Cunningham had a dress made in Vancouver and it fastens at the side with a zipper! Zippers are fine on galoshes, but not on a dress. I can't believe she'd go in for such a fad. I told her it would never stay shut and she was only setting herself up for an embarrassing situation, but of course she won't listen to me."

Polly grinned. Nothing had changed; Aunt Jean and Mrs. Cunningham had been rivals since they were girls.

"She'll be the next to get one—wait and see," whispered Uncle Rand to Polly as Aunt Jean was taking out the plates. "Now, tell me what subjects you're studying."

Polly sighed, but she had to be polite. She recited all her subjects.

"So many new things to learn," said Uncle Rand. "It makes me wish I were starting school all over again."

"Tell us about your roommates," Aunt Jean urged, coming back into the dining room with a blackberry pie.

There was no escape. Polly had to list her roommates and say where they were from. Then Uncle Rand asked her about her teachers.

Finally, Noni said, "Enough questions, now. I think Polly's tired. Let's have a song or two, and then she can go to bed." They gathered around the piano. Polly belted out the tunes, the familiar words cancelling out everything that had happened this horrible week.

Polly opened her eyes and stretched. She was in her own comfortable bed, the same arbutus tree gleamed in the sun outside the window, and, best of all, her beloved Tarka dozed at her feet. As soon as she moved, he wormed his way up and pressed against her side, then flipped onto his back so Polly could rub his tummy.

The only sound was the swish of the sea and a raven's hoarse croak. There was no clanging bell, no rigid schedule, and no crowd of noisy girls. She was *alone*, and she had the entire day to do as she pleased.

As usual, Polly made tea and toast for herself and Noni, and carried it upstairs on a tray.

"Ah, hen, what a treat! All week I had to go down and make my own breakfast." Noni patted the bed. "Come and sit beside me."

Polly leaned against the pillow and nibbled her toast, tossing bits to Tarka. Her grandmother put down her cup. "Now, tell me what you *really* think of St. Winifred's."

Polly didn't want to think of school at all, but she had to answer. "I hate it," she muttered.

"What do you hate about it?" Noni asked calmly.

Polly spat out her words like hot coals. "I'm never alone and I hardly ever get to go outside. There are loud bells that tell us to do things. Our dorm floor is splintery, and my bed is lumpy. There are so many stupid rules—we can't even talk in the halls! It's crowded and noisy, and the food is horrible. In the school bathroom there's only one roller towel for all of us—it's disgusting! Our homeroom teacher is really mean. Miss Guppy is just as bossy as she was when Maud was there. I miss you and Tarka and everyone else on the island so much. And Noni, the drawing teacher told me I was a show-off!"

"Gracious, what a lot of things to hate! It's a shame about your drawing teacher. But I'm sure your other art teacher will be different. Isn't there anything you *like*?"

Polly thought hard. "Having indoor toilets."

Noni chuckled. "That must feel like a real luxury after the island. But there must be something else you like. What about the other girls in your dorm?"

"I like Eleanor," said Polly, "and Daisy's all right. But Rhoda is really spoiled and stuck-up." She took a deep breath. "Oh, Noni, do I have to go back?"

Now Noni looked flinty. "Polly, we've gone over this so often. I'm very sorry you don't like St. Winifred's, but you've only been there for a week. It'll take a while to get used to being in a large school, and to being so regulated. Of course you miss us—we miss *you* terribly. But we'll see one another every weekend, and I guarantee you'll like St. Winifred's better soon. Your—your father and Maud and I, and the rest of the family, would be so disappointed if you left. You would be disappointed in yourself when you were older—you would have given up this chance for an excellent education."

Her face softened. "Many things in life are difficult, but you already know that. You've always been my brave lassie—can you try to be brave now and give the school a chance?"

Polly sighed. *Of course* Noni would react like this. What would her grandmother think if she knew Polly was only there for a year? "All right," she muttered.

Noni kissed her. "Good for you. Now, why don't you make yourself a sandwich and go find Biddy and Vivien. It's such a beautiful day. You don't have to be back until dinnertime—ask your friends if they'd like to come."

––––––––

Biddy and Vivien were much more sympathetic to Polly's complaints about St. Winifred's. They sat on the beach, enthralled and horrified, as Polly told them about the rules and the ugly uniform, described the food and imitated the Hornet.

"You poor thing!" said Biddy. "It sounds like a prison."

"It is," said Polly. "I hate it!"

"I would hate it, too," said Vivien. "But Biddy and I aren't much better off, Polly."

She and Biddy shared a governess with Dorothy, another girl on the island. "We only have to go in the mornings," said Vivien, "but they last forever. Miss Peate is so boring, and she isn't very smart. I'm far better at math than she is."

"She has B.O.!" said Biddy. "And she files her nails while we're reading."

"At least you have the afternoons off," said Polly.

"Yes, but we both have to work," said Vivien. "I have to help Dad in the orchard, and Biddy has to babysit."

"I have to look after Shirley all afternoon and pick up the twins from school," said Biddy. "Neither of them minds me—they drive me crazy. Oh, Polly, everything has changed so much! I wish it were last year and we were still in grade seven."

The other two agreed. They sat there glumly until Polly said, "Well, at least next year I'll be back on the island all the time."

"Yes, you will," said Biddy. "I'm so glad you don't like St. Winifred's. I was worried that you'd want to stay." She jumped up. "Come on, we only have the weekend together! Can we take out your uncle's gasboat?"

The rest of the day went by far too fast. The sea was so calm that they were able to take the boat as far as Vivien's farm. Then they helped pick apples and ate their sandwiches under the trees. After lunch, they putted back in the boat, then rode their bikes to the lighthouse, with Tarka and Biddy's dog, Bramble, riding in their baskets as usual. Then they hung around Biddy's room, looking at movie magazines.

Polly stretched out on Biddy's bed and listened to the other two argue about who was prettier—Jean Harlow or Loretta Young. Being part of this cozy threesome again felt so safe.

"I wish we could *see* some of these movies," complained Biddy. "Will you be able to go to movies in Victoria, Polly?"

"Maybe," said Polly. "When Maud was there, the boarders were sometimes taken to them."

"Lucky you!" said Vivien. "It's so frustrating to live somewhere with no movie theatre."

Polly didn't want them to think there was anything good about St. Winifred's. "They only go on the weekends," she said. "I'm not a full-time boarder, so I'll never see one."

"Tell us about your roommates," said Biddy. "Are they nice?"

"Two of them are. Eleanor's really smart and Daisy's good at sports. She's trying to get on her house basketball team."

"Who's the third one?" asked Vivien.

"Rhoda . . . she's awful. She's really conceited and she boasts all the time. I can't stand her!"

"Do *they* like boarding school?"

"Eleanor likes the classes, and she's so practical she just puts up with the rest. Daisy is the sort of person who likes everything. And Rhoda . . . well, she seems to hate it as much as I do," finished Polly slowly. She didn't want to admit she had *anything* in common with Rhoda.

"Do you like Eleanor and Daisy as much as us?" asked Biddy.

Polly grinned. "Of course not! You two are my best friends."

Biddy and Vivien were eager to come for dinner. Noni and Aunt Jean had cooked Polly's favourites: roast chicken, roast potatoes, and

butterscotch pudding. None of them urged her to eat her vegetables
the way they usually did.

Then they made two teams for charades: Polly, Uncle Rand, and
Biddy against Vivien, Aunt Jean, and Noni. Vivien was such a good
actor that her team won every time. It was very late when Uncle Rand
drove the girls home.

Polly took Tarka out for his last walk of the day. She strolled
along the road while Tarka marked the bushes. The stars were a mil-
lion diamonds sparkling above her, and the moon made a silver path
on the sea. Polly had always found the night sky reassuring, as if she
were part of a wondrous mystery. Several times, she had tried to
paint it, but she hadn't yet captured its essence.

How could she go back to a place where she wasn't allowed to
stand and marvel under the stars?

―――――

Polly sat in the tiny stone church and listened to Uncle Rand preach
about the parable of the sower. He joked about what a dismal gardener he himself was, and everyone laughed. Polly listened proudly.
Once, Uncle Rand's sermons had been so obtuse that no one could
understand them. But after Polly had told him that, his preaching
became simpler.

At coffee time, everyone came up to Polly and welcomed her
home. They kept asking her how she liked school. All she could do
was smile and murmur "Fine."

Mrs. Mackenzie, Alice's mother, wrung Polly's hand like a rag.
"I hope Alice is keeping out of trouble," she said.

Polly tried to answer just as sternly. "Alice is *never* in trouble! In
fact, she was just made president of her class."

"That's hard to believe," said Mrs. Mackenzie.

Polly escaped from her and bumped into Chester's parents. "Why, Polly, how nice to see you back on the island!" said his mother.

"We telephoned Chester last night," his father told her. "He's really enjoying being back at school, and he's trying out for the debating team."

St. Winifred's had absorbed Polly so much that she'd forgotten Chester was also in Victoria, boarding at St. Cuthbert's.

A warm memory flooded her mind, of sitting with Chester at the lighthouse and watching the whales. Then he had kissed her! That seemed like years ago, not months.

She wondered how far away Chester's school was from hers. There was no chance she'd ever see him, however; he was as imprisoned as she was.

"Is Chester coming home for Thanksgiving?" she asked in a carefully neutral voice.

"Of course!" said his mother. "He'd never miss my pumpkin pie. And it's his fifteenth birthday that weekend, so we'll have a cake, too."

Fifteen! Polly couldn't believe Chester was almost that old. He would probably be much more interested in girls his own age than in her.

Mrs. Hooper had been off for the weekend, but now she rushed up and enveloped Polly in one of her energetic hugs. "I made a chocolate cake for you," she said. "Look for it in the pantry. And take lots of cookies, as well. You'll want them for your tuck box, the way Maud used to. How's she liking university?"

"She loves it," said Polly.

"The house seems so lonely with you *both* away. At least your grandmother and I have Tarka to keep us hopping."

"I hope he's behaving," said Polly. "Remember he needs a lot of walks, or he'll chew things."

"Don't you worry. We're taking good care of him."

Tarka is my dog! thought Polly. I *should be the one taking care of him.*

———

After lunch, Polly spent a blissful few hours on the beach, drawing the view of Walker Island across the pass. But then Noni called her to come and pack.

Late that afternoon, Polly stood on the boat deck, holding Mrs. Hooper's cake and cookies in a large box. Noni and Aunt Jean and Uncle Rand and Tarka were already tiny figures in the distance. She waved until the steamer went past the point.

Mrs. Cunningham stood beside her; she was travelling to Victoria to visit friends. "Let's go inside, dear," she said to Polly. "We'll sit in the lounge and you can tell me all about your new school."

Polly had to spend the whole of the trip talking about St. Winifred's.

CHAPTER FIVE

A DISAPPOINTMENT

"THIS IS *SCRUMPTIOUS!*" SAID DAISY, CRAMMING MRS. HOOPER'S cake into her mouth. "Thanks, Polly!"

The Fearless Four were sitting in the dining room. Each dorm was allotted an evening before bedtime when they could dig into the tuck boxes they kept in the kitchen. Their evening was Monday; Polly was glad of that because the cake was still fresh.

"The cookies are great, too," said Eleanor. She inspected her own box. "I'm going to throw out these they're so stale."

"Tell us about your weekend, Polly," said Daisy.

Polly didn't want to talk about the island with them; it made her miss it too much. "There isn't much to tell," she said. "I just saw my family and my dog and my friends, and we took out the boat, and then my friends came for dinner."

"I bet you were glad to see your mum and dad," said Daisy sadly. "I really miss mine."

Polly flushed. "I . . . umm . . ."

Eleanor rescued her. "Polly lives with her grandmother," she said quietly.

"Oh!" said Daisy. She was too polite to say any more, but Rhoda asked, "Where are your parents, then?"

Polly wished she could leave the room. "My mother died when I was two, and my father lives in Kelowna," she muttered. There was no point in explaining he was in Winnipeg at the moment.

"Why don't you live with *him*?" asked Rhoda.

Polly couldn't answer. "She just doesn't," said Eleanor. "Let's tell Polly what *our* weekend was like."

"Yesterday was *so* tedious," said Rhoda. "We had to walk in a crocodile to church. Everyone stared at us. In the afternoon we had to talk about God and stuff with Miss Guppy. It was incredibly boring."

"Saturday was okay, though," said Eleanor. "They took us to the beach after lunch. When we got back, we could do what we wanted." She smiled at Daisy. "We played a *lot* of basketball! Dais here is a pretty fast dribbler. Rho's pretty good, too."

Daisy smiled back. "Sorry, El, but I need to practise if I want to get on the team."

Dais? El? Rho? Suddenly, the other three seemed best chums.

"This cookie is kind of bland," said Rhoda. "Our cook puts nuts and raisins in hers."

"Don't eat it, then," retorted Polly.

Now I've caught her! she thought as Rhoda mumbled that it wasn't that bad and finished the cookie.

"Rho, will you help me wash my hair tonight?" asked Daisy. "I can never get all the soap out of it."

"Sure! I'll lend you some of my special shampoo."

"But Rho, I thought I was going to help you with those history dates tonight," said Eleanor.

"Oh, right. Sorry, Dais, we'll have to put off the hair washing until after the history test."

Polly turned her back on them and put away the remains of the food. How could they be so accepting of Rhoda? And how had they become a trio in only two days? She wondered if Eleanor had shown them the hideaway.

"Thanks again, Poll!" said Daisy. "We really missed you, but I'm glad you returned bearing food!" She raised her glass of juice. "Here's to the Fearless Four!"

Polly clinked her glass with the others.

———

By the end of Tuesday, Polly had had a first lesson in all her courses except her extra art class. In literature they were studying *As You Like It*. Noni had read some Shakespeare to Polly, but never a whole play. Polly was relieved when she found the rich words easy to understand.

Her piano teacher, Miss Austen, was young and friendly. She told Polly she'd teach her to play some jazz as well as classical. Now Polly was allowed to miss the first twenty minutes of prep to prac-tise in one of the piano rooms in the gymnasium. The first time she went, Alice was in the other room practising her singing. She was so good that Polly stopped playing her scales to listen to her.

This morning Mrs. Horner had stomped into history muttering "Numbers one to twelve" before she even reached her desk. Polly had finally managed to memorize the kings, but she got two dates wrong and received ten out of twelve. Half the class failed, and the Hornet was disgusted. The girls who had failed had to stay in at break and go through the list while she drilled them.

At lunchtime, Rhoda was in tears. "I *hate* her!" she sobbed. "She told me I'd never catch up in British history because I'm an American. What about the other girls? *They* aren't American, but they failed, too! We have to miss break again tomorrow and do the test again. I'll *never* learn everything by then!"

The others tried to calm her down. "Don't worry—I'll keep helping you," said Eleanor.

"We all will," said Daisy. "We'll quiz you tonight after lights out. You won't be allowed to go to sleep until you know all the kings!"

I'm much better at memorizing than Rhoda, thought Polly with satisfaction.

Tuesday afternoon was Polly's first house meeting. She assembled in a classroom with the twenty or so other girls who belonged to Sussex. She wondered if anyone would mention her order mark. At least she wasn't the only person with one now. Many of the names on the other house charts had numbers beside them.

Sussex's house captain was one of the prefects, a large, blustery girl named Babs Cook. First she welcomed the new girls. Then she went on to describe all the activities this term: house competitions in grass hockey, basketball, tennis, and drama. "I expect everyone to do her bit in trying out for these," she told them. "So far we've earned ten points, which is a very good start. We won most of those points in debating last week. The rest were earned by Pauline Osborne for receiving the posture award. Attagirl, Pauline!"

Everyone clapped and Pauline sat up even straighter. Then Babs frowned. "Unfortunately, four members of Sussex have already received order marks, which have been deducted from those points. I'm very disappointed that these girls have let us down so early in the term. Edna, Audrey, Mary, and Polly, would you please stand?"

Polly had to hold the edge of the desk she was quivering so much. She listened to the other three explain why they'd received order marks; then it was her turn.

"Miss Netherwood gave me the order mark," she murmured. Then her voice grew stronger. "But all I did was draw a cube!"

"You must have done more than that, or she wouldn't have given you one," said Babs. She appraised Polly. "I was thrilled to learn you would be in Sussex, Polly. Your sister was the best house captain we ever had! We won the cup last year because of her inspiration. I'm going to try my best to follow her example, and I want you to, as well. From now on, every time you wonder how to behave, think of Maud and do what she would do."

Polly sat down, fuming. Like everyone else at St. Winifred's, Babs was talking about Maud as if she were a saint.

———

When another letter arrived from Maud that day, Polly forgot her anger as she rushed out to the steps to read it.

Maud and Ann were trying to get into a sorority. "It's called 'rushing,'" Maud wrote. "We get asked to teas and lunches, and we butter up the girls so we'll be invited to join. So far, we like Delta Gamma the best."

The rest of the letter was about Robert. "He's the bee's knees!" Maud gushed. "He has long eyelashes like Clark Gable. I see him every day. We meet between classes for coffee, and we're going out again this weekend. Ann says I'm stuck on him, and she's right!"

Maud had never had a beau before. She had never drunk coffee before, either. She seemed so grown-up.

"I tried the church Miss Guppy recommended, but I didn't like it at all," wrote Maud. "Don't tell the Guppy, but I'm not going again. Robert and I talk a lot about religion. He's making me look at God in a new way. I had a nice letter from Daddy, but I haven't heard one word from *you*. I'm sorry I can't be on the island for your birthday, Doodle. I hope you're all right. Write to me at once and let me know how you like school."

Why hadn't *she* heard from Daddy? Polly wondered. And how could she write to Maud? She couldn't lie and say she liked St. Winifred's, but if she said how much she hated it, Maud would be so disappointed in her.

That evening in prep, Polly slipped a piece of paper on top of her math homework and scribbled "Dear Maud." She pondered a moment, then began: "I'm sorry I haven't written to you yet. Here is what school is like."

Polly proceeded to list the names of her roommates. She told Maud how the Fearless Four had set up an obstacle course in the dorm and jumped from one bed to the other until Rhoda crashed through a mattress and Mrs. Blake stopped them. How they had smuggled chocolate up from Daisy's tuck box to celebrate when Rhoda passed the history test. How one warm evening Eleanor and Polly had led everyone out onto the fire escape. They had whispered on the stairs, daring one another to go down, but no one had had the nerve. Polly told Maud how she and Eleanor had snuck off to their hideaway again, where they sprawled on the moss and talked about their dogs. She went on to write about how a boarder had got locked in the bathroom, and how some boys in a car had passed them on their walk and honked and hooted at them.

Then she signed the letter. There! She had managed not to say whether she liked school. Instead, she had turned St. Winifred's into a story, like the boarding-school novels Maud used to devour. Maud would assume Polly was having as jolly a time at school as she had had.

Polly's gloom lifted after school on Thursday. Today was her first extra art class. She started whistling as she left her classroom.

"Stop that at once," called out a prefect.

But Polly whistled under her breath the whole way out of the building.

The art class was right after tea. Polly waited in a classroom with five other girls. They were all older than her, and they were all day girls except for Dottie.

"Miss Falconer is new," one of them explained to her. "Last year we had Mrs. Simon, but she left because she was having a baby."

"My parents told me Miss Falconer is famous," said Dottie. "She's even exhibited in San Francisco!"

Polly's anticipation grew. She had never met a real artist.

"Here she comes!" said one of the girls.

A small, trim woman carrying a basket flew into the room. She had messy grey hair tied into a bun and she wore a woven cape and a red wool tam. Her blue eyes twinkled.

She put down the basket and took off her cape and hat. Underneath was an embroidered purple smock. Polly immediately wanted one just like it.

In a light, musical voice Miss Falconer said, "Hello there, girls! Sorry I'm late." She looked around the room. "This isn't a very suitable space. Never mind—it will do for today. Arrange these desks into a circle, will you? That's better! Take a seat and let me get to know you all."

They gazed in amazement as the woman boosted herself nimbly up onto the teacher's desk and perched on the edge, swinging her legs. They were sheathed in lacy grey stockings; her shoes were red, with silver buckles.

"I'm Miss Falconer, but of course you know that. Now tell me *your* names, and about your experience in art."

Dottie, Margaret, Jane, and Katherine introduced themselves. They had all taken art for years, some of them in classes outside the school.

"Now for our little one!" Miss Falconer smiled. "You must be Polly. How long have you done art?"

Polly flushed. "I've been drawing and doing watercolours for three years. My grandmother taught me."

"Good for her! Let me tell you a little about me. I've been a professional artist for thirty years—don't start guessing how old I am! My favourite medium is oil, but I also do a lot of sculpture. I conduct many classes, and I'm delighted to have the opportunity to teach you, as well."

She smiled even more warmly. "Let's call this course *'special art'*! *You* are all special because you want to create. That's what humans are meant to do. We're going to try many mediums this term—drawing, watercolour, oil painting, pastels, clay work, and collage. I want you to sample everything, and then you can learn what you like the best."

Painting in oils! Clay! Something mysterious called 'collage'! Polly was so excited she thought she might be sick.

"Today we're going to draw leaves," said Miss Falconer, digging into her basket. "Everyone take a sheet of paper, and a hard and a soft pencil." She pulled out a handful of colourful leaves. "Choose a leaf and draw it any way you feel like—but try to use each pencil. If you finish your drawing, do the leaf again from a different angle."

Polly chose a large yellow leaf. For the next hour, she forgot everything but how it looked. Hating St. Winifred's, missing the island . . . they both went out of her head as she explored each leaf vein, hole, and notch with her pencil.

Miss Falconer came around and gave quiet suggestions to each of them. "You might want to try adding the shadow on the table—see? Did you notice how the stem widens at this point?"

When she got to Polly, she watched her for a long time. Polly continued to draw, trying not to feel self-conscious. Miss Falconer moved on without saying anything.

For the last part of the class, they gathered around each girl's drawing while Miss Falconer commented on it, pointing out what was strong and weak in each one. She told Margaret she had an excellent sense of design, and she suggested that Jane try a smaller leaf with less detail. She encouraged the girls also to make comments.

Polly was amazed at how different everyone's was. Dottie's leaves were dark and wild. Jane's drawing was so precise and careful that she hadn't even finished one leaf. Margaret, on the other hand, had filled her page with dozens of leaves. Polly liked Katherine's the best: she drew one huge leaf that bent and curled so realistically it looked as if it could be lifted off the page. Polly wanted to say how much she liked Katherine's drawing, but she couldn't make her mouth form the words.

Finally, they stood around Polly's desk. Her heart pounded so hard she was sure the others could hear. Their drawings were so experienced, like ones in a book. Hers seemed so childish in comparison.

Polly had drawn three leaves, one shaded heavily with the soft pencil, one delicately defined with the hard one, and one with both dark and light lines. She'd tried to make that one seem as if it were dancing in the wind.

"Wow!" said Dottie. "I can't believe someone so young can draw so well!"

"You have a strong, confident line, Polly," said Miss Falconer. She pointed out a wide curve. "Do you see how she doesn't hesitate, everyone? And you've put so much motion into your drawing—this leaf looks as if it's twirling. Well done, little one!"

Polly was stunned. Miss Falconer had pointed out something in *her* drawing as an example! And she and the others really liked it!

"You are all special . . ." Polly *felt* special, as if a spark inside her had kindled.

Then Miss Falconer looked anxious. "Sit down again, girls. The reason I was late was that I had to discuss something with Miss Guppy. Now I need to consult with all of you about it. I'm afraid my busy schedule is making it tricky for me to teach you during the week. Thursday afternoon was my only free spot, but now I've discovered that one of my most regular students wants that time for sculpture lessons."

Now her expression was pleading. "I'd like to switch special art to Saturday afternoons. We could have it at my studio, which is a much more productive space than here. And we could make the class longer—three hours instead of two. I wouldn't charge any more for the extra time. If you aren't able to do this, I'll have to cancel my other student, which would be such a shame. What do you think? Are you all able to attend on Saturdays? I know that two of you are boarders, but Miss Guppy said you could come on the streetcar. "

"That would be fine!" said Katherine. "I'd much rather have a longer class."

"I'll have to ask my parents, but I'm sure it's no problem," said Jane. Dottie and Margaret also agreed.

Polly's head whirled. If she went to the Saturday classes, she wouldn't be able to go home for the weekends!

"That's excellent, girls," said Miss Falconer. "What about you, Polly?"

"I don't know yet," Polly whispered. She felt as if someone had given her a wonderful present, then snatched it away.

"Oh, dear . . . we would miss you so much if you couldn't attend. Let Miss Guppy know as soon as you've decided, and she'll telephone me."

That evening Polly was summoned to Miss Guppy's study.

"I'm sorry Miss Falconer has had to change the class," she said. "Of course this means you'll now have to board full time. I know you didn't want that, Polly, but you'll soon get to enjoy it."

The Guppy didn't look sorry at all; she looked like a cat that had just finished a bowl of cream.

"I haven't decided anything yet," said Polly tightly. "I'm going to talk to my grandmother about it."

"Well, it's up to you. Let me know on Monday. But you'd be a foolish girl indeed if you lost this opportunity. Miss Falconer talked to me before she left. She says you're very talented for your age, and she hopes you decide to stay on."

For all of Friday, Polly was in a fog of misery. She didn't even cheer up when she got a letter from Daddy. He told her he was bored in Winnipeg, but soon they would be together again. "I hope that boarding school is better than you expected," he finished. "I know you will be my brave girl and take advantage of this wonderful opportunity to learn and grow. Please write and tell me all about it."

Polly couldn't write back to Daddy. She couldn't think. All she wanted was to curl up on her bed with Tarka and weep with disappointment.

CHAPTER SIX

A NOT SO HAPPY BIRTHDAY

POLLY KNEW SHE HAD TO TALK TO NONI ABOUT HER DILEMMA, but she couldn't bear to bring it up until Saturday morning.

"Oh, Noni, I don't know what to do!" she wailed. After she'd told her, Noni handed her a handkerchief. Polly blew her nose and waited.

"I already know," said Noni. "Miss Guppy telephoned me yesterday and tried to persuade me to let you stay on the weekends."

"She phoned you? But she said it was up to *me* to decide!"

"That's what I told her, Polly. Now, let's discuss this calmly. I've heard of Frieda Falconer. I've even gone to one of her exhibitions in Vancouver. She's an excellent artist, hen. I can't believe she's agreeing to teach you!"

"I really liked her," said Polly. "She's friendly and interesting and she praised my drawing! She's going to teach us oil painting and pastels and even working with clay. But oh, Noni, how can I not come home every weekend? I know there's no boat on Saturday nights, but couldn't I just come on Sundays?"

"You know that wouldn't work, hen. You'd just have to go back a few hours later."

Polly pounded the bed with her fist. "I *hate* St. Winifred's! It's bad enough to have to stay during the week!"

Noni took her hand. "I don't have to tell you how much I'll miss you if you become a full-time boarder. We all will! But try to think about this clearly. You'd be home for Thanksgiving, your half-term holiday in November, and Christmas—that's once a month. And what an opportunity for you. To study with such an accomplished artist."

"So what should I *do*?"

Noni looked grave. "That's up to you, hen. Tomorrow you'll turn thirteen. I think you're old enough to make your own decision. I promise you I'll accept it, whatever it is."

"But—"

Noni waved away the rest of her words. "Why don't you go to your room and make a list? Write down all the pros and cons, and tell me your decision before lunch. Then you can enjoy your party." She kissed Polly's forehead. "And I have a wonderful surprise for you!"

Polly didn't feel at all old enough. She climbed onto her bed and squeezed Tarka so hard he jumped off.

She didn't need to write a list; there were only two considerations, and they both involved giving up something. Either she lost being on the island every weekend, or she lost the opportunity to have lessons from a real artist who was inspiring and supportive and made her feel special.

What would Noni want her to do? And Daddy, and Maud? Polly knew the answer. But was that what *she* wanted?

I can go to art school after I graduate, she tried to tell herself. *Then*

I'll learn all the things Miss Falconer is going to teach us. And I'm only going to stay at the school for a year, anyway.

It was no use. Polly's deepest desire was to be an artist. How could she turn down such an opportunity?

She trudged downstairs and found Noni in the dining room, setting the table for the party. "I've decided," she said woodenly. "I'll be a full-time boarder so I can take special art."

"Oh, hen!" To Polly's surprise, her grandmother's eyes were teary. "I'm so proud of you. You're putting your future needs ahead of your present comfort. That's a true sign of growing up."

"I don't *want* to do it!" cried Polly. "I just can't help it."

"In many ways I don't want you to, either. You're very young to be away from home so much, and I'll miss you terribly. But you've made the right choice. Think of how lucky you are to receive such good training so young. I wish *I'd* been able to study art. You'll be very glad one day that you've made this decision." Noni hugged her. "What a brave, sensible lassie you are! Now I must telephone Miss Guppy and talk about the extra fees. You'll need more clothing for Sundays, as well." She bustled to the telephone.

Polly fled to the beach with Tarka. Already she regretted her decision.

Polly sat at the head of the table with a mound of presents in front of her. She gazed at the smiling faces of her family and friends, and tried to smile back. Then she noticed that there was an empty chair.

"Surprise!" Maud pranced into the room from the kitchen and engulfed Polly in a hug.

"*Maud!* I thought you couldn't come!"

Maud pried off Polly's arms and added a small present to the pile. "I thought I couldn't, either, but then my class was cancelled. Noni and I decided I'd surprise you."

"How well you look, Maud!" said Aunt Jean.

Biddy and Vivien gaped at her as she sat down. Maud glowed with self-assurance. She wore a blue suit that emphasized her curves. Her thick bob of hair was curled into even waves. Around her neck was a strand of pearls, and she even wore earrings.

"How's university treating you?" Uncle Rand asked.

"Let's talk about that later," said Maud. "This is *Polly's* day! Aren't you going to open your presents?"

Opening presents, blowing out thirteen candles, and enjoying her favourite cake lifted Polly's gloom for a time. Maud's small box revealed a set of the china dogs that Polly collected. Biddy and Vivien had pooled their money and bought her some green barrettes. Aunt Jean had knitted Polly her annual sweater—this year it was pink. Mrs. Hooper had wrapped up a movie magazine, which Biddy and Vivien immediately seized. Daddy had sent some handkerchiefs all the way from Winnipeg. They were embroidered with her initials. Gregor and Sadie had sent a book called *National Velvet.*

Then Noni handed Polly a blue velvet box. Inside was a short strand of pearls. "Oh, Noni, they're beautiful," breathed Polly, running the cool beads through her fingers.

"They belonged to my mother," said Noni. "I offered them to *your* mother once, but she didn't want them. They're only to be worn for special occasions."

"Thank you!" said Polly. She'd never owned anything so grown-up. Daddy had bought Maud her pearls in the days before the crash, when he had a steady job. Now Polly had some, too!

"Time for bumps!" shouted Vivien. She and Biddy and Maud seized Polly and bumped her on the carpet thirteen times. Polly laughed so hard she thought she'd throw up her cake.

———

After the guests went home, the family had a light supper. Maud chattered about university all through the meal.

"Well, you certainly seem to like it," said Aunt Jean, after Maud had regaled them with stories about her courses and the residence and frosh dances and rushing for the sorority. "Are you sure you're eating enough, chickie? You've slimmed down."

Maud chuckled. "I needed to, don't you think? Yes, I'm getting plenty to eat. The food's as terrible as it was at St. Winnie's, but Ann and I buy sausages and cook them over the fireplace in the lounge."

"I don't know how you have time to study with all those activities," said Noni.

Maud shrugged. "I only have five courses—that seems so few compared with school."

Polly listened to her answer Uncle Rand's question about her history professor. She didn't mind sharing Maud with the others; she'd have her all to herself later.

"Polly, aren't you going to tell everyone your decision?" Noni asked.

Polly was trying not to think about it. "I've decided to be a full-time boarder, because I want to take special art and it's only on Saturdays," she muttered.

Maud beamed at her. "You're going to board full time? That's swell, Doodle! The boarders have so much fun on the weekends. You'll love it."

"Polly's art teacher is Frieda Falconer," Noni told them. "She's a well-known Canadian artist."

"What a wonderful opportunity, chickie!" said Aunt Jean.

"But it will be hard for you not to come home," said Uncle Rand gently.

Polly gave him a sad smile. He was the only one who understood.

—————

As usual when Maud was home, she came into Polly's room and sat on the bed to chat.

"How's school?" she asked immediately, as Tarka demanded that she rub his tummy. "I enjoyed your letter, but you didn't tell me how you liked it."

What could Polly say? Maud had loved boarding school. She wouldn't understand any of the things Polly hated about it.

Polly shrugged. "It's okay, I guess."

"Are my friends looking out for you?"

Polly nodded.

"Tell me more about your roommates! Who's your homeroom teacher?"

Polly didn't want to waste one minute talking about school, but she had to tell Maud all about the Fearless Four and the Hornet.

"I miss St. Winnie's sometimes," said Maud, "but it's fabulous to be so free. There are no bells and no rules, and I can wear my own clothes. We have a nightly curfew, but apart from that I can do what I want."

Maud's face was thinner, which made her long nose and strong chin stand out even more confidently. "You look so happy," Polly said.

"I am! Oh, Doodle, everything was so *hard* before! Being so poor, all the trouble about Daddy, moving here . . . Now Daddy is almost free, and I adore U.B.C. And . . . oh, Poll—I think I'm in love! But don't tell Noni about Robert yet. I'll write to her about him. I may bring him home for Thanksgiving. Then you'll be able to meet him." She spoke as if that were an enormous privilege.

"I like your hair," said Polly. "How did you get it so even?"

"It's called a 'marcel wave.' Ann did it with her curling iron." Maud appraised Polly. "Doodle, don't you think it's about time you cut *your* hair? It would wave naturally, not like mine."

"Cut my hair? But Daddy—"

"Daddy wouldn't care. He didn't mind when *I* got a bob. Do it, Poll! I could cut it for you tomorrow."

"No!" Polly frowned. "I like it long and so do Daddy and Noni." As soon as she said that, however, she thought of how she was the only one at school with long hair.

"You're so pretty, Poll, but you'd look even prettier with a bob. Will you at least think about it?"

"Oh, all right. Maybe I'll do it one day, but not yet." They grinned at each other. "By the way, Maud, Miss Guppy told me to remind you to write to her."

Maud looked guilty. "I keep putting it off. I went to her church and I hated it! All they talked about was how sinful we were. I . . ." Maud hesitated.

"What?"

"Well, it's hard to admit this after how certain I was before, but I don't feel the same about religion as I did at school. Robert has to go to church with his family, but he told me he's an agnostic."

"What's *that*?"

"It means he doesn't know for sure if God exists. We have long arguments about it. I don't agree with him—I *absolutely* believe in God. But the Guppy's God is so black and white. I think he's a lot more mysterious and complicated. But I can't tell her that."

"Why don't you just write her a short note and don't say anything about religion at all," suggested Polly.

"I guess I could, but I know she'll suspect something." Then Maud laughed. "But you know what, Poll? She's not in charge of me anymore!"

Polly shuddered. "You're lucky."

"Are you all right about deciding to be a full-time boarder?" Maud asked. "You're so attached to the island I know you'll miss coming home."

"I don't want to do it, but if I want to be an artist I *have* to," said Polly.

"Good for you! Daddy would be so proud. Have any of the girls asked about him being cleared?"

"Not yet. But some of them know, I think. They give me strange looks."

"Just ignore them. I've told Ann all about Daddy, and I'm sure lots of my other friends know, but they're too polite to mention it. Oh, Doodle, in a few months we'll see him again!"

After Maud left, Polly pulled Tarka up to lie on her pillow so she could breathe in his skunky smell and stroke his soft ears. She wouldn't be able to cuddle with him again until Thanksgiving.

"Oh, Tarka, I *hate* turning thirteen!" she whispered. Already it seemed like an unlucky number.

———

Miss Guppy pumped Polly's hand so hard it hurt. "Good for you, my dear!" she barked. "You won't regret this. I'll telephone Miss Falconer right away and let her know. You're going to love being here all the time, I promise." She gazed at Polly hungrily, like a spider that had caught her prey.

Alice approved, as well. Polly told her on Monday, when they were both supposed to be practising. "That's absolutely the best decision!" she said warmly. "We're so lucky, aren't we?"

"What do you mean?"

"We both know what we want to do when we grow up, and we're already getting good training for it." Twice a week, Alice went to singing lessons.

"I guess you're right," said Polly slowly, "but I wish I didn't have to stay on the weekends to do it."

"You'll get used to it," said Alice. "The boarders get taken to concerts and plays sometimes—even movies." She thumped Polly's back. "Cheer up, Goldilocks! This is good news, not bad!"

That night Polly had another cake and candles before bedtime. The Fearless Four had asked the school cook to make it for a surprise.

"I'm so glad you'll be with us all the time now, Poll," said Daisy, after they had sung to her. "Now we're *really* the Fearless Four!"

Polly tried to share their enthusiasm.

———————

The next day after school, Mrs. Blake took Polly downtown on the streetcar to buy her the clothes she needed for Sundays. "You need a navy wool dress," she told her in the store.

"How about this one?" Polly held up a dress with yellow polka dots on its short sleeves and collar.

Mrs. Blake examined her list. "I'm afraid not, love. It says long-sleeved, with no coloured trimmings." She found a dress that was so plain that it made Polly feel erased. At least she liked the shoes, which had something called "Cuban heels."

"Can I get silk stockings?" she asked hopefully.

"No silk stockings until the lower fifth," said Mrs. Blake, picking out some wool ones.

Polly wouldn't be here then. Buying this dress was just as much a waste as having bought the rest of her uniform.

Before, they went back to the school, they had tea at the store restaurant. They munched on scones and jam while Mrs. Blake told Polly that she had a two-year-old boy.

"But who looks after him?" Polly asked. "Your husband?"

"His father is dead," said Mrs. Blake briskly. "Johnny stays with my landlady, and I see him on my days off. I wish I could find a job where I could come home at night, but I'm lucky to have one at all these days."

"That's terrible!" said Polly. "You must really miss him."

"I think of him every moment . . . but that's just the way things are." Mrs. Blake smiled. "Maybe one day I'll bring Johnny to school to meet you all."

How could she be so cheerful all the time? Polly wondered. She squirmed. Having to be a full-time boarder seemed so trivial a problem in comparison. The closer Friday came, however, the more miserable she felt about not being able to go home.

CHAPTER SEVEN

A VERY LONG WEEKEND

On Friday Daisy, Rhoda, and Eleanor eagerly told Polly
all that was to happen the next day.

"First we have prep," said Eleanor.

"Prep on a Saturday?" said Polly.

"It's only for an hour," said Daisy. "Then we can do what we
want for the rest of the morning. After lunch, they take us somewhere—to the beach or shopping. But that's when you'll be at your
art class, Poll."

"The matron cooks us supper and we all help," said Rhoda. "Last
week Mrs. Blake made us something called 'toad in the hole'—it was
scrumptious! But this weekend Miss Poirier's on, so it will probably
be something ghastly."

At breakfast the next morning Polly looked around the dining
room. "Where's Miss Guppy?" she asked. The headmistress wasn't
there.

"She goes out on Saturdays—I don't know where. But she comes
back after supper."

"Tonight she's taking us to a concert," said Daisy.

"It sounds boring," said Rhoda. "I'm not going."

"I am," said Eleanor. "Are you, Poll?"

"I guess so," said Polly.

At least they were allowed to wear their own clothes today. Polly had put on her oldest skirt and blouse, to be ready for art.

After prep, Daisy led them over to the gym. They took turns throwing baskets and tried climbing the ropes. Daisy and Rhoda were much better than Eleanor and Polly.

"Race you to the playing field!" said Daisy.

They collapsed at the far end of the field and lay on their backs. The other three began pointing out cloud animals.

"There's a horse," said Rhoda. "Did you know that I take riding lessons at home? I won second prize in a jumping competition last year."

"Really?" said Daisy. She and Eleanor asked Rhoda questions, but Polly refused to be impressed. Instead, she wondered what Biddy and Vivien were doing this morning. Would they be walking Bramble? Would they take Tarka along?

"You're awfully quiet, Poll," said Eleanor.

Polly swallowed her threatening tears and tried to think of something to say . . . "Guess what? Mrs. Blake has a little boy!"

They all sat up. "*Really?*"

Polly told them what she knew.

"What a shame she's on her own," said Daisy. "Did she say how her husband died?"

Polly shook her head. "We could ask her sometime."

"She's so nice," said Rhoda. "We're lucky to have her instead of the Crab." That was what everyone called Miss Poirier.

"Are you ready, Polly?" Dottie came up to the lunch table. "We should leave for Miss Falconer's in five minutes."

"Should I bring anything?" Polly asked her. "I have a sketch-book and pencils and my watercolours."

"Miss Guppy said that all our supplies are provided."

How free it felt simply to walk down the driveway! They made their way to the streetcar stop. When the streetcar arrived, they boarded at the front, paid their fare, and found two seats. The car rattled away from the school.

Polly was in awe sitting beside someone from the upper sixth form. But Dottie seemed a jolly girl, relaxed and friendly. "I knew your sister," she said. "She was so perfect she must be hard to live up to."

Polly nodded; at last someone recognized that. "Maud's wonderful, but we're really different from each other," she said shyly.

"Of course you are! My older sister couldn't be more different from *me*—she wants to be a nun! She isn't even Catholic, but she's going to convert. My parents are fit to be tied."

Dottie chattered all the way, and all Polly had to do was listen. Finally, they reached their stop. Dottie consulted her directions. "Let's see . . . we go three blocks down here, then turn right . . . now left . . . here's Morris Street . . . and here's number 32. It looks like her house faces the sea."

They stopped in front of a ramshackle cottage on the water side of the road. Honeysuckle draped the porch, where several pots overflowed with purple asters.

"Come in—come in!" said Miss Falconer, opening the door. "The other girls have already arrived." She wore red slacks and a loose yellow tunic. A cigarette dangled from her fingers. Polly smiled; that reminded her of Aunt Jean.

Miss Falconer led them through untidy rooms to the back of the house, which was a large studio. Beyond it was the water, with steps leading down to a log-covered beach.

"Gosh, what a view!" said Dottie.

Polly stared hungrily; it was so soothing to see the sea again.

"Yes, we're very lucky to live here."

The five girls glanced at one another, but no one was brave enough to ask why Miss Falconer had said ".we."

"Now, let me show you around." The walls were lined with bright paintings. Polly examined them curiously: some were landscapes, but many were simply swirls of colour.

"Those are called 'abstracts,'" Miss Falconer explained, "and here are some of my sculptures." Clay figures of birds and animals and people covered the floor and windowsill.

Some of the paintings and many of the sculptures were nude figures. Jane turned crimson and Dottie suppressed a giggle. Polly just stared. Never in her life had she seen depictions of unclothed bodies.

"I've managed to clear this table for you," said Miss Falconer. "Everyone take a seat, and I'll tell you what we'll do today."

Just like last week, they were to work on their own and then critique one another. Miss Falconer had set up a still life of fruit in a bowl. She handed out sticks of charcoal. "You won't be able to erase, so think carefully before each mark you make," she told them.

Polly had never used charcoal. She started with one of the apples, observing it so intently that it filled her mind. Then she drew its whole circumference in one long stroke. As she continued, her hands and face and blouse became smudged with black.

"I can't start," said Jane. "I'm too afraid of making a mistake."

"Just plunge in, dear," said Miss Falconer. "There *are* no mistakes! You don't have to make an exact representation."

What would Miss Netherwood think of that? thought Polly as she gleefully experimented with lines and shading. Beside her, Katherine was pressing so hard she kept breaking her charcoal.

Once again, Polly forgot about everything but what she was drawing. Once again, her work was heartily praised. At the end of the class, something deep and quiet inside her said she had made the right decision.

Miss Falconer laughed. "Look at my dirty girls! Go and wash up, and I'll bring you tea."

After they'd dusted their clothes and scrubbed off the charcoal, they sat in front of a fireplace at the far end of the studio. Miss Falconer poured them tea and passed around a plate of buns filled with chocolate. She showed them pictures of charcoal drawings from a book. Polly longed to leaf through the rest of the pages, and the many other volumes of art that filled a bookcase and spilled over the floor.

"Whom do we have here?" said a booming voice. A man came into the studio. He was bald, with a long, deeply lined face.

"This is Mr. de Jonge," said Miss Falconer. "Frans, these are my students from St. Winifred's—Dottie, Margaret, Jane, Katherine, and Polly."

Mr. de Jonge solemnly shook each of their hands.

"Would you like some tea?" Miss Falconer asked him.

He poured himself a cup and took two buns, but remained standing. "I'll take these upstairs. I need to finish this chapter before we go out tonight. I am charmed to meet you, young ladies!" He spoke with an accent, and his hooded eyes showed amusement.

"Mr. de Jonge is a novelist," Miss Falconer explained proudly, after he'd left. "His writing room is on the top floor, away from all my messes."

No one knew what to say. Finally, Dottie asked, "Does he rent it from you?"

"Rent?" Miss Falconer laughed merrily. "Oh, no, Mr. de Jonge *lives* here. We're a couple."

Dottie bravely broke the silence. "I hope you don't think this is rude, Miss Falconer, but why do you have different last names?"

"Because we're not married," said Miss Falconer calmly. "I know that's bohemian of us, but we've never seen the point of marriage." She paused. "It's best if you don't tell Miss Guppy, however. She won't want her young ladies exposed to such immorality."

Dottie grinned and Jane looked nervous. Polly was both shocked and thrilled. This was like one of Aunt Jean's romantic novels!

"Don't worry, Miss Falconer. We won't say a word," said Dottie.

Now they all shared a secret; they gazed at one another with importance.

"Isn't she remarkable?" said Dottie on the way home. "I wonder what the day girls will say to their parents. Mine wouldn't like it, but I just won't tell them. Will you?"

"Umm, I don't know . . ." said Polly. Noni would definitely disapprove, but perhaps Daddy wouldn't care.

"I think Miss Falconer is really brave going against convention like that," continued Dottie, "and she's an awfully good teacher. We're lucky to have her, aren't we?"

Polly nodded, feeling as if she had just visited a new and beautiful country.

Walking through the stone gates of the school felt like passing from summer into winter. Polly trudged up to the dorm to change out of her grimy clothes.

The other three were sitting on Rhoda's bed, poring over a photograph album.

"Hi, Poll!" said Daisy. "Rhoda's showing us some snaps of her holiday in France. How was art?"

"What did you *do* there?" asked Rhoda, making a face. "You're filthy!"

"Charcoal drawing," said Polly shortly.

"Was it fun?" said Daisy.

Polly just nodded. "Fun" seemed such a tame word to describe the afternoon.

"What exactly *is* 'charcoal'?" said Eleanor. "How do you use it?"

Polly explained that she didn't know what it was made of. Then her voice warmed as she told them about sketching the fruit.

"That doesn't sound very hard," said Rhoda. "In *my* art class we did still lifes with oil paints."

"Does Miss Falconer have a nice house?" said Daisy.

"Yes . . . she has a big studio that overlooks the sea. And guess what . . . she lives with a man and they aren't married!"

"Wow!" The others listened avidly while Polly described Frans.

"Isn't that against the law?" said Daisy.

Eleanor laughed. "It's not against the law—it's called 'common law.' A couple on our street live like that. My mother is friendly to them, but no one else is."

"It's not *right*," said Rhoda. "I can't believe Miss Guppy would let you take art from someone like that, Polly."

"Miss Guppy doesn't know," said Polly, "and don't you dare tell her, Rhoda! What does it matter? What Miss Falconer does is her own business, not anyone else's."

Rhoda shrugged. "Why would I tell her? I still think it's wrong, though."

"*I* think it's really interesting," said Eleanor. "I wonder why some people don't get married."

"Miss Falconer told us they'd never seen the point of it," said Polly.

Everyone was silent, digesting this new information.

———

The Crab crabbily cooked scrambled eggs for supper. The girls helped wash and dry the dishes. Then Miss Guppy appeared at the door. She had a strange, intense look in her eyes.

Polly realized where she'd been all day. Maud had told her that, every Saturday, Miss Guppy attended a different church from the one the school went to on Sundays, a church where people were "born again." Sometimes she took a few of the girls with her. When Maud was here, she herself had been born again. She had driven Polly mad by trying to convert her, as well.

Polly smiled. What would the Guppy think if she knew that Maud was loosening her beliefs?

"Those of you who are attending the concert, change into your best clothes," ordered Miss Guppy. "In half an hour, two taxis will arrive to take us downtown."

Polly changed once again. She put on clean white socks, and held back her hair with her new barrettes.

"You look so pretty in that dress," Daisy told her.

Polly flushed. She *felt* pretty in the green print dress she wore to church at home. She wished she could wear her fitted blue Sunday coat, as well, instead of this shapeless grey one.

"How do you like *my* dress, Dais?" Rhoda asked. "It's from a department store in Seattle."

Rhoda had changed her mind about coming. "I don't want to be here all by myself," she told them. "But I wish we were going to a movie instead of a recital. I read in Mrs. Blake's paper that *Hopalong Cassidy* is playing."

Nine boarders had chosen to go. Miss Guppy inspected them in the hall. "Very nice, girls. Now, I'm sure you all know how to behave at a concert, but let me remind you—no talking, not even whispering, until it's over. Sit perfectly still, and only clap when everyone else does. Is that clear?"

"Yes, Miss Guppy," they chorused.

Polly didn't say that she'd never even been to a concert.

Alice was squished beside her in the taxi. "I'm so excited!" she told Polly. "My singing teacher said that this group is really good."

The girls spilled out of the taxis and followed Miss Guppy into the theatre. Someone handed them programs, then they walked up to the second level and took their seats in the balcony.

Below them, a piano player and two violinists played opera selections. A majestic woman with a powerful voice joined the three musicians. Polly liked the music, but she found the singing too dramatic. She couldn't take her eyes off the singer, however; she wore a blue sparkling dress that was cut so low you could see her bosom!

To their astonishment, Miss Guppy produced a box of chocolates at intermission. The group stood in the upper lobby and sampled them. Polly let one melt in her mouth, savouring its creamy sweetness.

"Do you like the concert, Polly?" Alice asked her. "I think it's terrific!"

"Sort of," said Polly. "But why does the singer have to go so high? It hurts my ears!"

Alice laughed. "That's just opera. That's what I'm going to do one day, you know!"

"You are?" Polly gazed at her with awe. Then she chose another chocolate, wandered over to the railing, and watched all the people milling below her.

"Hi, Polly!"

A boy in a school uniform stood beside her. Chester! Polly swallowed her chocolate so fast she almost choked.

"What are *you* doing here?" she gasped.

Chester grinned. "Same as you! I'm on a school outing. We're not allowed to stay, though. Some of the fellows were making fun of the singer's—well, umm . . . anyway, we were fooling around, so we have to leave after intermission."

Polly giggled. "Her dress *is* kind of low!"

She was so happy to see him her legs were wobbly. Chester looked so spiffy in his navy blazer, white shirt, and red tie.

"How do you like St. Winifred's?" he asked.

"Polly Brown!" Miss Guppy's bark was so loud that people turned their heads. She advanced towards them.

"Oh-oh!" said Chester. "See you at Thanksgiving, I hope!"

He fled before Miss Guppy arrived.

Her face was thunderous. "Who was that boy you were talking to?" she quizzed.

"Just Chester," whispered Polly.

"And who is 'Chester'?"

"He's a boy from home. He goes to St. Cuthbert's."

Miss Guppy grabbed Polly's arm and yanked her back to the other girls. "You are *not* to talk to boys, even if you know them! Do you understand, Polly?"

"Yes, Miss Guppy," muttered Polly.

All through the second half, the other girls nudged her and grinned. Polly couldn't smile back. The concert was ruined. Why *shouldn't* she talk to Chester? They were friends! But she had been snatched away from him as if he were an alien species.

"Who was that boy?" whispered Daisy after lights out. It was the Crab's night on, so they had to keep their voices low.

"Chester Simmons," said Polly. "I know him from the island—we went to school together."

"Is he your *boyfriend*?" asked Rhoda in a mincing voice.

"No!"

"*I* have a boyfriend. His name is Frank, and I think he really likes me. The day before I left, he rode his bike over to my house to say goodbye."

"Don't be silly, Rho—none of us are old enough to have boyfriends," said Eleanor calmly. She yawned. "Let's go to sleep."

But Polly tossed for hours. Her mind raced with everything that had happened that day. Of *course* Chester wasn't her boyfriend! But she had to admit she'd had special feelings for him since she was ten. How wonderful it had been to see him, and how cruel to have their conversation cut short! But Chester had said he hoped to see her at Thanksgiving. Maybe she would have the courage to ask him to do something, like go for a walk or a boat ride.

Polly went over every detail of being at Miss Falconer's. She pondered the novelty of living with someone and not being married. What *was* the point of marriage? Uncle Rand might say it was something to do with God. Sadie, who had married Gregor in August, might say it was to wear a beautiful dress and have a joyful party afterwards. Noni would say it was about commitment.

Do I want to get married? Polly wondered. She decided that she did. Then she thought of the loving way Miss Falconer had talked about Mr. de Jonge. Perhaps you could be committed to someone even if you *weren't* married.

Her mind went back to the class again and she fell asleep sketching an apple.

———

The next morning, Polly was called into Miss Guppy's study. Once more, Miss Guppy told Polly she was never to talk to boys on a school outing.

"But I didn't know he was going to be there!" said Polly.

"Don't talk back, young lady. That's no excuse. While you are at school, I am your guardian. I want you to promise me you will never do this again."

"Yes, Miss Guppy," muttered Polly. *What a stupid fuss over nothing!* she thought as she got ready for church.

The twenty-eight boarders walked in a crocodile down the hill to St. Matthew's Anglican Church. Polly thought they looked like nuns, in their identical outfits: navy-blue dresses, maroon blazers, mustard-coloured felt hats, and white gloves. As her roommates had warned, everyone in the congregation stared when the girls trooped up the aisle and slid into the front pews.

The service was much as it was on the island. Instead of mild

Uncle Rand leading it, however, a lugubrious rector named Canon
Puddifoot preached as if his own words made him tired.

If only this were home! Polly thought. Aunt Jean would be sitting
beside her, commenting on someone's hat, while Noni shushed her.
At coffee time, Polly and Biddy and Vivien would giggle in a corner.

As the congregation came out of church, a scruffy man
approached them and held out his hand. "Please, can you spare a
penny or two?" he asked. "I'm so hungry!"

"Poor thing," said Eleanor. "I wish we could help him but I gave
all my change to the collection."

Polly looked around: Miss Guppy was talking to Canon Puddifoot. She dug in her pockets and found a nickel. They went up to the
man and Polly held out the money.

"Thank you, Miss!" he said.

"You're welcome," said Polly. The man's desperate expression
reminded her of Daddy when he had been so poor.

"I'm sorry that's all we have," said Eleanor.

"Eleanor and Polly! Get into line at once!" bellowed Miss Guppy.

They scurried over and joined the crocodile. "I will see both of
you in my study immediately after lunch," snapped the Guppy.

"What did you *do*?" whispered Daisy on the way back.

"Nothing worth fussing about, but she'll think so," said Eleanor.

Sunday lunch, at least, was a welcome change from the rest of
the week's food: roast beef and Yorkshire pudding. For dessert there
was treacle tart and cream. Polly gobbled up two helpings to cushion
the coming lecture.

"What did you two think you were up to, talking to a tramp?"
thundered Miss Guppy as soon as they had closed the door. "Did you
give him money?"

Polly gulped and nodded.

"He was hungry," said Eleanor.

"He was a dirty, disreputable beggar!" spat the headmistress. "You are not to speak to *anyone* when you are out, do you understand? Polly, I thought I had already made that clear."

She told them they were not allowed to have any dessert or treats from their tuck boxes for the whole week. "If I ever catch you speaking to strangers again, there will be far more serious consequences," she finished.

The Guppy's stinging words had been much more severe than the punishment. "She makes me feel so guilty, when we did nothing wrong!" said Eleanor, once they were back in the dorm.

After lunch, they had to lie on their beds for a full hour to nap or read. Then they were sent downstairs to sit in the dining room and write letters home. Polly scribbled short notes to Noni, Maud, and Daddy. She yearned to tell them about Miss Guppy's unfairness, but all she wrote was how interesting special art had been. "I can hardly wait to see you again," she ended each letter, blinking away tears.

Mrs. Blake was on duty today; she and Miss Poirier alternated on Saturdays and Sundays. "How is your little boy?" Polly asked her.

"Thank you for your interest, love. Johnny is thriving—he's talking in sentences now."

Mrs. Blake sent them upstairs to sort out their laundry and polish their oxfords for tomorrow. Each boarder had a laundry bag marked with her name. Polly's gloom lessened as she shoved her charcoal-coated clothes into it. At least next week she could go back to Miss Falconer's again.

It was another crisp, clear day. Polly wished she and Eleanor could escape to their hideaway, but for an hour before dinner all the boarders had to gather in the sitting room with Miss Guppy. She read them a passage from the Bible, then quizzed them about it.

"Why did the same people always answer?" said Daisy, while they were waiting for dinner.

"That's the Guppy's special group," Polly explained. "Some of the girls call them 'the Elect.' Maud belonged to it. Be careful not to join it if the Guppy asks you."

"*I* never would," said Rhoda. "It's bad enough having to go to church every week! At home we only went at Christmas and Easter."

"You did?" The others looked at Rhoda curiously, but lots of things about her were different; that was probably because she was American.

After dinner, they had free time in the sitting room. Polly played chess with Eleanor.

"You're good!" said Eleanor.

"My father taught me," said Polly sadly. She thought of the tramp again. Did he get enough money for a meal?

Gwen Pritchard strummed a ukulele and crooned "Cheek to Cheek." Two girls got up and danced while others sang along.

Polly was relieved when Mrs. Blake announced that it was time for the junior dorm to get ready for bed. The weekend had seemed more like a month than two short days.

CHAPTER EIGHT

A VERY LONG TERM

THE REST OF THE CHRISTMAS TERM PLODDED BY IN ITS TEDIOUS sameness. By Thanksgiving, Polly had received two more order marks: one for being late for French and another from Miss Netherwood. Polly had been trying to think of drawing as math, something unpleasant she simply had to get through. It had nothing to do with *real* art, nothing to do with the absorbing, wondrous world she entered every Saturday.

But one afternoon, while they were supposed to be cross-hatching an apple, she felt defiant. At first her apple was exactly like the one Miss Netherwood had demonstrated on the board, its form shaded in tiny crossed lines. But then Polly added a flowing stem and leaves. She drew a table for the apple to sit on, a window framing the sea behind it, and a leaping whale.

Polly gazed at the result with satisfaction. *This* would prove to Miss Netherwood that drawing the same apple as everyone else was a waste of Polly's talent!

When Miss Netherwood saw the drawing, however, she was not impressed. "Polly Brown! What *do* you think you're doing? You are deliberately ignoring my instructions! I'm giving you an order mark."

At least the rest of the Fearless Four had received order marks by now. There were so many rules that they couldn't help breaking them. Eleanor had passed a teacher on the stairs. Daisy had been caught with a hole in one of her stockings, even though she had inked her leg underneath the hole. Rhoda could never remember not to talk in the hall.

Order marks only applied to school. In the boarding house, there were different punishments. When Rhoda giggled during evening prayers, she had to sit on a chair at the side for the rest of the week. The members of the junior dorm were not allowed into their tuck boxes for two weeks after Miss Poirier found the hoard of cookies they'd hidden behind the bathtub. On several nights the Crab caught them talking after lights out and ordered them downstairs to get barked at by Miss Guppy. Polly despised the Guppy's satisfied look when she made Daisy cry.

Each time Polly had to walk in a crocodile, every time the loud bell summoned her somewhere, every day that she sat in her stuffy classroom and glanced longingly at the grass and trees outside, she yearned to escape.

Her roommates had fewer complaints. Daisy and Rhoda had both got on their house basketball team. Now they were best friends. Every day after school, they chose games and practised together.

Polly and Eleanor had also become a pair. They retreated to their hideaway whenever they could, although now that the weather had turned colder and wetter, they didn't go as often.

"How can you bear it here?" Polly asked her one day, when the rain sluiced down and they were stuck in the dorm after classes.

Eleanor shrugged. "It's not that bad. I like the courses, and the other girls and some of the teachers are so *interesting.*"

Polly wished she could share Eleanor's rational way of examining everything as if it were a science experiment.

Special art was the life raft that rescued Polly every Saturday. Now they were doing oil painting. Even in her sleep, Polly dipped her brush into the luscious colours. Whenever she passed Dottie, Jane, Katherine, or Margaret, they exchanged smiles, as if they were part of a secret society. "How lucky you are!" Noni and Daddy wrote, after Polly described in detail what she'd done in art that week.

Every once in a while, Polly remembered she'd be taking art for only a year. Then she felt sad. But that made her appreciate Miss Falconer's classes even more.

Thanksgiving was late this year because of the general election. Polly waved eagerly as Kingfisher Island grew closer and closer. Beside her, Alice glowered. As soon as they had got on the steamer, she had turned into the cranky Alice who hated coming home. Polly had hoped Chester would be on the boat, too, but there was no sign of him.

The three tiny figures Polly had spotted on the wharf grew larger and clearer. Finally, after a whole month away from the island, Polly was in Noni's arms. Then she scooped up Tarka and kissed his wriggling body all over. Tarka started squealing.

"What a racket!" said Aunt Jean, giving her the next hug. "I've never heard him make that strange noise!"

"He missed me, didn't you Tarka-boy?" Polly kissed Uncle Rand. She gazed at her family, her eyes swimming.

"There, there, hen," said Noni. "Being away for so long has been hard for you, I know. But now you're home for three whole days, so let's just enjoy one another."

"Polly, I really need your help decorating the church tomorrow morning," said Aunt Jean. "Mildred is trying to take charge of it, but I told her we had to wait for you because you have such a good eye."

"I've just read a book you might like," said Uncle Rand.

Alice was led off by her stern mother. Polly walked home safely enclosed in her family. Arbutus bark crunched under her feet, and the lamps in Noni's windows gleamed through the dusk—"the gloaming," Aunt Jean called it. At least home never changed.

———

But it had. Maud arrived the next day at noon—with her new beau! "Why does *he* have to come?" Polly had protested when Noni had told her last night.

"She wants us to meet him. It seems very soon for that, though he sounds like a pleasant lad. We must make him feel at home."

Polly couldn't stop staring at Robert. He didn't at all resemble Clark Gable, and he wasn't nearly as handsome as Chester. His nose was bumpy and his eyes were too close together. He sat quietly in the living room as everyone appraised him. Patiently, he answered their questions, informing Noni that he was studying engineering and Aunt Jean that his father was an accountant.

"What religion are you?" asked Aunt Jean.

"My family is Presbyterian," he told her.

"That's what we were in Scotland!" said Aunt Jean approvingly.

But then she bridled as Maud patted Robert's knee. Maud just smiled complacently, as if Robert were her prize sheep. That's what he was like, Polly decided, a mild-mannered sheep with fair curly hair.

"We're going to take the rowboat to Boot Island," said Maud.

"I'll make us a picnic. See you at dinner, everyone!" She pulled Robert out of the room.

"Well!" said Aunt Jean. "She's being awfully forward with that young man, don't you think, Clara?"

"Maud is eighteen, Jean. I'm sure she's old enough to know how to behave properly." But Noni looked worried.

"Of course she is!" said Uncle Rand. "And Robert seems like a sensible chap."

"She was touching him inappropriately," said Aunt Jean, "and now they've gone off alone for the whole day!"

That meant Polly wouldn't see Maud until bedtime. She pushed Robert out of her mind as she called Tarka and ran down the road to Biddy's.

———

Biddy and Vivien were sitting on Biddy's bed, deep in a discussion about Donald, a boy who worked for Vivien's uncle.

They greeted Polly warmly, but then went back to talking about how Vivien could get Donald's attention. Polly tried to divert them. "Last week, Louise Curtis in the lower fifth hung out of her classroom window by her hands!" she told them. "Another girl dared her. Luckily, it was only the first storey. We all thought she'd be expelled, but Miss Guppy can't afford to expel anyone—she needs the money too much."

"That's interesting," said Biddy vaguely. "I know, Viv—you could offer to wash Donald's shirts."

"I did," said Vivien sadly. "He told me he does his own washing."

Polly and Biddy had been best friends ever since Polly had come to the island. Vivien had arrived later, and she had always been the third wheel. But now, it seemed, that was Polly's role. "Do you want to go for a walk on the beach?" she asked them.

"No, thanks," said Biddy. "Vivien's going to try a freckle cure on my face. You're welcome to stay, of course."

Welcome to stay? Biddy had never had to say that; Polly had been in and out of her house freely since the day they met.

They went down to the kitchen to look for vinegar and oatmeal. Polly watched for a few minutes. Then she muttered, "I have to go now," and fled.

───────

Polly spent the rest of the afternoon on the beach with her watercolours. She was so absorbed that she didn't notice how cold her hands were until she had trouble holding the brush.

She inspected her four paintings, which were drying on a log. After doing oils, it was difficult to get used to watercolours again, but two of the paintings were quite good. She decided to take them back to school and show them to Miss Falconer.

All during dinner, Maud talked about Delta Gamma, the sorority that had accepted her. "I'm learning bridge!" she told them. "We play every afternoon at the D.G. house. Robert is coaching me," she said with a smile. "He and his parents and I have a game every Sunday before dinner."

Polly felt something under the tablecloth. She thought Tarka was begging, and looked down to scold him. It was Maud—she was rubbing Robert's leg with her foot!

Robert politely asked how Polly liked St. Winifred's. "Maud must be a hard act to follow!" he joked, but Polly didn't smile.

Finally, it was time for bed. Robert was sleeping in the small room on the main floor. When Polly came back from the privy, she glanced towards the bedroom door—and stopped short.

Maud and Robert were kissing! His hand was on her bottom! Their mouths stayed together for a long time.

Polly coughed, and the couple sprang apart. "Good night, sweetie!" said Maud, before she and Polly climbed the stairs.

"Doodle, I'm too tired for a chat," Maud said when they reached the top. "Let's talk tomorrow, all right?"

Polly was so shocked that all she could do was nod.

———

Polly never did get a chance to be alone with Maud. All during the Thanksgiving service and the bountiful meal that followed it, Maud's attention was entirely on Robert.

Biddy had smiled at Polly in church, but when Polly joined her and Vivien at coffee time, the other two were planning to spend the afternoon at Vivien's. "You can join us," they said, but Polly told them she was busy. She could tell that they didn't really want her there.

Alice came up and eagerly started a discussion about school. "I can hardly wait to get back, can't you? Do you want to go to the beach this afternoon?"

Polly shook her head; she would have to talk about St. Winifred's the whole time.

Instead, Polly helped Noni cover some of her shrubs with sacking for the winter. "This is kind of you, but don't you want to spend time with your friends?" she asked.

"They don't like me anymore," said Polly.

"Oh, hen!" Noni picked some dead leaves off Polly's sweater. "I'm so sorry they're leaving you out. It's natural that Biddy and Vivien would turn to each other. You're in different worlds now. Yet you and Biddy have always been such close friends. Why don't you try seeing her alone?"

"She only wants to be with Vivien."

Noni sighed. "How hard it is to be young. But don't look so gloomy. Tell me more about your art classes. What did you do last week?"

———

Maud and Robert were planning to have another Thanksgiving dinner with Robert's parents, so they left the island for Vancouver early Monday morning. Polly was glad to see them go. She put Tarka into her bike basket, rode to the lighthouse, and watched the waves dash against the rocks. Tarka snuffled over the sandstone, looking for otter doo to roll in.

Polly sat on the same log where Chester had kissed her. Not a disgusting kiss, like Maud and Robert's; a magical one. She touched her forehead, as if the kiss were still there.

The sea air smelled so fresh. There were no whales at this time of year, but a seal bobbed lazily near her. Overhead, some gulls attacked a bald eagle, which chittered them away. How could she bear to leave this tomorrow?

On the way home, she passed Biddy, her little sister Shirley, and Bramble coming out of their drive. "Polly!" called Biddy.

Polly stopped and they stared at each other. Tarka hopped out of the basket and rushed up to his mother. The two dogs chased each other down the road, Shirley shrieking after them.

"I'm sorry we didn't see each other much this weekend," muttered Biddy. "How's school?" she asked, but not as if she were really interested.

"Terrible as usual," said Polly, "though I like my Saturday art class. And guess what? My art teacher, Miss Falconer, lives with a man she's not married to!"

That got Biddy's full attention. *"Really?* Tell me more! Shirley, get out of the ditch!"

They caught up with Shirley and walked along the road, chatting all the way. Noni was right. When Vivien wasn't there, Polly and Biddy were still friends.

———

As soon as they all got back to school, the Fearless Four continued planning their skit for the boarders' Halloween party the next Saturday. They were acting out *Cinderella*. Polly was the main character because she was the only one with long hair.

In the drama cupboard, Polly had found a raggedy dress that she would uncover to reveal a long white satin gown that Mrs. Blake had shortened for her. Rhoda was an ugly stepsister and Eleanor was the prince. Daisy had two roles: the other sister and the fairy godmother. She had also written the play.

The party was in the dining room, with all the chairs pushed back, and pop and cookies for later arranged on the tables against the wall. The first performance was by the upper dorm, whose five members acted out being the Dionne quintuplets. Then the west dorm performed a lively cancan; they looked so glamorous in their fancy dresses and bright lipstick. The long dorm did a scene from a Shirley Temple movie. The east dorm came dressed in their Sunday coats, labelled either Italy or Ethiopia. With a loud cry and uplifted fists, the Italy group rushed the Ethiopia group and pinned them to the ground.

That was clever, Polly thought. And their skit was about current events, so they'd probably win.

Finally, it was the junior dorm's turn. To Polly's relief, she had very few lines; even so, she found it hard to gaze lovingly into Eleanor's moustached face without giggling. Daisy did an efficient job of whisking from one costume to the other. But Rhoda was the one who stole the show. She had the room roaring as she complained about her warts, or galumphed around in her oversized shoes.

To their amazement, they won! That meant they were allowed to go to a movie of their choice. Next Saturday afternoon, Mrs. Blake took them to see Laurel and Hardy's *Bonnie Scotland* at the Capital Theatre. Polly hadn't seen a movie since she'd lived in Winnipeg. She was as absorbed as the others, but watching the antics of Stan Laurel made her ache for Daddy; he had often imitated him.

The Fearless Four had now gained respect in the upper fourth classroom for being the only boarders. "You must have such larks!" Ivy told them one day at break.

"We do!" said Daisy. "We have pillow fights and sneak food into the dorm."

Polly didn't want Ivy to think that being a boarder was fun. "But the food is terrible, and we have to go to bed at nine o'clock!" she told her.

"Don't listen to Polly," said Rhoda. "The food isn't that bad, and we talk for ages after lights out."

"I wish *I* could be a boarder," said Ivy. "I've begged my parents, but they won't let me."

Rhoda looked smug. "That's too bad. You're missing a really good time."

Ivy walked away. "Why did you tell her that?" Polly asked Rhoda. "You said boarding school was like being in an army!"

"I don't think so anymore. Last week my parents were talking to Miss Guppy and she told them I've adjusted really well." Rhoda appraised Polly. "Maybe you're just too young for boarding school, and that's why *you* haven't adjusted."

Polly bristled. "I'm only a few months younger than you are, Rhoda!"

"I guess I'm just more mature, then," said Rhoda.

The bell for the end of break rang before Polly could think of a retort.

———

Polly still didn't contribute much to the long conversations after lights out, but she listened with interest one night when Daisy said, "Wasn't it awful when Edna Cooper fainted during assembly? She almost hit her head!"

"I wonder why people faint," said Eleanor.

"I bet I know," said Rhoda. She paused dramatically. "I bet Edna got her monthlies!"

"Really?" Daisy was scared. "Is that what happens when you get them? You faint?"

Now Rhoda sounded uncertain. "Maybe . . . I haven't started yet, so I don't know."

"Of course that's not what happens," said Eleanor. "I started menstruating last month, and I certainly didn't faint."

"You've had your period? Why didn't you tell us?" demanded Rhoda.

"I didn't think it was anyone's business," said Eleanor.

"You're the first one!" said Rhoda. "Unless you've started, Polly."

"Uh-uh," muttered Polly, glad it was dark so they couldn't see her hot cheeks.

"Tell us what it's like, El!" urged Rhoda.

Eleanor proceeded to tell them. She was as reassuring and calm as usual. Polly shuddered, however. She didn't want to take part in this strange grown-up ritual, but she had no choice.

Polly and Alice—and Chester, as well—were on the boat, going home for the half-term holiday in November. Polly sat with the other two in the lounge, listening to them chat about the inter-school debating competition. Chester had his back to Polly. He probably liked Alice more than her; after all, they were the same age.

Finally, Chester turned around. "I hope your headmistress didn't ream you out for talking to me at the concert," he said.

Polly grimaced. "She did! But I don't care."

"How do you like school so far?"

"I hate it—except for special art."

"You'll get used to it," said Alice.

That didn't help. Polly *was* used to it now, but it didn't mean she liked it any better.

"Why didn't you come home for Thanksgiving?" Alice asked Chester.

"My parents decided to visit Victoria, instead. We had a good time, but I'm excited about being on the island again."

"I'm not," said Alice glumly. They both looked at her with sympathy.

Maud was not able to come home this weekend. Polly was almost glad, since all Maud's letters were about two dreary subjects: Robert and the D.G.s.

Biddy wasn't there, either. She'd gone with her family to visit her relatives in Comox. Polly went for a bike ride with Vivien, but all she wanted to talk about was Donald. She listed for Polly all the indications that meant he liked her. "I think George likes Biddy, too," she said. "He keeps staring at her in church! Don't *you* have anyone you're sweet on?"

Polly shook her head.

"That's because you never see boys. Poor you . . . I'd *hate* to go to a girls school!"

Polly didn't want to tell her about Chester. The silly way Vivien giggled about Donald seemed so trivial compared with the special connection that she and Chester had. And they were just *friends*, Polly told herself firmly.

All the same, she felt a thrill that he was on the island, as well. She watched out for him wherever she went. Chester smiled at her in church, but she was disappointed when he walked away with his parents and didn't stay for coffee time.

At Sunday dinner, all that Polly's relatives could talk about was how Mr. and Mrs. Wyatt, the owners of the island hotel, had just put it up for sale.

"What are they thinking?" said Aunt Jean. "They'll never sell it in these hard times!"

"Addie Wyatt told me her father is ill. They're going to live in Vancouver and take care of him," said Noni. "But I agree with you, Jean. No one is going to buy it, and who will tend it after the Wyatts leave? It would be such a shame if it became derelict."

"Perhaps you should buy it back, Clara," suggested Uncle Rand.

Before she had come into her husband's money, Noni had once owned the hotel herself. "Buy it back?" She shook her head. "That would be far too much work. I'm too old!"

"You could hire someone to run it," said Uncle Rand. "There are plenty of couples who would jump at the chance."

"But why would Clara want to spend all that money?" asked Jean. "Really, Rand, you're very impractical sometimes."

As usual, the adults' talk buzzed around Polly, while she thought about far more important matters . . . like Chester's smile.

———

Too soon, Polly was back at school. After the house meeting one week, Babs took her aside. "Polly, you've received more order marks this term than anyone else! What would Maud think of you?"

"Sorry," muttered Polly. "I don't get them on purpose." *And I don't give a fig what Maud thinks,* she added to herself. *Maud doesn't care about me anymore—all she cares about is Robert.*

It was another soggy November day. The rain had thundered down all week and they were confined indoors, even for break. Polly felt like a caged animal. On days like this at home, she could snuggle with Tarka in front of the fire. Here, all the rooms were cold and drafty. Despite her woolly layers of tunic and blazer, she never felt warm.

On Monday she had sat in history and daydreamed about what she'd make in special art that week: now they were working with clay. She hadn't heard a question from the Hornet, and received an order mark. The next day she received another one when she dropped her math homework in a puddle.

Polly had now received eight order marks; that meant she had a conduct mark for the first five. But the numbers against her name in the hall no longer embarrassed her. The punishment for her conduct mark had been to clean all the classroom blackboards; that wasn't onerous.

"Let's see if we can think of how you can *gain* points for Sussex!" said Babs chirpily. "Why don't you try out for house basketball or debating or the school play?"

"I don't like any of those things," said Polly haughtily. What a prig Babs was, and how stupid houses were! She wasn't even going to be here next year, so why should she bother to gain house points? She tried to ignore the hurt look on Babs's face.

———

Polly cheered up when they began rehearsing Christmas carols for the school concert. That meant that soon she'd be able to go home for three whole weeks! And in early December, Noni and Aunt Jean came to Victoria for the weekend to do their Christmas shopping. Polly was allowed to spend all of Saturday with them. She hated missing special art, but she couldn't *not* see her family.

"Robert's mother wrote to me and asked if Maud could spend Christmas with them," said Noni as they ate their lunch at the hotel restaurant. "I don't know what she was thinking! It's not at all proper when they aren't even engaged. Maud has also asked me. But I've told her she has to come home."

"Good!" said Polly. "Are Gregor and Sadie coming, too?"

Aunt Jean shook her head. "They can't until New Year's. That's the problem with being a clergyman—Christmas is the busiest time of the year."

"Is there anything special you'd like for Christmas, hen?" Noni asked.

"I'd love some pastels," said Polly.

"And you need a new dress," said Aunt Jean. "You're getting so tall, chickie, that one is looking skimpy." Then she grinned. "There's something else you need, young lady—a brassiere!"

"Don't make her uncomfortable, Jean," said Noni. She smiled at Polly, as well. "But you *are* getting a figure, hen. After lunch we'll buy you a brassiere."

Polly blushed. Her chest was growing as fast as her height. A few weeks ago, Rhoda had rudely pointed out that Polly needed a brassiere. It would be a huge relief to get one, but how embarrassing to talk about it.

She had to bring up another awkward topic. "Noni, Daddy's planning to arrive on the island on the third of January. Is that all right?"

Polly braced herself for the frown that always appeared on Noni's face whenever Polly mentioned Daddy. Then, as usual, Noni replaced it with a brittle smile. "Of course, Polly!"

"You must be so excited about seeing him again," said Aunt Jean.

Polly could only nod. "Excited" was too mild a word; every time she thought of being in Daddy's arms again she wanted to explode. If only her family were looking forward to seeing him at least a bit!

On the second-last day of term, the Hornet handed out their report cards. Polly had done well in all her subjects except math, but at least in that she received a C+. Then she stared at the bottom of the sheet of paper. She had failed drawing!

"Polly has consistently ignored instructions in class," wrote Miss Netherwood. "She shows no talent for the exercises, and is recalcitrant when offered assistance. There is no point in submitting her work to the Royal Drawing Society, and I recommend that she withdraw from the course."

Polly's cheeks burned. Miss Netherwood was lying. Lately, Polly had done everything she was supposed to, and of course she was talented! And what did "recalcitrant" mean?

She read the comments again with mixed feelings. To fail something was humiliating, but perhaps she wouldn't have to take drawing anymore.

That evening Miss Guppy spoke to her. "I simply cannot understand, Polly, why someone who is supposed to be so good at art can fail drawing. Miss Netherwood is convinced, however, that you will never pass the requirements for the certificate. I could ask her to let you stay, as long as you try harder."

"I *do* try!" said Polly. "Miss Netherwood just doesn't like me."

"Don't be saucy, young lady. You are not to blame a teacher for something that's your fault."

"Do I have to keep taking it?" Polly asked. She waited, knowing how the Guppy hated a student to get her own way.

"Very well," said Miss Guppy finally. "I'll ask Mrs. Partridge to give you extra math in that period—you can certainly stand to improve there."

Polly skipped up to the dorm. Extra math was boring, but she didn't care. No more Miss Netherwood! And tomorrow, after the concert, she was going home.

CHAPTER NINE

DADDY AT LAST

CHRISTMAS WAS A HAPPY BLUR. POLLY RECEIVED HER PASTELS and a new dress and many other presents. But all through the celebration, she could only think of one thing: Daddy was coming!

Gregor and Sadie arrived in time for Hogmanay. Polly hadn't seen them since their wedding in August. "Pollywog!" cried her cousin, smacking her cheek. "You've turned into a young lady!"

"Hi, kiddo," said Sadie. She appraised Polly. "Gregor's right—you're looking very grown-up."

Polly crossed her arms. Why did everyone have to notice her bosom? It was rude.

Maud crushed Sadie in a hug. "I have so much to tell you!" After tea they disappeared for a long walk. *Poor Sadie,* thought Polly. All she would hear about was boring Robert.

At midnight, after Gregor had knocked on the door as the "First Footer," they all went outside with their champagne and toasted the new year. Polly was allowed half a glass. She savoured it slowly. The night was so still she could hear faint cheers and bells and boat whistles through the darkness, even from Walker Island across from them.

She stared at the radiant moon. What would 1936 bring? First of all Daddy. That was the best. Then two more terms of school—ugh—but also two more terms of special art. In June, she'd have to tell Noni she wouldn't go back. Noni would be so disappointed; so would Daddy and Maud. *But I'm not changing my mind!* vowed Polly. June was a long way away; she didn't have to worry about it yet.

The next day they celebrated Maud's nineteenth birthday. Robert telephoned after lunch, and she talked to him for ten minutes. Noni scolded her. "You know how expensive calls are, Maud!"

"Sorry, Noni," said Maud. She yawned. "I think I'll go and lie down before my party." Maud had slept in every morning, and she had a long nap every afternoon.

"Poor lass, she's worn out with all her studies," said Aunt Jean.

But Polly was puzzled. Maud's boundless energy had never been diminished by working hard.

―――――――

At long last, the day came when Polly and Maud walked to the wharf to wait for Daddy's boat.

"It's really *you*!" Polly cried as they ran into his embrace. What a change from the shabby father she had hidden in the woods a year and a half ago! Daddy's suit was worn but clean, and his grey hat sat tilted at a jaunty angle. His handsome face with its distinguished long nose was clean-shaven. Last time, he had been so broken in spirit that Polly had felt like his parent instead of his child. Now, although Daddy looked sheepish and apprehensive, he grinned as he had in the old days.

"I have my girls back," he said, his voice breaking. "And how beautiful you both are! Yes, yes, you're beautiful, too," he added as

Tarka jumped up. He studied them greedily. "I see you're wearing the necklaces I gave you."

"I never take mine off!" said Maud.

Polly fingered the silver heart. "I'm not allowed to wear mine at school, but I always wear it at home."

They began to walk along the road. Then Daddy stopped and rubbed his hand over his face the way he always did when he was nervous. "I want to apologize to you, my darlings."

"You already did," said Maud. "There's no need to again."

"I wrote to you, but that's not the same. I'm so sorry, Maud and Polly, that I put you through what I did. I'm sorry I stole the money and I'm sorry I abandoned you. Most of all, I'm sorry I lied."

"That's all over with now," said Maud briskly. "Right, Poll?"

"Right!" said Polly. If only Daddy would stop talking about the past! His words opened wounds she thought had healed a long time ago.

"Do you forgive your old father?" Daddy asked them.

"Of course we do!" said Maud. "We've told you that in our letters, Daddy. You've made your confession, and now you're free. Let's leave all that behind us now."

Daddy chuckled. "Yes, Boss. How about you, my Polly-Wolly-Doodle?"

It had taken Polly longer to forgive Daddy than it had Maud. Now, however, all the sorry business about his theft seemed far away. "I forgive you *utterly*," she whispered.

Daddy's eyes glistened. "I know you wrote me that, but I had to hear it in person. Thank you."

He picked up a hand of each. "All right, let's go and face the dragons!"

They walked to the house hand in hand, swinging their arms.

When they passed the Cunninghams' place, Polly lifted her head proudly. Mrs. Cunningham would be watching from behind her lace curtains, but here was Daddy, free to be out in the open at last! As they approached Noni's house, however, Polly started to worry.

Noni was waiting on the porch. "Hello, Daniel," she said quietly, holding out her hand. "I'm very glad to see you again. Please come in and join us for tea." Her words sounded rehearsed.

Daddy sat awkwardly on the sofa, like a prisoner who longed to escape. Maud and Polly guarded him on each side, and Tarka perched proudly on his lap. Polly clenched her hands when Aunt Jean eyed Daddy's frayed cuffs and the cracked polish on his old shoes.

Uncle Rand made a formal little speech about how glad they were that Daddy had been cleared. Aunt Jean tittered. Gregor grinned foolishly and Sadie looked so sorry for Daddy that Polly wanted to shake her.

"What are you planning to do now?" asked Noni.

"I'll go back to Kelowna and resume my old job."

"And what was that?"

Polly squirmed. Couldn't Noni make her voice warmer?

"I've been laying bricks," said Daddy. He returned Noni's stony expression just as stonily. "Just as my father did," he added firmly.

"Where will you live in Kelowna?" asked Uncle Rand.

"Where I did before, in a boarding house." Daddy turned to Noni again. "I'm hoping that Maud and Polly can visit me at Easter. There's an extra room."

Noni looked frightened. "Easter? But we want to see them, too!"

"Of course you do. How long a break do you get then, girls?"

"Two weeks," Polly told him.

"I'm not sure," said Maud. "It depends when my exams are."

Daddy smiled at Noni. "Then how about if they stay with me

after Easter, for the second part of Polly's holidays? Polly could come for a week and Maud for as long as she can manage."

"That would be all right," said Noni, giving him back a strained smile.

They had Daddy for only two days; he planned to leave on Sunday. The family left him alone with the girls, except for meals. The first day was clear and crisp. They bundled up and went for a long walk.

Maud chattered non-stop about U.B.C. Polly was content just to hold on to Daddy's large hand.

Daddy heard all about Maud's courses and Delta Gamma and far too much about Robert for Polly's taste. "I joined the Players' Club," said Maud. "They're doing *She Stoops to Conquer* in March and I have a tiny role! That's unusual for a freshman. And Robert got on the rugby team!"

"I'm glad that you're having such a good time, Maudie," said Daddy. "What about you, Doodle? How do you like St. Winifred's?"

Polly answered carefully. There was no point in telling Daddy how much she hated school. He would be so worried and so disappointed. She tried to sound enthusiastic, which wasn't hard when she talked about art.

"How lucky you are!" he told her, picking up a stick and throwing it for Tarka. "Maybe you'll be a real artist one day!"

"Oh, I will!" said Polly with surprise. She had known that for so long it seemed unnecessary to say it.

"And I'm going to be a lawyer!" said Maud.

Daddy grinned. "What smart girls I have! The best thing that happened to you was to come and live with your grandmother. You wouldn't have had such a good education if you hadn't." His words sounded automatic, as if he had been repeating them to himself for years.

Maud and Polly were silent. "It *wasn't* the best thing," said Polly slowly. "We would rather have lived with you."

Daddy rubbed his face. "Girls, I . . ."

"Let's not talk about any of that," said Maud briskly. "It's over now. Daddy, did I tell you that I'm thinking of becoming a Quaker? There's a girl in my residence who's one. I went to a service with her and I really liked it. They just sit still until someone feels like speaking."

"A quacker? Funny . . . you don't look like a duck."

Maud leaped upon him and began tickling him the way she used to in Winnipeg. Polly attacked Maud. They were a threesome again, almost as if the preceding years hadn't happened.

"Hi, Polly!" Biddy and Vivien were standing on the road ahead. Polly suspected they'd planted themselves there on purpose. She hadn't seen them much this holiday, although she and Biddy and Biddy's brother Luke had inspected one another's presents on Christmas Day the way they always did.

"Come and meet my father," called Polly.

"Hello there!" said Daddy, shaking their hands. "I've heard a lot about the two of you!"

They just stood there clumsily, staring at Daddy as if he had risen from the dead. *Which he has in a way,* Polly thought, *since for a long time everyone thought he was dead.*

———

"What's *wrong* with everyone?" Polly asked Maud in her bedroom on Saturday night. "They treat Daddy as if he's a criminal!"

"He is," said Maud quietly.

"Don't *say* that!"

"Poll, listen to me. Daddy stole some money. He confessed, but no one can forget that he did it. And no one's used to him yet. The family hasn't seen him since he and Mother were married, and your friends have never met him at all. It's just too new. And it's too strange for them, since they thought Daddy was dead."

"I can see why Biddy and Vivien would be shy with him," said Polly. "But it's more than that with Noni and Aunt Jean and Gregor. They disapprove because he stole the money, but it's as if they know a secret about him . . . and Daddy knows they know. They don't seem to *like* him."

"They never did, Doodle. There was some kind of quarrel a long time ago, but we'll probably never find out what it was." Maud yawned. "I'm so tired. Go to bed now, Poll, and don't worry what everyone thinks of Daddy. The only important thing is that *we* love him."

Polly smiled at her and said good night.

———

Daddy told them he wouldn't attend church. "Everyone will stare at me, and that will embarrass you all," he said at breakfast.

Noni looked relieved, and gave Polly and Maud permission to stay home with him.

Outside it was rainy, but inside they huddled around the fire and played chess. Polly could hardly concentrate. In a few hours, Daddy would be gone.

Maud, as well, seemed restless. "This is boring," she said, putting down her pawn. "Poll, I have an idea—let's bob your hair!"

"No!" said Polly. But she glanced at Daddy to see his reaction.

He chuckled. "Doodle, were you wanting to cut your hair?"

"Maud thinks I should," mumbled Polly.

"Do *you* want to?"

"I might," said Polly slowly, "but what about you, Daddy? You always said you loved my long hair."

Daddy hugged her. "I always did. But I would love your hair any way it was, because I love *you*. If you want to cut it, it's fine with me."

"Really?"

"Really. It's your hair, after all. You're lucky to have so much of it," he added ruefully. Daddy's thick hair used to hang over his forehead. Now the front of his scalp was almost bare.

"So, do you want to, Poll?" asked Maud. "I'm good at cutting hair—I do Ann's all the time."

Polly hesitated. Her long hair had been part of her all her life. But she was thirteen now. It would be swell to look more grown-up, and she was tired of being the only one at school without a bob.

"All right," she whispered.

"Good for you! Let's go into the kitchen so we don't get hair all over the carpet."

Polly sat on a stool in the middle of the kitchen with a towel draped around her shoulders. When Maud approached her with the scissors that Noni used to cut flowers, Polly wanted to change her mind—but it was too late. Already the cold blades were against her neck and long strands of hair were drifting onto the linoleum.

Polly closed her eyes tightly and tried not to cry as the scissors snipped away. This was a huge mistake! She would look awful, and everyone would tease her, and her hair would take forever to grow out again.

"There!" said Maud finally. She shook the towel out the back door, then wiped off Polly with it. "Oh, Doodle, you look *beautiful*!"

"You really do," said Daddy.

Maud ran out and returned immediately with a small mirror. "See for yourself."

Polly stared at the strange girl in the mirror. She had *her* face, but it was framed with soft waves of blond hair. It made her eyes look bigger. Her neck felt cold, but her head felt delightfully light and free.

"Well? Do you like it? Say something!" Maud actually sounded frightened.

"I—I *do* like it! Oh, Maud, thank you!"

Maud was sweeping up Polly's hair when someone knocked loudly on the kitchen door. Polly opened it to a dripping wet Alice.

"Hi, Polly—I love your bob! I ran over from the parish hall," she puffed. "Can I meet your father?"

Polly didn't have time to answer; Alice had already pushed her way in. "Hi, Mr. Brown!" she said, sticking out a hand.

Daddy chuckled. "Well, hi to you, too. Whom do I have the pleasure of meeting?"

"I'm Alice Mackenzie, a friend of Polly's from St. Winifred's."

Daddy asked her more questions and she gazed at him hungrily between answers. *She wishes he were* her *father*, Polly realized. Poor Alice—she'd probably never see her own father, who had left her when she was a little girl. At least Daddy was in Polly's life, even though it wasn't all the time.

———

Polly had forgotten that her grandmother also liked her with long hair. When Noni returned from church, she gasped and put her hand to her heart.

"Polly, what have you done?" she cried.

Polly led her over to the sofa. "Maud cut my hair, Noni," she said. "Do you like it?"

Noni was trembling. "Since you ask, I have to tell you that I do *not* like it! How could you do this without my permission?"

"She had *my* permission, Mrs. Whitfield," said Daddy quietly. "And Polly's thirteen. She's old enough to wear her hair the way she wants to."

"She's just like Una," whispered Noni.

"What do you mean?" asked Maud.

"Your mother. *She* cut her hair without asking me." Noni took out her handkerchief and wiped her eyes. Then she stood up. "If you'll excuse me, I'm going up to my room for a while."

Polly's own eyes stung. Maud put an arm around her shoulder. "Don't worry, Doodle. She'll get used to it."

"It's just the shock," said Daddy. "You *do* look different." He grimaced. "And it seems that we've brought back a difficult memory for your grandmother."

Polly felt so guilty that she could barely eat her lunch. It helped, however, that the rest of the family raved about her new hairstyle.

"You look like Jean Harlow!" teased Gregor.

"She does not, Gregor! She still looks like our own dear Polly, only a wee bit more grown-up," said Aunt Jean.

At the head of the table, Noni was silent. That afternoon Polly knocked on her door.

"Come in," said the gravelly voice.

"Are you asleep?" asked Polly.

"No, I'm just reading." Noni gazed at Polly, then began to weep. "Oh, hen, come and kiss me. I'm sorry I was so sharp. You hair actually suits you very well. And your father is right. You're old enough to do what you want with it."

Polly ran to the bed and climbed up beside Noni. Noni's tears ended as abruptly as they had begun. "Listen to this," she said. She began to read a poem by Coleridge.

Polly was so relieved Noni had stopped crying that she almost fell asleep.

———————

"Are you okay, Boss?" Daddy asked that afternoon. Maud had taken some aspirin because she had a headache.

Maud shrugged. "I guess so. I keep getting headaches and I'm so tired and queasy all the time. I thought I might have the flu, but I don't feel *really* sick—just sickish."

Daddy looked worried. "Perhaps you should see a doctor. Is there one on the island?"

"Just Dr. Cunningham, and he's such a stick. If I still feel like this when I get back, I'll go to the university doctor."

"Good," said Daddy. "You must have been working too hard last term." He grinned. "Or playing too hard! You take better care of yourself this year, all right?"

They were having a last walk in the rain. Polly clung to Daddy's arm. In a few hours he would have to leave! "Do you want to see the cabin?" she asked him.

Daddy smiled. "My hideaway? Sure! Anyway, there's something I want to talk to you two about and it's getting too wet to stay out."

The three of them—four, counting Tarka—pushed through wet bushes to the cabin. Polly hadn't been in it for a long time. Water was dripping from the roof, but they squatted on stumps in a dry area.

Daddy looked around and shuddered. "At least I don't have to hide anymore. It's been such a relief to see you openly. It was generous of your grandmother to let me come."

"I wish she would be friendlier, though," said Polly.

"Don't worry about that, Doodle," said Daddy. "You know that Una's family has never liked me. We had a terrible quarrel."

"What was it about?"

"You're not old enough to know yet. One day I'll tell you—I promise." He cleared his throat. "There's something I *will* tell you, girls. I have—well, I have a lady friend in Kelowna."

"You *do*?" said Maud. "Who is it?"

"Her name is Esther. Her mother owned the boarding house I live in. Esther and I became friends, and then we began walking out. While I was in Winnipeg, Esther wrote to me and told me her mother had died. She wants me to help her run the boarding house."

"What does that mean?" asked Maud. "Will you get married?"

Married! Polly couldn't absorb any of this.

Daddy laughed. "Not right now, although I'd certainly like to one day. No, at the moment it will be strictly a business arrangement. Esther is a fine lady. I think you'd both really like her—she's kind and smart. It's best if you don't tell the family here about her, though. They probably wouldn't approve."

"But why not?" asked Polly.

"Because Esther's Jewish."

"I have a friend at varsity who's Jewish," said Maud. "She's really nice."

"I'm glad you're friends with her, Maud. But I don't think your family here would be friendly towards Esther. They can be narrow-minded—especially your grandmother."

Polly flushed, as if *she* were responsible for Noni's opinions. She wished Daddy was wrong, but she knew he wasn't. Noni had stubborn prejudices; she *would* disapprove.

Polly disapproved for other reasons. Now that Daddy was finally back in her life, she didn't want to share him with anyone else.

"Does Esther know about what happened to you?" asked Maud.

"She knows all about it, Boss," said Daddy. "I told her before I left for Winnipeg this summer, and I told her my real name. She was shocked that I stole the money, of course. But she understood how desperate I was—that I did it for you. And she admired me for confessing."

The three of them sat quietly. This enormous change—*Esther*—dropped into the silence like a stone into a pool.

Then Maud smiled. "Well, Daddy, now we *both* have sweethearts! I'm excited about meeting her."

Polly gulped. "So am I," she lied.

"And so is Esther!" said Daddy. "I talk about my girls all the time, and she can't wait to meet you." He gave them a yearning look. "If we ever do get married, and if we make a go of the boarding house, perhaps . . ."

"What?" asked Polly.

Maud seemed to know what he meant. Daddy passed his hand over his face. "Nothing. Just wishful thinking."

Polly seethed inside. What weren't they telling her? But she didn't want to spoil Daddy's last few hours by making a fuss.

"Now, let's do some planning," said Daddy. "Easter is April 12. Let's say you visit us during the week of April 20. I'll write to your grandmother nearer the time and we'll arrange it. You two can meet in Vancouver and go on the train to Kelowna. After your visit, Maud can go back to U.B.C., and Polly can take the boat straight to Victoria from Vancouver. Do you think you can get away then, Maud?"

"I'll try," said Maud. "I'd really like to meet Esther and see Kelowna. How big a city is it?"

Polly didn't hear the answer. She wanted to visit Daddy, but she wanted him all to herself.

"I'm going to walk Tarka," she told them, and fled.

When Polly and Maud arrived at the wharf to see Daddy off, Chester was standing there with his parents. "Hi, Chester," said Polly shyly. "This is my father."

"Well, well, it's very nice to meet you!" said Chester's mother nervously. Her husband mumbled a greeting, but he acted as if Daddy belonged to another species.

Chester, however, treated him like anyone else's father. "How do you do, sir?" he said, shaking Daddy's hand and looking him in the eye.

Polly glowed; what a gentleman Chester was! She stepped away from the adults, and as she'd hoped, Chester followed. He stared at her with such clear admiration that Polly blushed.

"What's the matter?" she asked him.

"Your hair," said Chester. "It's . . . it's so pretty!"

"Oh!" Polly blushed even more deeply. "Are you waiting for someone to arrive?" she mumbled.

"No, I'm going back to school early. There's a football tournament I want to see."

That was too bad; Polly had looked forward to more time with him on the boat.

"Polly! Daddy is saying goodbye!" called Maud.

Polly hurried over and buried herself in Daddy's coat. She drew in his familiar smell and her eyes filled. She wouldn't see him again for months.

"Goodbye, my precious darlings," Daddy told them as the steamer approached. "I'm so glad I'm part of your lives again."

He waved to them until the boat drew out of sight.

Gregor and Sadie had gone, as well, and Maud was leaving the next day; she and Robert were going skiing on Hollyburn Mountain.

"By yourselves? That's not proper," said Aunt Jean at dinner. "In my day, a young woman and a young man were never alone without a chaperone."

Maud became Maudish. "It's perfectly proper, Aunt Jean, and it's only for a day. Things have changed a lot since you were a girl—this is the thirties!"

Noni frowned at her. "There's no need to be rude, Maud. We're all delighted that you have a beau, but you and Robert *must* observe the proprieties. Do you understand what I mean?"

"Yes, Noni." Maud lowered her head. Then she winked at Polly and dug into her venison.

As usual, Polly had eaten no venison. When she was younger, she had tried to be a vegetarian. Now she'd decided that was too hard, but she still couldn't bear to eat the gentle creatures she saw every day on the island.

Noni cleared the plates and brought in a platter of Christmas cake and cookies. "These are so yummy," said Maud. "Can I take some back with me?" She was in high spirits tonight, teasing Aunt Jean about her new hat and telling them a hilarious story about rehearsing for her play.

No one had mentioned Daddy since his departure. At first Polly resented this. Then she was shocked to discover that she was as relieved at his absence as everyone else seemed to be. Everything was the same again. They were gathered around the family table, content with one another's company.

I miss him, but I'm glad he's gone, thought Polly guiltily. It had been wonderful to see Daddy . . . but also unsettling. Anyway, she would see him again in April. Now she just wanted to savour her family and her last precious days on the island before school began.

Three days later, Polly watched the island fade into the mist. Her prison sentence had resumed; she wouldn't be able to come home until the half-term break in March.

"Tell me everything, Polly," said Alice eagerly as they settled in the lounge. "How was it seeing your father after so long? He's so handsome!"

Polly smiled. "Yes, he is."

"It's such a shame you can't live with him," said Alice.

"Live with him?"

"Don't you want to? He's your father! But I suppose you can't, being that he stole that money," she said bluntly.

"Let's not talk about it," Polly said quickly. She remembered the queer look Daddy had given them in the cabin. Was that what he had almost said? If he and Esther got married, did he mean to have Polly and Maud live with them?

Once Polly would have given anything to be back with him . . . but surely she belonged with Noni now.

"Okay, we won't talk about it! Polly, did you know that Kay Winston has a pash on the school gardener? This week she's going to sneak him a note!"

Polly had to spend the rest of the journey talking about school.

PART TWO

TWO MORE TERMS

CHAPTER TEN

THE EASTER TERM

TWO MORE TERMS IN THIS DREARY PLACE . . . HOW COULD SHE endure them? Polly wondered.

She was pleased to see Eleanor and Daisy again, and touched by how glad they were to see her. But Rhoda immediately informed Polly that her bob should be longer in the back and that Polly's new dress, which she had worn back to school, was old-fashioned.

Polly had to put up with several days of rhapsodies about her short hair. They all kept coming up to her and saying they loved it. That was flattering but embarrassing, and she got tired of saying "Thank you."

At least there was special art again on Saturday. Miss Falconer explained that now that they had sampled many mediums, they were spending all of this term on drawing. "If you can draw, you can do anything," she told them. She set up a still life and told them to simply gaze at it for at least ten minutes before they began drawing. "The first part of drawing is *looking*. Observe every line and space and shape, and feel them, as well. Don't begin until you are absolutely ready."

This was real *drawing!* thought Polly happily as she finally picked up her pencil. No longer did she have to endure Miss Netherwood's dry classes. Now she could draw from her heart as well as from her head.

———

A week later, Polly knelt in church as the congregation prayed. She was supposed to bow her head like everyone else, but she kept staring at the rector. In their second class of the term, Miss Falconer had explained the proportions of the face. Then they had drawn one another. Polly had fixed her eyes on Dottie while she tried to reproduce each eyebrow and nostril and ear.

Canon Puddifoot was standing there for so long it was a good opportunity to examine him. Sure enough, his mournful face fitted Miss Falconer's formula. His eyes were in the middle, and his ears reached from the top of his eyebrows to the base of his nose. Polly's fingers itched to draw the long lines of his drooping cheeks.

"Let us pray especially for our ailing king," the canon finished. "May his suffering soon be relieved, and may his family be consoled at this time of his passing."

Polly was disappointed when they all stood up to sing; she hadn't finished imagining how she would sketch the canon's gleaming bald forehead.

Before Sunday lunch, Miss Guppy called Polly into her study. "What do you mean, young lady, showing such disrespect during the prayers? Why wasn't your head bowed?"

"Sorry," muttered Polly. "I was thinking of something else."

"You are always thinking of something else! Next week you will sit beside me. I'm very disappointed in you, Polly. You've been back at school for only ten days, and you are not applying yourself. Why is that?"

"I don't know," mumbled Polly.

She wished she had the nerve to tell Miss Guppy that aside from art, school grated on her even more this term. She was glad to be free of Miss Netherwood, but now she had to sit by herself in the library and do endless math exercises. She and Eleanor had received two order marks each for having a race down the school hall when they thought no one was looking. The Crab had caught Polly reading in an empty bathtub after lights out, and had made her go to bed an hour earlier the next night.

"Maud would be very disappointed in you," finished the Guppy, as she always did.

Polly thought of Maud and Robert kissing. What would Miss Guppy think of perfect Maud if she knew about *that*?

At evening prayers on Tuesday, Miss Guppy was pale. To everyone's astonishment, she was wiping tears from her face. "I'm very sorry to have to tell you, girls, that our beloved king has died. Even though we have expected this news, it is a sad loss."

The next day, all the teachers talked about King George V. Most of them, like Miss Guppy, spoke of England as "home"; they were all as upset as she was.

Polly tried to feel sad. All her life she had seen pictures of the king, on stamps and coins and photographs on school walls. Last year, Noni had bought a special mug for the silver jubilee, with the king's moustached face and the queen's regal head of silver curls painted on its side. It felt important to hear about such an esteemed person's death, but she couldn't *really* feel sad about someone she had never met.

"It's so weird that someone who lived in England also ruled Canada," said Rhoda. "Who will be king now?"

"Edward, the Prince of Wales," Daisy told her. "He's so handsome!"

"My grandfather saw the king once," Eleanor told them. "He reviewed Grampa's troop in England during the Great War."

"Why is it called 'the Great War'?" asked Rhoda.

"Because there will never be another one," said Daisy.

Eleanor looked sombre. "There might be. That's what my dad says. I sure hope not—maybe my older brothers would have to fight in it."

Panic fluttered in Polly. Another war? Would Chester have to fight? Would Gregor? Maybe Daddy would! She tried to calm herself. Surely Chester would be too young and Daddy too old. And surely Eleanor's father was wrong. She decided to ask Uncle Rand the next time she was home; he knew everything.

In composition, they were asked to write something about the king. Eleanor wrote about her grandfather. Rhoda wrote about not having a king in her country, and Polly wrote dutifully about what a great king he was. She didn't say that she wasn't sure why.

Daisy's essay was so good that she was asked to read it aloud. She described how miserable the king's dog must be feeling; then Polly felt sad for the first time.

The following Tuesday was a school holiday for the king's funeral. The lucky day girls could stay home, but all the boarders had to go downtown in the morning and attend a service at the cathedral. They arrived at eight-thirty to get a seat. Two hours later, when the service began, over a thousand people filled the vast space. Polly was so hot she thought she would faint, but they weren't allowed to take off their blazers, hats, or gloves. As usual on their outings, she looked for Chester in the crowd, but he wasn't there. Finally, the congregation sang "Abide with Me" and "O Canada," and they could escape into the cool air.

"You will always remember this day, girls," Miss Guppy told them on the streetcar going back. After lunch the boarders were invited to gather in the sitting room and listen to the funeral in London on the radio. The Fearless Four chose to go over to the gym and shoot baskets, instead.

Polly was trying to stay out of Rhoda's way this term, and usually she succeeded. Rhoda had decided she was going to earn the most points of any girl in her house. After school she was busy playing a sport or rehearsing for a play. In the dorm she chattered to the other three instead of Polly. If she made a mean remark, Polly ignored her.

One rainy afternoon, however, they were stuck in the dorm together. One of the prefects had taken Daisy to the dentist, and Eleanor was in the library.

Polly bent her head over her book. Rhoda was knitting a square that would be part of a blanket for the Red Cross; she gained a house point for each square she completed.

"Would you like to borrow some wool and needles, Polly?" she asked in a simpering voice. "If you began knitting squares, you could make up for some of the order marks you've received."

Polly didn't answer. For a few minutes Rhoda was quiet, as well. Then she said, "Polly, stop reading. There's something I've always wanted to ask you."

Polly looked up suspiciously. "What?"

"Why don't you ever talk about your father? We know you live with your grandmother, and that your mother is dead and your father lives in Kelowna. But I heard you telling Eleanor you saw him over the holidays. Does he live on the island now?"

Polly stiffened. "My father still lives in Kelowna. He was just visiting me."

"But why doesn't he live with you all the time?"

Polly stood up. "He just doesn't. That's all you need to know, Rhoda. The rest is none of your business!"

"The rest of *what*?" asked Rhoda.

But Polly was already on her way out of the dorm.

———

Once again, Polly was standing in Miss Guppy's study with the door closed. The headmistress was holding a large white envelope. It had been slit open.

"This is addressed to you, Polly," she said. "As you know, you are allowed to receive mail only from the approved people on your list, so I had to open it." She handed the envelope to Polly, grimacing as if it contained something alive. "Look what I found!"

Polly pulled out a decorated cardboard heart outlined with white lace. Inside, it said "Happy Valentine's Day, Polly."

"Who is this from?" Miss Guppy asked sternly.

Polly stared at the card. At the bottom was a tiny drawing of a whale.

She could say she didn't know. But the Guppy had a remarkable ability for ferreting out the truth. "It's from Chester Simmons," whispered Polly.

Miss Guppy exploded. Polly shivered as the harsh words soaked her like a cloudburst. St. Winifred's students were *never* to receive letters from boys! Girls Polly's age were much too young to correspond with boys at all. Miss Guppy was going to inform the headmaster of St. Cuthbert's what Chester had done.

On and on she ranted, while Polly fingered the valentine for comfort. It was so beautiful, with its lace and bright flowers, even nicer than the one Chester had given her three years ago. And he remembered the whales!

"I'm sorry, Miss Guppy," said Polly when the storm of words had ceased, "but I didn't know he was going to send it."

"You must have encouraged him in some way," said Miss Guppy, "just as you did at the concert. You are far too young to be making eyes at boys, young lady! I'm going to write to your grandmother and inform her of your behaviour."

Noni won't care, thought Polly. It cheered her up to think of how she and Aunt Jean and Uncle Rand would laugh about it at the dinner table.

Miss Guppy's voice was winding down now; the lecture seemed almost over. Polly waited to be dismissed, pressing the valentine to her chest. In a few minutes, she could run up to the dorm and savour it.

The headmistress finished with her usual words: how ashamed Maud would be. She paused.

"Now, give me back the valentine."

"But can't I keep it?"

"Certainly not!" Miss Guppy snatched the valentine and tried to rip it.

"*No!* Please, don't!" cried Polly.

The lace wouldn't tear. Miss Guppy picked up some scissors from her desk and sliced the red heart into many pieces. "There!" she said, dropping them into the wastepaper basket.

Polly was so horrified that for a few seconds she couldn't move. Then she raced out of the study and up to her dorm.

The others were already in their nightgowns. They stood around Polly's bed while she sobbed into her pillow. "I hate her—I hate her!" she kept saying. Finally, she choked out the whole story.

"You poor thing!" said Daisy.

"You got a valentine from a *boy*?" said Rhoda.

"She had no right to open your private mail," said Eleanor.

"What did it *say*?" said Rhoda.

Mrs. Blake came in to tell them to get ready for bed. She stroked Polly's back, while the others told her what had happened.

"I *hate* her!" said Polly again.

"I shouldn't say this, love, but I have to agree that Miss Guppy was much too strict," said Mrs. Blake. "All you can do is try to stay out of her way."

"I do, but I keep getting into trouble!" said Polly.

After lights out, Polly tried to reconstruct the valentine in her mind. She pretended it was under her pillow as she sobbed herself to sleep.

All Maud's letters were about Robert, and all Daddy's were about Esther. Esther had made new curtains for the boarding house. It was a marvel, said Daddy, how she managed to cook such thrifty, tasty meals for everyone. She and Daddy had painted the dining room green, and Esther had got paint in her hair. Now Daddy called her "the Green Giantess."

In his last letter, he'd sent a snap of the two of them in front of the house. Esther was as tall as Daddy. She had a long bony face and a wide smile. And she did look kind. "She can hardly wait to meet the two of you," Daddy kept writing.

Polly had such mixed feelings. She still wasn't used to this new person in Daddy's life, but she was glad he was so happy.

In February, Maud wrote Polly a short note saying she had stopped seeing Robert. "He's not the person I thought he was," she said. "He's turned out to be intolerant and judgmental, and I don't want to have anything more to do with him."

Polly was relieved that Robert was out of Maud's life. Together they had been a soppy couple who had excluded her. Still, she couldn't help feeling a bit sorry for Maud. She had enjoyed having a beau to show off.

"Poor Maud," said Noni the next week when Polly was home for half-term break.

"There are lots of other fish in the sea!" said Aunt Jean. "Our Maud is so bonny she won't have any trouble finding another young man."

"I'm worried about her, though," said Noni. "I don't understand why she didn't want us to come to Vancouver." The family had planned to spend Polly's holiday there, but Maud had told them she had so much work to do that she couldn't take time off for a visit.

Polly was both hurt and disappointed. Maud *always* wanted to be with her! And the only part of Vancouver Polly had ever seen was the train station. She'd been excited about exploring such a big city.

Chester came up to Polly after church. "I'm sorry I got you into trouble." He grimaced. "I got into trouble, too. What a stupid fuss they all made! It was just a valentine."

"I'm glad you sent it, though," said Polly shyly. "It was beautiful. But Miss Guppy cut it up!"

"Never mind." Chester hesitated. Then he said in a rush, "You look pretty today, Polly." He hurried away before she could respond.

In special art, they continued drawing, with pencils, charcoal, and ink. Polly began looking at everything more carefully, from faces to trees to the sky. "'Try to be one of those on whom nothing is lost,'" Miss Falconer told them. "A writer named Henry James said that. Mr. de Jonge has his words posted over his desk. It's excellent advice for artists, as well as for writers."

She encouraged them to carry small sketchbooks and a pencil wherever they went. Polly kept hers in the pocket of her blazer. She didn't dare take it out during class, but in her free time she drew her roommates or the school buildings or a teacup or a flower. To capture the school on paper helped distance its grimness.

One Saturday at tea, Miss Falconer asked the older girls if any of them wanted to choose art as a career. "If you're going to the Vancouver School of Art, we'd better start sending in applications for those of you who are graduating."

They all shook their heads. Jane wanted to become a nurse. The others didn't plan to have careers, although two of them were hoping to go to university.

"I'm sure I'll still do art, but only as a hobby," said Dottie. "I'll be too busy having babies! After I meet the right man, of course," she added with a blush.

"What a waste," said Miss Falconer quietly.

Then she looked at Polly. "How about you, little one? It's probably too soon for you to know, but do you think you might want to become an artist?"

Polly nodded so vigorously she spilled her tea.

"Would that be all right with your family?"

"Yes. They already know I want to go to art school instead of university."

"I'm so glad, Polly. I'll give you the best training I can for the next four years, and then I'll help you put together a portfolio. With your talent, I'm sure you won't have any problem being accepted."

"Oh, but . . ."

"What?"

"Nothing," mumbled Polly. She couldn't say that she was leaving at the end of this year. Miss Falconer would be so disappointed.

Spring in Victoria was more colourful than spring on the island. The cherry trees on the edge of the playing field burst into pink froth, then the gardens blazed with tulips. The weather grew so warm that they switched to their summer uniforms: checked maroon cotton dresses, and sandals and short socks instead of scratchy wool stockings and heavy oxfords.

Polly was enjoying botany. Every week they were allowed to gather bluebells and other wildflowers from the woods, bring them into the classroom, and draw them. One afternoon Miss Linton, usually a calm young woman, looked agitated.

"Put your pencils down, girls, and pay attention. Today I'm going to teach you about pollination."

She turned to the board and drew a large flower. "This is called the 'pistil' and these are called the 'stamens,'" she said tightly. "The stamens produce pollen, which is transferred to the top of the pistil, which is called the 'stigma.' Then seeds are made at the base of the pistil, in the 'ovule.'"

She turned around from the board, her face pink. "Any questions?"

Eleanor put up her hand. "Does the pollen always go to the same plant's stigma?"

"A very good question, Eleanor. No, the pollen is often transferred to a different plant, by bees or the wind. That is called cross-pollination."

Rhoda thrust up her hand. "Miss Linton, it seems to me that flowers are like people! The stamens are—"

Miss Linton cut her off, but several girls started giggling. "Rhoda Spiegel, that's enough! I'm giving you an order mark for rudeness. If anyone else finds this amusing, she will get one, also. Now, please copy this drawing into your notebooks."

Polly was confused. Why was Miss Linton so upset, and why did some of the girls have smirks on their faces?

———

That evening after lights out, the Fearless Four were sitting on the top of the fire escape, as they had done several times since the spring weather arrived.

"Miss Linton was really unfair today," said Eleanor to Rhoda. "Your question was perfectly justified. It's remarkable, really, how similar different species are. Flowers *are* like people!"

"They are?" said Daisy.

"How?" said Polly.

Eleanor smiled. "Don't you know? Rho, you must, or you wouldn't have asked that question."

Rhoda nodded. "I've known since last year. My mother told me."

"Know *what*?" said Polly. It was irritating how smug Rhoda was acting. Eleanor was almost as bad.

"I found out just before I came here," said Eleanor. "My brother Ralph and I discovered a book called *Married Love* in Mother and Dad's bedroom." She looked solemn. "Do you want me to tell you, or would you rather ask your parents?"

"Tell us before we push you off the fire escape!" laughed Daisy.

In her usual precise way, Eleanor told Polly and Daisy exactly why flowers were like people.

"Oh!" gulped Daisy, when she'd finished. "Well, I sort of knew that."

Polly realized that so did she. When she thought of the animals on Biddy's farm, it all made sense.

"Do we have to do it, too?" asked Daisy.

"Not unless you want to, and not until you're married, of course," said Eleanor.

"My mother says it's a beautiful way of celebrating the love you feel for your husband," said Rhoda.

Despite Rhoda's loftiness, Polly relaxed at her words. And Polly wouldn't be married for years and years, so there was no point in worrying about it now.

She looked longingly at the smooth lawn below. The air was so soft and warm. "Let's go down!" she suggested.

"Good idea!" said Eleanor. They had often thought of this, but no one had ever dared.

"What if we get caught?" asked Daisy.

"We won't," said Polly. "The Crab is off, and Mrs. Blake is reading in her room, the way she always does. And the Guppy is out—her car isn't there."

"Shall we?" giggled Rhoda.

"Yes!" said Daisy. "Come on, troops!"

They slipped down the stairs in their bare feet. Then they danced around on the lawn and played a silent game of tag, covering their mouths to keep from laughing.

How wonderful to feel cool grass again, thought Polly. The full moon was so bright it was almost like daylight. For the first time, she felt as free at school as she did on the island.

Then a car drew up into the parking lot. They were frozen in its headlights like frightened deer.

"*What* do you think you are doing?" barked the Guppy.

Five minutes later, they were standing in her study. An hour of extra prep on Saturday morning . . . eating silently at a separate table for a week . . . no tuck boxes for a month . . . the list of penalties went on and on.

At least Polly wasn't the only one in trouble this time. Their shared resentment made them more of a group than ever. They even had a good time doing their extra prep. Eleanor did it quickly for all of them, then they played hangman for the rest of the hour. Millicent Price, the prefect who was supposed to be supervising, ignored them. She was too busy writing a letter to her beau.

In early April, Maud wrote and said she was not coming to the island for Easter. Instead, she was going to spend it with Daddy and Esther, then stay on for Polly's week there.

"My classes will be over then and I'll be very busy studying for exams," she wrote. "I'm longing to see you, Doodle," she ended, adding many X's and O's.

If so, why wasn't she coming home?

Chapter Eleven

What's the Matter with Maud?

On Easter Monday, Uncle Rand and Aunt Jean left to visit Gregor and Sadie in Chilliwack. "Poor Sadie," said Noni, after they saw them off. "She's about to receive far more advice than she wants on being a minister's wife."

For the rest of the week, Polly and Noni were on their own. Biddy had once again gone to Comox with her family. This time she had taken Vivien with her. They had already left by the time Polly arrived home.

She had seen Alice a few times, but all Alice wanted to do was talk about school. Polly was always happy to be alone with Noni, but her grandmother was distracted by worries about Maud.

"I simply don't understand why your sister wouldn't come home for Easter," she kept saying. "This is the second time she's stayed away."

"I guess she just wanted to spend more time with Daddy," said Polly sadly.

"That must be it, but we're her family, as well," said Noni. "It's as if Maud's avoiding us. Do you think she's angry at us for some reason? Can you ask her if anything's wrong?"

Polly promised she would.

Noni was also fretting about Polly travelling to Kelowna by her-self, especially since it was an overnight trip. "If Maud had come home as she was supposed to, you could have gone together," she said. "Perhaps I should go with you."

"Oh, Noni, I've never gone alone on a train—please, can't I try it?"

Noni smiled. "That's my plucky lass! Very well, hen—I don't want to baby you."

Polly could tell she was relieved. If Noni came along, she'd have to stay overnight with Daddy and Esther.

Daddy had telephoned and assured Polly she would be perfectly all right. "Just remember you have to change trains in Kamloops," he said. "The porter will help you. We'll all be at the Kelowna station to meet you."

The following Monday, Noni and Polly travelled to Vancouver and spent the rest of the day with friends of Noni's. The three adults sat in the living room, talking about the past. Polly was so bored she went into their den and read from start to finish the book she had packed for the journey.

Finally, it was time to go to the train station. Noni came on board with Polly and settled her in her seat, fussing as if she were a little girl. When the porter appeared, Noni pressed some money into his hand and asked him to take special care of her granddaughter.

Polly flushed; how humiliating! But the porter, a chubby man named Jim, grinned. "She'll be in good hands," he said. "I have a granddaughter the same age."

"Don't talk to strangers," warned Noni, hugging Polly goodbye. "All aboard!" called the conductor.

Noni hurried off the train. Polly clutched her new purse and waved out the window at her. Here she was, travelling to Kelowna all by herself!

The seat beside Polly was vacant, but a couple sat across from her and asked where she was going. Polly answered so shortly that they left her alone after that.

Since Polly had already read her book, she spent the first few hours looking out the window. After the train left the city, the train went along a wide, muddy river. "That's the Fraser," said Jim, walking by. Now they were in lush farmland surrounded by mountain peaks.

Memories flooded back of the last time Polly had been on this route, but going the other way: that miserable journey almost four years ago, travelling with Maud and awful Mrs. Tuttle from Winnipeg to Vancouver.

The river became narrower, rushing between steep canyons. Jim came back and turned Polly's seat into a bed. Last time, she and Maud and Mrs. Tuttle had had a suite with its own bathroom. This time, Polly had to go to the end of the sleeping car to use the toilet. Then she climbed through her canvas curtain and zipped it shut. She struggled out of her clothes and into her nightgown. The lurching space felt cozy and safe, like being in her own cave.

She lay awake for a long time, worrying about tomorrow. What would Esther be like? What if Polly didn't like her? Could she tell Daddy that? Would he stop seeing Esther if Polly wanted him to? Finally, her swaying berth rocked her to sleep.

The next morning Polly felt very grown up as she dressed and washed and followed Jim's directions to the dining car. She ate a huge delicious breakfast of eggs and sausages. People smiled at her and she smiled back. The conductor sat down with her for a while; she told him where she was going and answered his questions about the island.

At Kamloops, Jim helped Polly collect her things, get off the train, and board another one for Kelowna. He was switching trains, too, so he'd be with her all the way.

Polly sat in her new seat and watched the dry rolling hills outside. Now she was bored, and her legs were twitchy from sitting for so long. She got up and lurched along the train cars until she reached a lounge. A woman and a little girl were sitting there.

"Are you travelling all by yourself, dear?" the woman asked.

Polly decided to ignore Noni's instructions. She sat down and chatted to the woman, then helped the little girl colour a picture with crayons. They were also going to Kelowna, to visit the woman's parents. She was so friendly that surely she didn't count as a stranger.

After the train stopped at Vernon, Jim found Polly and told her it was time to go back to her seat. The train rumbled beside a long lake. Just as it slowed down, Polly noticed a lot of rough men in a clearing, sitting around a fire and cooking. Then the train steamed up to a small station, and Polly stepped down the stairs into soft, fragrant air.

"Polly! Doodle!" Daddy's and Maud's arms both hugged her at the same time.

"And this is Esther," said Daddy proudly.

"How do you do, Polly?" said Esther, bending down to shake her hand. "I'm so glad to meet you at last!"

Esther seemed even taller than in the photograph. She had wavy brown hair. Her voice was warm but shaky, and she seemed frightened. Frightened of *me*, Polly realized.

She smiled and said, "I'm glad to meet you, too."

Daddy looked relieved. "Now we're all together at last." He picked up Polly's suitcase. "Follow me, Doodle. Our house is only a short walk from the station."

Polly followed him along the wide main street and down a side one. Kelowna seemed a much smaller city than Victoria. "What's that wonderful smell?" she asked.

"Fruit blossoms!" said Daddy. "Kelowna is full of orchards. The apricots are in full bloom, and the cherries, pears, and peaches have just started."

They reached the boarding house, an ugly grey building on a corner. Its paint was peeling and some of the roof shingles were missing.

"Look, Polly, there's the lake," said Esther, pointing down the street. "We're lucky we're so close to it."

Polly caught a glimpse of the blue water she had seen from the train. She wished they could go there instead of into the dark house, which smelled of cooking and damp. "Show Polly her room, Maud," said Daddy.

Maud led Polly to a second-floor room with two beds in it. It was just as shabby and musty as the rest of the house, but beyond the large window were green hills, pink and white flowery trees, and the lake.

"Oh, Polly, it's been so long since I've seen you!" said Maud. "You're almost as tall as I am." She made Polly press her back against hers and measured their heads. "Not quite!" she laughed.

Maud looked different, too. She was chubby again, even fatter than she had been at boarding school. Her face was puffy, and her stomach bulged against her loose sweater. Her laughter was strained, and her eyes were as worried as they had been in the days when she had shouldered so many responsibilities.

Something *was* wrong. Polly remembered her promise to Noni, but there wasn't time to ask. A bell tinkled, Maud whisked her downstairs, and they joined the boarders for lunch.

———

Three men lived in the house: Mr. McMillan, Mr. Lane, and Mr. Hirsch. They grunted hello to Polly and bent over their plates, much more interested in eating the ample meal than in talking. Mr. McMillan was elderly, with a bush of white hair and fierce, tufty eyebrows, like an owl's. Mr. Lane and Mr. Hirsch were young men who worked in a bank. They were so much alike they could have been brothers, with their sleek, dark hair and thin moustaches. *Perhaps the bank requires them to look like that,* Polly thought.

She was so busy drawing the boarders' faces in her mind that she almost didn't hear Esther ask her if she wanted more chicken. "No, thank you," said Polly.

A delicious apple pie followed the chicken. After he'd wolfed down a huge piece, Mr. McMillan wiped his mouth vigorously and burped. Polly suppressed a giggle. "Thank you, ma'am," he said, standing up. "Very tasty, as usual."

He went upstairs, and the two younger men thanked Esther and went back to work.

"That was fast!" said Polly, who had barely started her pie.

Daddy laughed. "They always eat and run. But that means we get more time to ourselves."

"They're so easy," said Esther. "But men are always easier than women. Mother and I had a widow once, and my, how she complained! I had to wait on her as though I were her servant. After she left, we decided we'd have just male boarders. The only problem is that they eat more."

"Where was your mother from?" Maud asked her. "Did she always live in Kelowna?"

"Oh, no, Mother was from Vancouver. That's where I grew up, but when my father died ten years ago, she and I moved here to live with her brother. Then *he* died and we inherited this house—and now it's mine."

Maud kept asking Esther questions in a brittle voice Polly knew from the past. It was the falsely polite tone she put on when she was nervous and wanted to cover up how she really felt.

Polly pondered her sister as Esther talked and Daddy made comments. Perhaps Maud didn't *like* Esther and was trying to conceal it for Daddy's sake. It was hard to find anything not to like about Esther, though. She was shy with them, but her manner was open and friendly.

"What do you think of Kelowna?" Polly asked her.

Esther flushed. "The lake and the hills and the orchards are so beautiful. But I've always felt isolated. In Vancouver we had a close-knit circle of family and friends, but until I met your father, I didn't have anyone like that here."

"Why not?" asked Polly.

"Because Esther is Jewish," said Daddy quietly. "People can be incredibly narrow-minded, Doodle. They're polite to Esther on the surface, but she's never asked to any of the ladies' functions. Neither was her mother."

Polly squirmed as she remembered how Noni had barred Mrs. Osaka from the Kingfisher Women's Auxiliary just because she was

Japanese. Why were people like that? Polly had never met anyone who was Jewish, but Esther seemed just like everyone else.

"I think I must be the only Jew in Kelowna," said Esther. "But enough about me. We haven't even heard how Polly's journey went. Did you enjoy travelling on the train all by yourself?"

Polly told them all about it. "There were a lot of men eating outside near the station," she said. "Who are they?"

"That's what's called a 'hobo jungle,'" said Daddy. He sighed. "The poor fellows can't get work, so they have to subsist on what they can find. I lived like that once." Then he grinned. "But not anymore!"

Polly answered their many questions about the family and school. Just as in her letters to Daddy and Maud, she tried not to complain about St. Winifred's. She told them how the Guppy sat with her legs spread apart, and was relieved when Maud laughed.

"This afternoon I'll take you to the lake," Maud said.

"Too bad it's not warm enough for swimming yet," said Esther.

"You'll have to come back in the summer and try it," said Daddy. "Isn't it swell that we can visit each other whenever we want?"

Daddy seemed as happy as Polly remembered from her early childhood. He'd lost the haunted look he'd had when he didn't have enough money to take care of them, and he no longer acted as guilty as he had in January. She grinned at him.

"Get over here, Doodle," he said, opening his arms.

Polly climbed into his lap, even though she was thirteen. She lay back and breathed in Daddy's familiar smell of clean cotton.

"There, isn't this nice?" said Daddy, smoothing her hair. Esther smiled warmly at them, and Polly melted. She was back where she belonged, in Daddy's embrace.

But then she glanced at Maud. She had tears in her eyes: not happy tears, but tears of misery and terror.

Okanagan Lake was as vast as a small sea. Its colours shifted constantly, from bright blue to dark blue to almost black. Polly longed to capture them in paint.

She tried to find a chance to ask Maud what was wrong, but Maud strode ahead of her as if they were in a race. The path went under huge pine trees that smelled like honey. Polly wanted to linger, but Maud hurried them back to the house. Then she went upstairs to study.

Polly helped Esther peel carrots for supper. "Tell me about Kingfisher Island," Esther said.

Unlike many adults, she was a good listener. Her face was rapt as Polly described the deer and ravens and whales.

"It sounds like paradise!" Esther said. "You must really miss it at boarding school."

"I do," said Polly sadly. "The worst is being inside so much. But I—" She closed her mouth. Esther was so easy to talk to Polly had almost told her she wasn't going back in the fall.

Once again, the three boarders rushed through their meal and fled to their rooms. Maud and Polly and Esther did the dishes. Then they all sat in the living room and listened to the radio while Daddy fixed a lamp and Esther mended. At ten o'clock, Daddy kissed them goodnight. Polly hesitated in front of Esther; then she kissed her, as well.

"Is anything wrong, Maud?" Polly asked as soon as they were in bed.

"Of course not!" said the brittle voice.

"You seem so . . . different, as if something's bothering you," persisted Polly.

"I'm absolutely fine, Poll."

"But why didn't you come home for Easter? Noni was really upset."

"I'm sorry she was, but I needed to study."

"You could have studied at home."

"Polly, would you please leave it! Go to sleep now."

Polly had wanted to talk about Esther, but now she didn't dare. There was no way of penetrating Maud's armour when she got this stubborn. She seemed to feel she had fulfilled her sisterly duty by showing Polly the lake. For the next few days, she stayed in her room except for meals.

Daddy and Esther were too busy to spend much time with Polly. On some days Daddy laid bricks for various people in town, and on others he repaired the house. Esther shopped for food, prepared meals, and cleaned. Polly realized how little money the two of them had. There was no one to help with the constant work, their clothes were clean but shabby, and everything in the house was threadbare.

She thought of her comfortable life in Noni's house and felt guilty. Some people, like Daddy and Esther, had to constantly struggle for money. Others, like those poor men she had seen, had none at all. Yet Noni had too much! It was so unfair.

Polly kept offering to help, but Daddy and Esther told her she was on holiday. She wandered along the streets and looked in store windows. She spent her allowance on trinkets for her family and bought postcards that she sent to Eleanor and Daisy and Biddy. The rest of the time she sat by the breezy lake and sketched or painted. Daddy told her to watch for Ogopogo, a twenty-foot monster with three humps that was supposed to inhabit the lake. Polly drew a picture of it that made him laugh.

Maud appeared for meals blotchy faced and red-eyed. "She

must be very worried about her exams," Esther told Polly. "She's done nothing but study since she arrived."

Polly had never known Maud to worry about exams. She was so clever that she learned things fast. Last term, she seemed to have spent the whole time either with Robert or playing bridge at the sorority, and she'd still received high marks.

"I think she must also be missing her young man," said Esther. "We were sorry to hear that didn't work out. Did you ever meet him?"

Polly told Esther about Robert. "I didn't like him much," she confessed. "But I didn't really know him."

Every day that week, the radio broadcast reports of a mining disaster in Nova Scotia. On Thursday, Daddy, Esther, and Polly sat riveted as they heard that two of the three trapped men had been rescued. But Maud didn't even come downstairs to listen.

"Polly, is something the matter with your sister?" Daddy asked Polly that evening after supper as they were walking by the lake.

"I don't know," said Polly.

"She's so quiet and reclusive and sad—not like our Maudie! Do you think she doesn't like Esther and is afraid to tell me? When I ask her if anything's wrong, she just gets irritated."

"I don't know," said Polly again. She smiled at Daddy. "*I* like Esther. I like her a lot."

Daddy put his arm around her shoulder. "I can tell you do. I'm so glad, my Polly-Wolly-Doodle! Thank you for telling me. But what about Maud? Could you ask her and let me know? And if that's not the problem, could you try to find out what is?"

Polly nodded reluctantly. Now *two* people expected her to quiz Maud! But how could she, when Maud barely spoke to her?

The next morning Daddy said firmly, "No studying today, Maud. You've been cooped up with your books far too much, and you're not spending enough time with your sister. Esther and I have to lay a new carpet in the hall. It's such a gorgeous day. Why don't you two take a picnic to the lake?"

"But—" began Maud.

"No buts. Let me be the boss for once, Boss." Daddy grinned.

Maud had no choice. Esther packed a basket of food and they put on their hats and set off for the lake.

———

Again, Maud walked so fast that Polly had to scurry to keep up with her. They went along the same lakeside trail as before.

Finally, Maud stopped. She looked up and down the beach, then led Polly to the shade under one of the pines. It wasn't nearly lunchtime, but Maud tore into the basket. "Oh, good—meat loaf!" She ate a sandwich so fast she almost choked. "Don't you want one?" she asked. "These are scrumptious!"

"I'm not hungry yet," said Polly. She drank some lemonade, instead, and watched a goose family swim by. The silence between her and Maud became so frustrating that she got up, took off her shoes and socks, and waded into the cool water.

When she returned, Maud was leaning against the tree with her eyes closed. Polly lay down on her back, put her hat over her face, and closed her own eyes. The sun was so warm, and the sand so soft . . . she wanted to doze peacefully, but her promise to Noni and Daddy was like an annoying fly buzzing around her. She *had* to find out what was wrong with Maud!

Polly forced herself to get up and sit beside Maud against the tree trunk. She would start with the easier of her two questions. "What do you think of Esther?" she asked.

"She's fine," murmured Maud, her eyes still closed. "She's good for Daddy, and I'm glad to see him so happy."

She said the words as if reciting something she had memorized. "Do you *like* her?" persisted Polly.

"Sure I like her. Poll, quit asking me so many questions—I'm trying to sleep."

Polly seethed. "Why are you so distracted, Maud? You act as if you're not really here! I just wanted to know. So did Daddy."

Maud opened her eyes. "Sorry, Poll, I didn't mean to snap at you. I really do like Esther, and you can tell Daddy that."

"Do you think they'll get married? Will Esther be our mother then?"

"They plan to," said Maud. "Then Esther will be our step-mother."

Polly giggled. "They act like they're already married! Daddy's always hugging her, and last night I saw them kiss!"

Maud smiled. "I've seen them kiss lots of times. It reminds me of when Daddy and Mother used to."

Polly began to relax. This was just like old times, when she and Maud talked about everything. "How did your play go?" she asked.

"I dropped out of it," said Maud.

"You did? But you were so excited that you had a role!"

Maud didn't answer. She leaned back against the tree and the awkward silence returned. A boat chugged by, and a dog barked from the road.

Maud opened her eyes again. She looked as if she were trying to think of something to say. "How's school?" she asked in a weary tone.

"Oh, Maud, school is *awful*!" Polly couldn't help spilling out the truth. In a rush, she told Maud how much she hated the rules and the bells and the food and the dreary routine. "And I can't seem to do anything right!" she finished. "I'm always getting into trouble, and I never mean to—it just happens!"

The old Maud—the one who had been head girl—would have frowned and told her to try harder. This new, strange Maud just sighed. "I'm sorry you don't like it, Poll. You just have to keep remembering what a good education you're getting, especially in art. Think of all you'll learn in the next few years."

"Oh, but I'm not going back!"

"What do you mean?"

"Miss Guppy and I have a bargain. She asked me to try St. Winnie's for a year, but she said if I didn't like it, I wouldn't have to go back. And I don't, so I won't! Noni will be upset, but the Guppy promised she'd take my side. Noni will have to get me a governess, or I'll share Biddy and Vivien and Dorothy's."

Maud the head girl returned. She sat up straight and faced Polly, fully present and bristling. "That is *absolutely* ridiculous! Listen to me, Polly Brown! If you don't go back to St. Winifred's, you'll regret it all your life! You want to be an artist, don't you? How can you do that if you don't keep taking art? And you're learning lots of other things you'd never be able to learn with a governess."

"I can do art on my own," mumbled Polly. "I don't need to take classes." She knew how unconvincing that sounded.

"Perhaps you can, but you'll never learn as much as you would with Miss Falconer. The way you talk about her, she sounds like a terrific teacher. Doodle, you just have to believe me. Not going back would be a huge mistake!" Then Maud looked smug. "But you'll have to. Noni would never let you stay home, no matter what the Guppy says."

"Shut up, Maud! I don't want to talk about it anymore!"

Polly turned her back, picked up a stick, and drew a leaf in the sand. She wished she'd remembered her sketchbook.

Drawing calmed her. There was no point in worrying about school when it seemed so far away. She glanced at Maud again, wondering if she was still angry.

Maud's face was shiny with tears, and her shoulders heaved.

"Oh, Maud." Polly moved closer and put her arm around her. "What's *wrong* with you? I know there's something—you have to say!"

Maud's tears came faster. She put her head on Polly's shoulder and shook with sobs.

Then she told her.

Chapter Twelve

Maud's Secret

"You're *what?*"

"I'm going to have a baby," repeated Maud. She pulled out her handkerchief and mopped up her face. "Oh, Polly, what a huge relief it is to tell you! I wasn't going to, but I just can't help it. No one else knows but Ann . . . and the doctor, of course."

"But—how—"

Maud took her hand. "Dear Doodle . . . do you know how babies are made?"

"I just found out," said Polly. "One of my friends at school told us." She flushed. "So . . . did you do that with Robert?"

"Yes."

Polly remembered Rhoda's mother's words. "Was it . . . beautiful?"

"It was at the time, but that's because I loved him. We should have waited until we were married—then I would have known he loved me."

"But Maud, I thought babies didn't *happen* until after you were married!"

"Your body doesn't know if you're married or not," said Maud bluntly. "If a woman has relations with a man, she may become pregnant. I knew that. I just didn't think it would happen to me. How stupid I was!" She took a bite out of another sandwich and offered one to Polly.

Polly shook her head. She was too full of questions to eat. "When did you *know* you were having a baby? Is that why you didn't come home? Does *Robert* know? When is the baby going to be born?"

"Hold off!" Maud laughed. She picked up the sandwich again. "Here, Doodle, you have to eat something. I get such cravings for meat I might devour the whole lunch! Just listen, and I'll tell you everything."

Polly nibbled on a sandwich while Maud related the whole story.

Maud had first discovered she was pregnant at the end of January. "Remember how I didn't feel well at New Year's? I went on like that, not *really* sick. But then it got worse. I was throwing up every morning, and I felt so tired and headachy all the time. So I finally went to the doctor, and he said I was three months pregnant. I was so shocked! I should have guessed, because I'd stopped having my monthlies, but I just put that down to having the flu or something."

The doctor had been very disapproving. "He treated me like a naughty child . . . he still does."

Maud had stopped feeling sick, but then she'd begun to gain weight. "Everyone at varsity thinks it's because I eat so much," she said. "I do!" She patted her tummy. "I wear loose clothes and two girdles. I worried that Daddy and Esther might notice, but Daddy just teases me about my good appetite. Esther's never met me, so she thinks my size is normal. I thought Noni or Aunt Jean might suspect, though. And I worried I'd break down and tell them. That's why I couldn't let them see me."

The first person Maud had told was Robert. "I assumed he'd want us to get married right away. We had talked about marriage, but not until we graduated. We'd talked about having children, too, but we were going to wait until we were both settled in our careers. Having a baby this early would be tricky, but we loved each other—at least, I thought we did—so I was sure it would work out."

Robert, however, had been furious. "He acted as if it were all *my* fault!" Maud said, her eyes filling once more. "He said his family would be horrified, and I had to give the baby away, and then we could go on as we had before. I told him if that was his attitude, I never wanted to see him again. I haven't spoken to him since."

"Give the baby *away*?" whispered Polly. "You won't do that, will you?"

Maud swiped at her tears. "I'd keep it if Robert had agreed to marry me. People would have gossiped about us having a child so early, and our families would have disapproved, but I wouldn't have cared if Robert had wanted it—if he loved me. But he doesn't. So I have to give up the baby, Poll—don't you see? How can I have a child on my own? How could I take care of it and still go to university? And can you imagine how upset Daddy and Noni would be? I'd be a disgrace to the family!"

Maud grimaced. "After Robert told me he didn't want it, I tried to get rid of it. I had hot baths, and jumped up and down, and drank castor oil. That made me throw up, but I was still pregnant."

Polly gasped. "You mean you tried to *kill* the baby?"

"It didn't seem like a real baby then," said Maud. "And why should I have to go through this when it's not my fault? But now I'm too far along to get rid of it. After I give birth, though, I'm definitely going to give it away."

"But—who would you give it *to*?" Polly croaked.

"It will be adopted, Doodle. There are lots of couples who can't have children and would give it a good home. The doctor told me about a place in Vancouver that takes in girls who are in trouble. I'll go there in May after classes end. The baby is due at the end of July. After he's born, someone will adopt him and I'll carry on as if nothing has happened."

"*He?*"

Maud smiled. "I'm sure it's a boy. Ann did this test she heard about, with a ring on a thread. She held it over my belly and it swung back and forth. That means it's a boy."

A boy! Like the little brother Polly had always wanted. But this would be her nephew, not her brother.

"Oh, Maud," she cried, "*Don't* give him away! You can't!" She thought wildly. "Maybe Noni could take care of him! I'll be back on the island next year—I could help her."

"Don't be silly, Polly. Noni would probably disown me if she knew I was pregnant."

"How about Daddy and Esther, then?"

"Of course not! No one wants to take in an illegitimate child."

"What does *that* mean?"

"A child who is born out of wedlock . . . a child who would always live with that disgrace. No, Poll, this is the only solution. I just have to wait it out until August, and then it will be over. I'm going to tell Noni I'm spending the summer with Ann in Portland, that I'm taking a course there. Ann has been an absolute brick about all this—I don't know how I could have survived without her. I'll give Noni her address, and Ann will forward me her letters. I'll send mine back to Ann, and she'll send them on to Noni. She won't like me being away for so long, but I'll come home in August and everything will be normal again."

Now Maud was in control, putting things tidily into boxes the way she always did. Polly couldn't speak. She lay down and put her head in Maud's ample lap. Maud stroked her hair while they listened to the waves break on the shore. How could they sound so ordinary, as if nothing in the past hour had been said?

Polly felt a twinge under her head. She sat up. "Maud, I felt something! Was that—"

Maud smiled. "That's the baby kicking. He's been doing it a lot lately." She put Polly's hand on her stomach. "Can you feel it?"

There was a small movement, like a minnow swimming under Maud's skin. Polly's eyes stung. Something alive . . . a little person inside Maud! "If you—if you *did* keep him, what would you name him?" she whispered.

"'Danny,'" said Maud at once. "After Daddy, of course."

"He'd be a grandfather!" said Polly. "Oh, Maud, you have to tell him." Maybe Daddy could persuade Maud not to give Danny away.

Maud looked wooden. "I'm never telling him. And you mustn't, either, Polly. You mustn't tell *anyone*—do you promise?"

Polly reluctantly promised. They sat under the tree for a while longer. Then they trudged back to the house.

———

The whole world had changed. Polly felt like a different person as she went through the motions of the rest of the day.

A *baby*! A baby inside Maud! Polly wondered how big he was, whether he had fingers and toes and hair. Her own nephew! *Danny.* But he'd never know her. He'd never call her "Aunt Polly" and she would never wheel him in his carriage or bounce him on her lap.

Daddy would never carry him on his shoulders the way he had done with Polly. Noni would never read him poetry. Worst of all, Maud would never feed him or sing him to sleep or watch him grow.

Polly couldn't bear it. "Oh, Maud," she said that night. "You can't give away your baby! You have to keep him." She began to sob.

Maud didn't comfort her. She sat up and looked stern. "Polly, stop it! I have to do what's best for *me*, not you. I shouldn't have told you—you're much too young to know. I'm giving up the baby and that's that, do you understand?"

"Yes, Maud," gulped Polly. "But will you let me know how you are?"

"Of course I will," said Maud more gently. "I'll write to you regularly and I'll telephone you when the baby is born. I promise. But *you* have to promise not to keep asking me to keep him, all right?"

"I promise," said Polly, because she had no choice.

"Good girl. Now, let's just carry on as normally as possible," said Maud briskly. "We're both used to keeping secrets. This is just another one, that's all." She smiled ruefully. "Shall we prick our fingers and swear not to tell, the way we did the last time?"

Polly couldn't return her smile. The last secret—the one about Daddy being alive—had been almost impossible to keep. This one seemed even more stupendous. How could Polly bear such a heavy burden?

———

Every night Polly lay awake for hours, trying to think of how Maud could keep Danny. But there was no solution. Her head ached with worrying about it, and she almost wished Maud hadn't revealed her secret.

But then she thought of how much worse it must be for Maud. It was so unfair. It wasn't Danny's fault that he'd been created.

Maybe we can find out who adopts him, and go and visit him, Polly thought. She decided she'd ask Rhoda if she'd ever met her real parents.

Telling Polly her secret seemed to have cheered up Maud. She came out of her room and took part in the outings Daddy had planned for the last few days: a visit to an orchard and a movie at the Empress Theatre.

"When can you come back?" Esther asked them the night before they left.

"In July, I hope," said Daddy.

"I can't come in July," said Maud carefully.

Polly tried not to look at her.

"I'm staying in Portland with my friend Ann. We're taking a course there."

"What sort of course?" Daddy asked.

"Cooking," said Maud quickly.

Polly knew she'd just thought of it.

"That sounds grand! I've always wanted to take a cooking course. Maybe you could teach me what you learned when you come back," said Esther.

"I'll be the official taster," said Daddy. "But Maud, university only goes until the end of April, right? Could you come for a visit sometime during May or June?"

"It's a long course," said Maud.

Polly marvelled at how confident she sounded.

"It runs from the beginning of May until the end of July. And then I should spend some time on the island. So let's say I'll come here for the last two weeks of August. Will that be all right?"

Polly winced at how disappointed Daddy was.

"The end of August! That's so far away." He sighed. "Very well, Maud. I know you're a busy young lady. I can't expect to see you all the time." He turned to Polly. "How about you, Doodle?"

Polly thought fast. She wanted to be at home, not here, for the news of Danny's birth. "How about if I visit for a week right after school ends? I'm sure Noni won't mind. I could come back again in August with Maud."

"That would be wonderful!" Daddy kissed the top of her head. He beamed at them, and picked up Esther's hand. "One reason I was asking when you could come was that we want you to be with us for a very special event. You tell them, honey."

Esther flushed. "Your father and I are getting married," she said shyly. Then she chuckled. "Since this is a leap year, I asked *him* . . . and he said yes!"

"Oh!" said Polly.

"When?" said Maud.

"Well . . . how about the end of August?" said Daddy. "Then you could both be here. I'll write to your grandmother and inform her. It will be a very quiet wedding—just a civil ceremony, and then we'll all go out for a bang-up meal. Aren't you going to congratulate us?"

"Of course! Congratulations!" said Maud, hugging them both.

Polly did the same, but her arms moved automatically, as if they belonged to someone else. Even though she had known that Daddy and Esther had planned to get married, this news was too much to absorb after Maud's.

Chapter Thirteen

The Summer Term

Being back at school seemed unreal, but the tedious routine was also soothing; it gave Polly space to absorb Maud's news.

I'm going to be an aunt—I'm going to be an aunt! she kept telling herself, as if that fact was a pinch to wake herself up. *I'm going to have a nephew named Danny.* Then sorrow replaced her excitement as she reminded herself that Maud was going to give Danny away.

Polly got Rhoda alone as soon as she could. "I need to ask you something," she told her.

Rhoda looked suspicious, but she shrugged and said, "Ask away."

"Have you ever tried to find out who your real parents are?"

"Of course not! How could I?"

"Isn't there a way you can?"

"I don't think so. And why would I want to know? Mom and Dad *are* my real parents. What an incredibly nosy question, Polly!"

She flounced away. Despite her feelings about Rhoda, Polly felt a twinge of guilt; Rhoda had seemed close to tears.

The problem of Danny overcame her guilt. If Rhoda couldn't

find her parents, that meant her real mother couldn't find *her*. So Polly would never be able to find Danny. All the way back to school, she had imagined how she would track down his adoptive parents and rescue him. She'd bring him back to Maud, and Maud would be so overjoyed she would keep him.

Every night, Polly lay awake and imagined Danny into reality. He would have Maud's brown eyes and hair. Polly would feed and burp him the way she used to Biddy's sister Shirley. She would dress him and bathe him—it would be like playing dolls. Danny would call her "Aunt Polly." When he was older, she'd read to him and teach him how to paint.

Then Polly would cry softly. She would never even *meet* Danny. He would grow up in a stranger's family, and never know he had a mother named Maud and an aunt named Polly. If only she could per-suade Maud to keep him! But she'd promised not to.

"Why are you so dozy this term, Poll?" Eleanor asked her. "It's as if you're not really here."

Polly shrugged, longing to tell Eleanor her secret and relieve herself of its weight.

"You've changed, little one," said Miss Falconer in the first special art class. "Even your art has changed." She was examining Polly's watercolour painting. Polly had based it on the tree she and Maud had sat under, where she had heard the stupendous news.

"This is more mature than your previous work, Polly," said Miss Falconer. "Do you see how you've captured the *feeling* of the tree? It almost seems ominous!" She patted Polly's shoulder. "Very fine work, little one—very fine indeed."

She turned to the rest of the class. "We're going to be doing watercolour all term, and I want you to paint with it on your summer holidays, as well. I look forward to seeing the results in the fall."

Polly flinched. She wouldn't be *here* in the fall.

Then a surprising thought nudged her: maybe she *would* be. Maybe she would come back after all. How could she possibly miss out on special art?

No! answered a voice in her head. *You* hate *St. Winifred's.*

"Is something wrong, Polly?" asked Miss Falconer. "You look so stern!"

Polly tried to smile. "Nothing's wrong," she said, but she put down her brush. She couldn't paint when her head was whirling so much.

The next evening, Polly was called into Miss Guppy's study. "Did you have a good holiday?" said Miss Guppy.

Polly nodded. What did the Guppy want? Was she going to ask if Polly had decided to stay on at school? Polly panicked: all of a sudden, she wasn't ready to decide that.

But Miss Guppy was asking how Maud was. "I've had only one letter from her the whole time she's been at university—but she must be very busy."

If only she knew! "She's fine," muttered Polly.

"Polly, dear . . ." *Dear?* Polly became suspicious, especially when the Guppy gave her a sickening smile and said, "I want to talk you about your spiritual life."

Polly tried to listen as Miss Guppy told her how disappointed she had been in Polly's behaviour the last two terms. "You seem to have made a bad start at St. Winifred's. I've been thinking about you over Easter, and I've decided your life has been so unstable—what with your father and all—that you need some grounding. Do you know about my special group of girls?"

Polly thought of the six girls called 'the Elect,' the Guppy's pets. All of them were boarders. They had tea with Miss Guppy every Thursday, and sometimes went to church with her on Saturday afternoons.

Maud had been one of the Elect. She certainly wouldn't be now.

"I don't usually ask girls to join us until they're in the fifth form, but I'm going to make an exception for you, Polly. First because you're Maud's sister, and second because you could greatly benefit from some spiritual guidance. Would you like to be part of our group?"

"No, thank you," said Polly firmly. "My great-uncle is a rector, so I already have spiritual guidance. This summer he's going to prepare me for confirmation."

"That's encouraging, but you need guidance at school, as well. You may feel shy because you would be the youngest, but I promise you the other girls will be thrilled to have you there."

"I'd rather not," said Polly.

"Are you sure? We have such a good time and have such interesting discussions."

"No, thank you."

The Guppy asked her several more times. Polly just kept saying no.

Then Miss Guppy was cross. "I think you're making a big mistake, young lady. I can't force you to join us, but I expect to see an improvement in your behaviour this term, do you understand? You're going to find that difficult without help from our Lord. Will you let me know if you change your mind?"

Polly nodded and escaped. She would *never* change her mind!

Gradually, Polly got used to her secret. It became a dull weight inside her that increased each time she got a letter from Maud, as if she, Polly, were growing something, as well.

True to her word, Maud kept Polly apprised of how she was feeling. "I'm too big to wear my girdles now," she wrote. "Ann and I went to a second-hand store and bought looser clothes. The baby is kicking so much he keeps me awake. It's the strangest feeling, as if he's trying to get out!"

Oh, Danny, Danny, moaned Polly.

Noni's letters kept asking about Maud. "She seemed fine when I saw her," Polly wrote back. It was easy to lie in a letter, but Polly would be going home for the long weekend in May. When she saw Noni in person, how would she be able to conceal the truth?

For the first few weeks of term, Maud's condition so distracted Polly that she managed not to get into trouble. She went to class, did her homework, and practised drilling and piano as if someone else were doing these things. Once a week the boarders were taken to swim at the Crystal Gardens. The warm water soothed Polly, but she hated the awful green bathing suits they rented. The only times she felt real were in art, or fooling around with the rest of the Fearless Four.

Her dorm mates were just as unsettled. Daisy had not made it onto the school lacrosse team. "You can try again," the others kept telling her, but she became mopey and dispirited. They felt rudderless without her cheerful confidence.

Rhoda had seen a lot of Frank during the holidays and wouldn't stop talking about him. They got so tired of hearing "Frank says . . ." or "Frank thinks . . ." or "Frank did . . ." that they told her she was allowed to mention his name only once a day.

Even the usually calm Eleanor was cranky. "Why do I feel so

angry all the time?" she wondered aloud, after she'd thrown her shoe across the room when her lace broke. "I'm never like this!"

"It's just your age, love," said Mrs. Blake. "Your emotions can't keep up with all the changes you're going through." She smiled at them. "Remember to tell me, girls, if you need any supplies."

They all looked uncomfortable, especially Polly. Just last week she had had to go to Mrs. Kent, the school nurse, to tell her she'd begun her monthlies. The nurse had given her a box of Modess and said Polly was excused from gym for three days. That was so embarrassing; everyone knew why she and two other girls were sent to the library to study, instead.

Maud had prepared her several years ago for this huge change in her body, but Polly still found it shocking. She remembered Maud's words: "Every month your womb prepares a kind of nest for a baby. If a baby doesn't come, the tissues that make up the nest are expelled from your body. Then your womb builds up a nest for the next month."

Polly tried to piece together all the information she had heard from Maud and Eleanor, as if she were putting together a hard puzzle. Maud had said she had stopped having her monthlies when she became pregnant. Now the egg that Robert had fertilized was growing in the "nest" inside Maud. Since Polly herself had started menstruating, the same thing could happen to her! This was interesting and even a bit thrilling, but when it came to things like Modess or doing *that* with a boy, it was just plain icky.

The weather was so clear and warm that Polly and Eleanor met in their hideaway several times a week. They stretched out on the warm moss and sometimes even slept; it was so peaceful just lying there. The school garden was dotted with ruffly rhododendrons, and the air smelled like lilacs.

Today Eleanor was talking about her parents. This Saturday they were visiting Victoria; Eleanor had invited Polly out to lunch with them.

"They'll be glad to meet you after all I've said about you." Eleanor paused. "Poll, are you *sure* you're not coming back in the fall?"

"I'm sure," mumbled Polly, although lately she had felt more and more unsure. Sometimes, when she couldn't sleep for worrying about Danny, she would make a list of what she would miss after she left St. Winifred's: special art, of course, and literature, and botany, and piano, where she was learning jazz . . .

"I wish you'd change your mind! We'll miss you so much! Especially me," said Eleanor. "You're the most interesting friend I've ever had."

And Eleanor, of course! added Polly to her list. *And Daisy, and Mrs. Blake . . .* "I don't want to talk about it," she said.

The next day during history, Eleanor threw Polly a note. Polly uncurled the tightly folded piece of paper while the Hornet was writing a list of dates on the board. "Let's sneak some food out of our tuck boxes and take it to the hideaway today!" the note said.

Polly turned around and grinned at Eleanor. "Okay!" she mouthed.

"Polly Brown!" The Hornet's gimlet gaze fastened on Polly's desk. She marched over and pounced on the note.

Whenever the Hornet got angry, a crimson flush crept up her neck to the top of her forehead. All the girls watched the redness rise while she examined the note.

"Polly and Eleanor, into the hall," she ordered. "The rest of you, copy down the dates on the blackboard."

The Hornet's sharp questions stung them. "What do you mean by a 'hideaway'?" she asked them. "Where is it?"

They had to tell. *Now for more order marks*, thought Polly wearily. But it was worse than that. Mrs. Horner marched them to Miss Guppy's office.

The Guppy had never been so furious. Her scornful words pelted them so relentlessly that Polly felt like ducking. Worst of all, she kept saying what a bad influence Polly was on Eleanor.

Finally, she wound down, looking as exhausted as the girls by her tirade. "You are each to receive three order marks," she decreed. Then she paused. "And you are not to go out with your parents this Saturday, Eleanor. I will telephone them and inform them that you are grounded."

"No!" said Eleanor. "You can't do that!"

"That's not fair!" said Polly.

"No sauce! Now, go over to your dormitory until it's time for lunch. I'm sure Mrs. Horner does not want to see you again this morning."

Eleanor lay on her bed and sobbed. Polly had never seen her cry before. She patted her friend's back. "It's totally unfair!" said Eleanor. "Mother and Dad will be so disappointed. I don't blame you for not coming back, Poll. This school is a prison!"

Polly agreed. How could she have even *considered* returning?

The others were just as infuriated when they heard. That evening, however, Eleanor was called down to speak to Miss Guppy. When she returned, she was triumphant.

"Dad told the Guppy she *had* to let me see them! She was furious, but she said she had 'no choice but to let me go.'" She imitated Miss Guppy's voice.

"Can *I* still come?" asked Polly.

"Yes! Dad told her that, as well. I can't wait to hear about the whole conversation from him."

———

"That headmistress of yours is certainly a battleaxe," laughed Mr. Ford, as they sat at lunch. "I told her I'd pull you out of school unless she let us take you out."

"But what did you *do*?" asked Mrs. Ford.

"We went into the woods," said Eleanor.

"We had a secret place there," said Polly sadly. Now their refuge had been snatched away.

"You went into the woods? That's *all*?" said Mrs. Ford.

They both nodded. "It's strictly forbidden," said Eleanor solemnly.

Mr. Ford chuckled. "I shouldn't be encouraging you to break the rules, but it doesn't sound like a very serious crime."

"And to not allow you to come out with us!" said his wife. "That woman seems far too strict. Are you sure you're happy at the school, darling? You don't have to go back if you aren't."

"I'm fine," said Eleanor. "I'm learning so much, and we have a lot of fun in the dorm—right, Poll?"

Polly nodded. To her surprise, she almost envied Eleanor for liking school again.

She gobbled up her delicious lunch, listening to Eleanor and her parents talk about their family. Eleanor grilled them about her dog, Breeze, and they assured her he was fine. They told her a funny story about her younger sister, Peggy, playing a trick on her older brothers.

The Fords were like Biddy's parents: a bit boring, but kind and comfortable and . . . *normal.* Imagine what they would think if they knew that Polly's father had stolen some money, and that her sister was expecting a baby!

Mrs. Ford smiled at Polly. "We've been ignoring our guest. Eleanor has told us you live on Kingfisher Island. We went there years ago. You must love it it's so beautiful."

"I do," said Polly.

"And you live with your grandmother?"

Polly could tell she wanted to know more. She explained that Daddy lived in Kelowna and was going to get married in August.

"He is?" asked Eleanor.

Polly realized she hadn't told anyone at school; Maud's news was so much more important that the wedding had faded in comparison.

Polly tried to keep her voice steady as she went on to tell them Maud was finishing her first year at U.B.C.

"That's where *I* want to go," said Eleanor.

"And that's where you're headed, Ellie, with marks like yours," said her father proudly. "How about you, Polly? Do you want to go to university like our bright young lady?"

Polly shook her head. "I'm going to the Vancouver School of Art."

"Good for you!" he said.

"Eleanor tells us you're always drawing," said Mrs. Ford, "and that you're taking special classes on Saturdays."

"So we have a future science teacher and a future artist at the table," said Mr. Ford. "What special youngsters you are! You already know what you want to do."

"Only until you're married and have children, of course," said Mrs. Ford firmly. "You won't need a career after that, although I suppose it's helpful to have something to fall back on in case you're left high and dry."

"Now, my dear, times are changing," said her husband, patting her hand.

The waiter brought their bill. After Mr. Ford had paid it, he said, "Eleanor, sweetheart, I'm afraid I have disappointing news for you. Your mother and I won't be home on the long weekend."

"But why?"

"We have to go to a wedding in Vancouver," said Mrs. Ford. "It's a colleague of your father's, so it wouldn't be suitable to take you children. Gerald and Ralph are going to look after you and Peggy."

"Oh, no, Mother! I hate it when they take care of us. They just sit around and have their friends in, and Peggy and I have to do all the housework."

"It can't be as bad as all that," said her father.

"It is," said Eleanor.

"It's only for three days," said her mother. "I'm so sorry, darling, but you'll still be at home. You can play with Breeze and see your friends."

Eleanor pressed her lips together and wouldn't answer.

Polly was embarrassed to be in the middle of a family quarrel. Then she had an idea. "I know! Why don't you come home with *me*, El? My grandmother would love to have you, and I could show you the island. You could meet Tarka!"

"Now, Polly, I'm sure your grandmother doesn't want the trouble of a guest," said Mrs. Ford.

"She won't mind one bit," said Polly. *And then I won't have to be alone with her*, she thought.

"The island is really fun on Empire Day," she told Eleanor. "People visit from the other islands, and there are races and a parade and a dance."

"I'd love to come," said Eleanor. She turned to her parents. "Please, can't I?"

They looked at each other. "Very well," said Mr. Ford, "but only if Polly's grandmother agrees."

"I'll write to her tonight," said Polly.

Polly stood at the side of the dancing in the recreation hall, tapping her foot in time to the fiddle. She grinned as Uncle Rand clumsily led Eleanor in a waltz. As usual, Aunt Jean was a wild dancer, whirling in and out of the others. Polly glimpsed Noni on the other side of the room, chatting with Alice's mother.

Alice herself was dancing with Chester! On the ferry he had chatted more to Alice than to her, and tonight he'd only given Polly a friendly "Hello." Didn't Chester like her anymore? Polly half wished he'd ask *her* to dance, but she'd never danced with a boy before; she'd probably step on his toes.

It had been an unusual Empire Day, split between mourning for the old king and celebrating the new one. "I don't approve of that young man," said Aunt Jean, as if King Edward VIII were her personal acquaintance. "He's a womanizer and a gadabout. Mark my words—he'll come to no good."

Polly had tried to enjoy the festivities. She and Eleanor had taken part in the egg-and-spoon race and the three-legged race, and had rooted loudly for Kingfisher in the softball game, even though the island team had lost. The weather was perfect for walking Tarka and going out in the boat. Everyone in the family had taken to Eleanor, and she seemed to be having a wonderful visit.

Polly, however, couldn't stop feeling anxious about Maud. Being home made Maud's predicament more real. Everyone kept asking about her, and Polly had to keep explaining that Maud had too much work to come home.

"How I miss her!" Aunt Jean kept saying. "The family doesn't seem complete without Maud and Gregor and Sadie here."

What if they knew? Polly kept thinking. Would they reject her? Would Noni really disown her, as Maud had said she would?

"I'm so worried about your sister," Noni had told Polly this morning. "She started out at university by having such a good time, but now all she writes about is her studies. Is she still upset about Robert?"

"I don't know," said Polly. She had hoped not to be alone with Noni, but her grandmother still expected her to bring her breakfast to her room every morning.

"Ann's mother has written me a very pleasant letter saying how they're looking forward to having Maud in Portland," said Noni. "But the course she and Ann are taking is so long, and we won't see Maud until August. That doesn't seem right. Do you have any idea why Maud wants to do this? It's as if she's avoiding us."

Polly just repeated "I don't know." She wondered how they had managed the letter; Ann must have written it. Noni was so worried that Polly yearned to tell her everything.

"Polly . . ." Noni seemed embarrassed. "Your father has written to tell me that he's getting married. How do you feel about that?"

"I feel glad!" said Polly. "He and Esther seem really happy, and I like her a lot."

"That's reassuring. But I wonder . . . could she be Jewish? Her last name sounds as if she might be."

"Yes, she's Jewish," said Polly. She waited for Noni's reaction, hoping that Daddy was wrong.

"What a shame," said Noni quietly.

Polly bristled. Why was Noni like this?

"*I* don't think it matters if Esther is Jewish or not," Polly said firmly. "She's just Esther."

"I suppose you're right, hen. Anyway, it's none of my business whom your father marries. I just hope—"

"What?"

"Well, I hope you will always regard the island as your home, Polly."

"Of course I will!" Polly forgot her anger as she gave Noni a hug.

Now the music changed to a waltz. "*There* you are, Polly!" Biddy came up and frowned, as if Polly had been trying to avoid her. Polly flushed. All weekend she had felt pulled between her two friends. Eleanor was friendly to Biddy, but Biddy regarded her suspiciously. She had shocked Polly by telling her that Vivien and her parents had suddenly moved off the island. Her father thought he could find better work in Sidney.

Polly smiled, trying to reassure Biddy that they were still friends. "It's too bad about Vivien," she said. "You'll really miss her."

"It's terrible! I have no one to be with except Dorothy, and she's so boring. But at least you'll be back next year, Polly. It will be just you and me again, the way it was before Vivien . . . and before you knew *her*."

Polly was silent.

"You *are* coming back, aren't you?" demanded Biddy.

"Yes, of course I am," said Polly quickly.

Eleanor approached them with two glasses of lemonade. "I brought you a drink, Poll. Your uncle is some dancer! Oh, hi, Biddy. Do you want me to get you a drink, too?"

Biddy just glared at her and walked away.

"Instead of painting this week, we're going to visit someone very special," Miss Falconer announced the next Saturday. They all piled into Miss Falconer's old car. Jane sat in the front and the other four squished into the back; Polly had to perch on Dottie's knee. They asked whom they were going to see, but Miss Falconer said she wanted it to be a surprise.

She drove downtown, and past the Empress Hotel into James Bay. Then she told them to look for Beckley Avenue. Margaret spotted it first. The car turned onto an unpaved road lined with shabby bungalows. It stopped in front of a rundown cottage. "This is it—number 316," said Miss Falconer.

Theirs was the only car on the road. They stumbled out; a group of children and dogs playing nearby turned to stare at them.

"Who lives here?" asked Katherine.

"Miss Emily Carr," said Miss Falconer. "I've wanted you to see her work for a long time. She just moved to this house, and I haven't visited her new studio yet. Now, girls . . ." She hesitated by the front door. "Miss Carr can be crotchety, so don't be upset if she seems rude. That's just her way."

Miss Falconer knocked and a chorus of yaps answered. A stout old woman in a shapeless dress opened the door. Four small dogs with grizzly hair swarmed at her feet. Polly bent to pat one. It resembled Tarka, but was much more whiskery.

"Come in, come in," said Miss Carr. Her voice was gruff. "How are you, Frieda?" She led them into a tiny studio. "Now, whom do we have here?"

Polly tried not to stare as Miss Falconer introduced them. Miss Carr's round face was sunburned. Tufts of white hair poked from the wide black band around her forehead. Her eyes were direct and bright as she examined them.

"So these are your fancy pupils!" she said in a mocking voice. Polly avoided her gaze and gave her attention to the studio. Every inch was covered with paintings: some hung on the walls and many more leaned against them.

"Oh!" gasped Polly, advancing towards a painting as if it were calling her.

"Look as much as you like," said Miss Carr, her voice warmer. "Frieda and I will get you some tea—if I can find the teapot, that is."

The two women left the room, and the girls walked around gingerly.

"What are *those*?" giggled Dottie, pointing to a cage on the table.

"Chipmunks!" said Katherine.

Polly rushed to the cage. Three chipmunks were nibbling on a bowl of nuts. She watched them for a moment, but the glorious paintings beckoned her back. Miss Carr painted forests and skies in swooping strokes, using the deep-green and bold-blue colours of the west coast. The paintings shimmered with light and energy.

"I've never seen anything like these!" said Dottie.

"That's because they're Modern Art," said Katherine solemnly.

"I don't like them," said Jane. "Trees don't look like this."

But they do, Polly thought, gazing at a painting in which a tree soared to the sky and became part of it. This was the *essence* of a tree, its freedom and wildness and power. Some of the paintings made Polly feel like flying; some invited her to walk right into their dark, wooded depths.

Miss Falconer came into the studio with a tray full of mismatched cups and a teapot. Miss Carr followed her with a crumbling cake on a plate. She set it down on the floor and shut the door to keep out the dogs.

"Help yourselves, young ladies," she said. "The cake is a bit stale and I've run out of milk, so you'll have to make do."

"Do you have any questions for Miss Carr, girls?" said Miss Falconer.

Everyone was silent until Dottie asked, "How do you decide what to paint?"

"How do *you* decide?" said Miss Carr.

Dottie laughed nervously. "Well, I paint something that I think is pretty—or something Miss Falconer asks us to."

"That's all very well, but you should try to paint what calls you. Trees and totems and skies—they all beg me to capture their reality, so I try to do that."

Since the other girls were still tongue-tied, Miss Falconer asked Miss Carr several more questions. Polly listened avidly, wishing she could write down the answers.

Finally, as she was sipping a cup of cold, bitter tea, Polly murmured, "Miss Carr, how do you make your paintings *move* like that?"

"I beg your pardon? You'll have to speak up, child—I'm a bit deaf."

Polly repeated her question in a louder voice.

Miss Carr smiled at her. "Movement is vital. If you really look at God's creation, you will see how it's always in motion. I try to let that movement get into my brush."

"That's why your paintings are so alive." Polly said the words softly, but this time Miss Carr heard her.

"Thank you—what is your name?"

"Polly."

"Thank you, Polly. Do *you* want to be an artist?"

Polly nodded.

"Well, here's some advice for you—for all of you. Be careful that you don't paint anything that isn't completely yours—that isn't in your own soul. You have to learn the mechanics, of course, but use them in your way, not someone else's."

They were all digesting this when the door burst open and a little girl in a yellow dress rushed screeching into the room. She grabbed Jane's leg, and Jane screeched even louder.

"Get it off—get it off me!"

It wasn't a little girl at all—it was a monkey!

"Oh, Woo, you bad thing." Miss Carr pulled the monkey away by its collar and fastened it by a chain to the table leg.

"This is Woo," said Miss Carr fondly. "She didn't mean to frighten you. She just gets excited when visitors arrive."

Woo chittered and scolded as they stared at her. She was about the size of one of Miss Carr's dogs, with large ears and thick brown fur that stuck out over the back of her dress. Her beady eyes were close-set beneath her wide jutting brow. Jane retreated to the far corner of the studio, but Polly edged closer and closer.

"Can I pet her?" she said.

"I wouldn't advise it," said Miss Carr. "She bites!"

"How does she like her new house?" said Miss Falconer.

"She loves it. She's taken over the plum tree in the back and spends all her time there, unless she's plaguing the dogs."

"I've never known anyone who has a monkey!" said Dottie.

"I used to have a white rat named Susie, but she died last year," said Miss Carr sadly.

"Now, girls, we must go," said Miss Falconer. "Emily, I can't thank you enough for letting us come."

"You're lucky you caught me. Woo and the dogs and I are spending all summer in the Elephant. You and Frans must visit us there."

Polly gaped. Did Miss Carr own an elephant as well as a monkey?

"Don't look so surprised, young Polly!" laughed Miss Carr. "'The Elephant' is what I call my caravan. I park it in the country and sketch from it."

She walked them to the front door and said goodbye. "Come and see me again in the fall," she told them. They could still hear the dogs barking and Woo screeching after she closed the door.

"I want you to always remember this afternoon, girls," said Miss Falconer. "Someday you can tell your children you met a brilliant Canadian artist."

"Really?" said Jane doubtfully.

"Really! We'll talk about her art next week, and maybe you'll understand it better."

Polly didn't dare to say that she already understood it. That sounded like boasting. She sat in a daze all the way back, trying to remember every one of Miss Carr's paintings and words. "Don't paint anything that isn't in your own soul . . ." Polly wasn't entirely sure what that meant, but the words opened up a window inside her.

CHAPTER FOURTEEN

POLLY'S DECISION

THE LAST FOUR WEEKS OF THE SCHOOL YEAR WERE PACKED WITH activities. The boarders were taken to the beach for picnics and to several concerts and movies. Four other girls schools arrived one Saturday for the drill competition. To Miss Gower's dismay, St. Winifred's came second, beaten by Ashdown Academy from Vancouver. Polly didn't care; she was just relieved that the dreary marching she'd done for three terms was finally over.

Rhoda got her certificate from the Royal Drawing Society; she'd received top marks for the first level. "Miss Netherwood says I show great promise," she boasted. "It's such a shame you had to drop out of drawing," she added to Polly. "You'll find it hard to be an artist without the good training I'm getting."

Polly ignored her. All she could think about was Maud. Now she had gone to the special home for "unwed mothers." She wouldn't tell Polly the address or telephone number. "I'll phone you around the end of July and let you know when I've had the baby," she wrote. "I'll say it in code, in case someone else is listening on the line. After that I'll come back to the island, and we'll all carry on as we did before."

At least Maud kept writing to Polly. The home sounded bleak and tedious, much worse than boarding school. There was a strict schedule of work and prayers and meals. Maud had to swab out bathrooms and dust furniture and peel vegetables. Polly could tell it was even worse than Maud's stoical words implied.

And where would she have the baby? Would she be alone? Polly wasn't sure how babies were born; would it *hurt* Maud? She looked in the school library for a book to explain childbirth, but found nothing.

Polly spent long hours after school wandering on the grounds. Now the roses were in bloom. They made her miss Noni's. For the first time, however, she missed Maud much more than she did her grandmother. Her sister seemed so far away, as if she were in another country, a country that excluded Polly.

"Is something wrong, Poll?" Eleanor asked, when Polly wouldn't go to the tree at the bottom of the field with her. Now that their hideaway was off limits, this was their new place to escape to.

"I just need to be by myself," mumbled Polly.

"Are you trying to decide if you'll come back or not?" asked Eleanor in her usual blunt manner.

"There's nothing to decide," said Polly. "I'm not coming back."

"Have you told the Guppy?"

"Not yet, but I will soon."

"Oh, Poll, *please* stay. I'd miss you so much!"

Polly tried to smile at her friend. "I'll miss you, too, El, but I hate it here. I don't want to talk about it anymore, all right?"

"All right," said Eleanor glumly, "but *I* think you're making a huge mistake."

The next Saturday, Miss Falconer asked them to take away all the art they had done so far that term, so they wouldn't have as much left to remove on their last day. Polly carried her large portfolio up to the dorm.

"What's that?" asked Daisy.

"It's my art," said Polly shyly.

"Can we see?"

Polly spread her watercolour pictures out on her bed.

"Golly!" said Daisy. "These are amazing!"

Eleanor examined each painting. She looked up. "These *are* amazing, Poll. I didn't know you were this good."

"Thanks," said Polly. She gazed at her paintings. Some of them she wished she'd done differently, but on the whole she was proud of them.

"*I* think they're kind of sloppy," said Rhoda. "Why didn't you mop up those drips? And this tree isn't in proportion with the one beside it. I hope you don't mind me telling you," she added.

Polly gazed at Rhoda's pretty, simpering face. She clenched her hands. "I do mind, Rhoda," she said slowly. Then her voice gathered speed. "They're *supposed* to be that way. The drips add to the effect and the tree isn't meant to be realistic—it's how I felt it. You don't know anything about *real* art, Rhoda. You're good at technique, but that's all."

"How dare you?" said Rhoda. "I'm just as talented as you are!"

"No, you're not," said Polly. "You just think you are, because you got that stupid certificate."

"You—you—" sputtered Rhoda, advancing towards Polly.

"Oh-oh," said Eleanor. "Come on, Dais—let's get out of here."

Polly and Rhoda faced each other. Then they began shouting.

"You're such a show-off!" said Polly. "Why can't you just accept that I'm better at art than you are?"

"Because you aren't!" said Rhoda. *"You're* the one who's a show-off! You think you're so special just because your mother is dead. But why won't you tell us about your father? There's something fishy about your life, Polly."

"My life is none of your business!" yelled Polly.

They continued to argue, getting louder and louder. Tears flooded down Polly's cheeks. Rhoda's face was crimson.

Then Mrs. Blake hurried in. "Girls, girls, what on earth is the matter? Calm down, both of you!"

"Polly said I was a show-off!" said Rhoda. She began weeping in such a melodramatic way that Polly wanted to slap her.

"I don't care what either of you said. Stop this immediately! Polly, you go and wash your face and sit on the front steps until supper. Rhoda, you stay in the dorm. I don't want either of you to speak to the other for the rest of the day."

Polly ran out. She splashed cool water over her face, then sat on the steps, trying to breathe steadily.

Eleanor found her there. "I hope you don't mind that we told Mrs. Blake, Poll, but we thought you might kill each other! Why do you let Rhoda bother you so much? I know she's spoiled, but she's not that bad if you give her a chance."

"I hate her!" said Polly.

"I wish you didn't," said Eleanor. "We'd have a lot more fun if the two of you got along."

Polly was relieved that she wasn't allowed to talk to Rhoda. At supper, the two of them carefully avoided eye contact with each other.

"Polly, how would you like to meet my little boy tomorrow?" Mrs. Blake asked her later. "I have the afternoon off and you could come home with me."

"Only me?" said Polly.

"Only you, love." Mrs. Blake smiled. "I think you need to get away from here for a while. Seeing Johnny will cheer you up—I promise!"

———

After Sunday lunch, Mrs. Blake and Polly took the streetcar to the end of the line. Polly stared out the window, waiting to be scolded for yesterday.

"Polly, love, I'm sorry you and Rhoda clash so much," said Mrs. Blake. "Have you ever considered why?"

"Because Rhoda is a spoiled brat," muttered Polly.

"That's not a helpful thing to say," said Mrs. Blake. "I can think of a better reason, but you won't like it. Have you ever considered that the two of you are quite a lot alike?"

"No! We're not at *all* alike!" said Polly.

"Calm down and give me a chance to explain. You are, actually. You're both very pretty, which gives you each a confidence not many girls have at your age. You're both talented at art, even though you approach it differently. And perhaps, Polly, you're a bit spoiled yourself! From what you've told us, your grandmother indulges you, does she not?"

"I'm not at all indulged! *Rhoda* is the one who is!"

"I knew you wouldn't like my reason. You don't have to agree, but over the summer will you think about what I've said? And will you resolve to get along with Rhoda from now on? I've asked her the same thing. You don't have to like each other, but you *must* start being civil to her. If you don't, I will have no choice but to tell Miss Guppy. I hope that when you see each other again in the fall, you and Rhoda will each have a new attitude."

Polly nodded because she had to. Underneath, however, she seethed at Mrs. Blake's words. Anyway, she wouldn't be here in the fall . . . so there was nothing she had to think about during the summer.

They reached their stop, then walked a few blocks to the white bungalow where Mrs. Blake boarded with a widow named Mrs. Turner.

The front door opened and a small boy rushed out. "Mummy— Mummy!" he shouted.

Mrs. Blake lifted him up and swung him around. Then she plastered his face with kisses and released him. "This is my Johnny!" she said.

Johnny was chubby, with a halo of brown curls. He hid behind his mother and stuck his thumb in his mouth while he stared at Polly.

"He's been waiting by the window," laughed an older woman who had followed him out. "Who is this, Martha?"

Polly smiled as she was introduced. Wait until the others found out she knew Mrs. Blake's first name!

Mrs. Turner left to go shopping, and Mrs. Blake and Polly had Johnny to themselves. They pushed him in the swing in the backyard and sat on the edge of his sandbox while he moved his truck around, mumbling gibberish to himself. Then Mrs. Blake took him into the kitchen and tenderly washed his hands and face. She made some tea and poured some milk for Johnny. "He's been drinking out of a cup since he was one," she said proudly.

Johnny perched on a tower of cushions, munching a cookie. He was a quiet little boy and didn't say much except "More, pease," holding up his cup. After tea, they went into the living room and Mrs. Blake read him a story. Then he fell asleep on her lap.

Polly couldn't keep her eyes off him—his high forehead, his dimpled hands, and the long lashes resting on his cheeks. She yearned to draw him. This could be Danny in a few years!

"You're so lucky to have a little boy," she blurted out.

"Why yes, I am!" said Mrs. Blake. "You seem to like children, love. I'm sure you'll have some in your life one day, as well."

Polly had to bite her lip to keep from telling. She could have a child in her life now—not her own, of course, but her *nephew*—if only Maud wasn't so determined to give Danny away. Maud had said it would be hard to bring up a child by herself. It must be hard for Mrs. Blake, too. She had to work to support Johnny, and she couldn't see him every day. But her peaceful face bent over her child was proof that it was worth it.

"When did your husband die?" Polly asked her. "Did he ever see Johnny?"

Mrs. Blake flushed. "No, he died before Johnny was born."

"Was Johnny named after him?"

"No!" Then her voice softened. "My son was named after my father."

Why did she sound so angry? wondered Polly.

Johnny must have heard his name. He woke up, and Mrs. Blake started bouncing him on her knee chanting, "This is the way the farmer rides."

"Will you watch him while I wash up the tea things?" she asked. "His toys are in that basket."

Polly emptied the basket on the floor, and Johnny began piling blocks. He wasn't as shy with her now, and let her help him when they fell over.

Mrs. Turner returned and soon it was time to go. Mrs. Blake had tears in her eyes as she hugged her son fiercely. "I'll see you in a few days, Johnny-cake," she murmured into his neck. She scarcely said a word all the way back.

———

That night, the others wanted to know every detail.

" 'Martha'!" said Rhoda. "It suits her."

Polly wanted to ignore her as usual, but she remembered Mrs. Blake's admonition. "It does suit her," she made herself answer. This was the first time she and Rhoda had spoken since yesterday. Polly noticed Daisy and Eleanor exchanging relieved glances.

"The poor thing," said Daisy. "Losing her husband before he even met Johnny!"

"I wonder why she left England?" said Eleanor. "Doesn't she have family there?"

"I don't know," said Polly.

"Hmm . . . I wonder if she *had* a husband," said Rhoda slowly.

"*What?*"

She hushed their protests. "Just listen a moment. She never talks about her husband, and she told us she came to Canada right after Johnny was born. My mother had a girl working for her who was having a baby, and *she* wasn't married. Maybe Mrs. Blake is the same. Maybe she just *pretends* she was married and that her husband died."

"She wears a ring," Eleanor pointed out.

"That could be so people won't talk about her. My mother's maid wore a ring, too."

Daisy looked puzzled. "Can you *have* a baby when you're not married?"

Polly winced, remembering asking Maud the same question.

"Of course you can," said Eleanor. "You're not supposed to, but sometimes people do."

"Oh."

They were all silent. Then Daisy said firmly, "Well, I don't care whether Mrs. Blake is married, and I don't think it's any of our business. Let's not talk about it anymore."

Polly, however, couldn't help pondering Rhoda's words. It all made sense. She would never find out, of course, and she could never ask. But perhaps Mrs. Blake was like Maud. Perhaps she had also "got into trouble" and left England because her family was ashamed of her.

It wouldn't be like that for Maud, thought Polly. She wouldn't be isolated the way Mrs. Blake was. Daddy and Esther would support her entirely—maybe they'd even take care of the baby for Maud. They could pretend it was theirs.

But what about Noni? She and Aunt Jean and Uncle Rand were much more proper.

Oh, poor Maud, and poor Danny! What was going to happen?

As the term drew to a close, Polly wondered when Miss Guppy was going to ask what Polly had decided. Would Miss Guppy bring up their bargain, or was that up to Polly? Perhaps she wouldn't even *let* Polly come back to school Polly had been such a disappointment.

But did she *want* to come back? Every day Polly noticed the things she hated: wearing a uniform, walking in line, the terrible food, all the stupid rules, never having time to herself, being inside too much . . .

And yet . . . every Saturday her heart broke at the prospect of never coming to special art again. Never watching and listening while Miss Falconer talked about what each girl had done, never learning so many new techniques, never laughing with the others over tea and cookies, never hearing Miss Falconer say "Fine work, little one!"

Polly had been trying to put into practice what she had learned from Miss Carr. Noni had taught Polly to paint exactly what she saw. But you didn't have to do that. You could paint the *meaning* of what you saw: the truth behind the object or tree or landscape in front of you, the truth that reflected the truth inside you. When Polly thought about this, she felt the way she sometimes did in church on the island or gazing at the stars: that there was something mysterious and wonderful in the universe that was just out of her grasp.

"Come and see me again in the fall," Miss Carr had said. If Polly didn't return to school, she would never meet Miss Carr again.

And she'd have to leave Eleanor and Daisy. She would miss them so much. Eleanor had told her that she'd invite Polly to stay with her in Nanaimo next Christmas, but they might feel like strangers by then. Next year her friends would have more escapades together, but Polly wouldn't be part of them. "The Fearless Three" didn't have the same ring as "the Fearless Four."

Polly thought of what else she would miss. She had really enjoyed literature and botany and piano this term. And it was a treat to be taken to movies and plays and concerts; she could never attend those on the island.

But Polly would be *home.* She'd be with Noni and Aunt Jean and Uncle Rand; and with dear Tarka, whom she ached for just as much as on her first day here. She'd be able to wander on the beach for hours, with no bell ordering her to be somewhere. She could renew her friendship with poor lonely Biddy, who was so eager to have her back. She could once again revel in the sea and the forest and the vast starry sky.

Maud and Daddy would be disappointed in her. Noni would be even more so, since she believed so much in Polly getting a good education.

I don't care! Polly tried to tell herself. *I hate this place, and I don't choose to go back! I'll just have to do art on my own.*

What to decide, what to decide? The question throbbed in her brain like a drum, as if she had a gigantic headache.

Then one morning she *was* sick. Her head pounded, her nose streamed, her throat ached, and she was hot all over.

"It could be a grippe," said Mrs. Blake. "To the infirmary with you."

For the rest of the week, Polly lay tucked up in the infirmary, a room at the top of the house. She was the only patient there and received all the attention from Mrs. Kent, the school nurse. Every few hours she put cool towels on Polly's forehead and brought her glasses of water and fresh handkerchiefs. The rest of the time she left Polly alone.

Polly tried to read, but mostly she escaped into sleep: a deep, soothing sleep in which she forgot all the turmoil of this year—of *all* the years since she'd left Winnipeg. She would wake up refreshed for a while, then plunge back into sleep's healing embrace.

On the fourth day, she sat up in bed feeling much better. Her temperature had gone down, her nose wasn't as stuffy, and her throat was fine. Best of all, she was starving.

"Good for you," said Mrs. Kent, after Polly had gobbled up three pieces of toast and jam. "I think you're on the mend. I want you to stay in here for the day, then you can go back to your dormitory."

The morning seemed very long. Mrs. Kent said Polly could get up, so she sat in her dressing gown by the window and watched the other girls go back and forth. This was fun for a while because they didn't know she was observing them. She gasped as she saw two upper sixth girls, Lucy Tarrant and Julia O'Callaghan, sneak behind the school building and light cigarettes. They were *prefects*!

Then Polly tried to read, but her book didn't interest her; nor did any of the magazines in the infirmary. She longed to draw, but she didn't have her sketchbook with her.

The question of whether she would stay at St. Winifred's rose in her mind again, as if it had been waiting for her to get better. Polly couldn't focus on it; she wished someone would simply decide for her. She couldn't worry about Maud, either; she was too sleepy. After lunch she went back to bed.

She woke up when she heard a familiar voice coming from the stairs: "Mrs. Kent? Are you there?"

Alice! Polly hadn't seen as much of her at school as she thought she would. Each was so involved with her own age group that their paths didn't often cross.

Alice came into the room. "Polly! What are you doing here? Are you sick?"

"I was," said Polly, sitting up in bed, "but now I'm better."

"Have you seen the nurse? I was running down the path and I fell and scraped my knee." Beneath her dress, Alice's knee was raw and bloody.

"Poor you!" said Polly. "I don't know where Mrs. Kent has gone. Why don't you wash it and I'll look for a bandage."

Alice grimaced as she picked out tiny pebbles from her wound, then soaped it. Polly found some gauze and tape, and together they managed to wrap it around Alice's knee.

"It really stings!" said Alice. "I'll wait for Mrs. Kent to come back—maybe she can put something on it so it won't get infected."

She hobbled over to a chair and sat down. Polly went back to her bed.

"Only a week left of school," sighed Alice. "Did you know I'm singing a solo at the graduation ceremony?"

"Good for you!" said Polly.

"Will you spend the summer with your father?" Alice asked her.

"Not the whole summer. I'm visiting him for a week straight from school. Then I'll be home until the end of August, then I'm going back to Kelowna. My father's getting married then." Imagine if Alice knew what was *really* happening this summer!

"He's getting married? That's swell! Do you like his fiancée?"

Polly realized she'd been so busy worrying about Maud that she'd hardly thought about Esther all term. "Yes, I do," she said. "They suit each other."

"Now that they're getting married, will you live with them?"

"No!" Why did Alice keep bringing this up? "I'll keep living on the island with my grandmother, of course."

"But your dad and your stepmother might want you to be with *them*! Who's your legal guardian?"

"My grandmother," said Polly. "At least, she *was*, and I suppose she still is, even though—"

"Even though your father's alive after all! I think that means *he'd* be your legal guardian. Maybe he'll *insist* you live with them."

"He hasn't said anything about it. And he and Esther haven't got much money—they probably couldn't afford to feed another person. Anyway, I want to stay on the island. Daddy would want what *I* want."

"I think you're crazy," said Alice. "How can you not want to live with your own father? I'd give anything to be with mine." She looked dreamy. "One day, Polly, I'm going to find him. I'm going to be the star in an opera, and he'll see my name on the marquee and come in. After the performance, he'll knock on my dressing-room door, and we'll be together again. Then I'll live with him, and take care of him when he's old."

Alice had told this to Polly before. It was such an unlikely fantasy that Polly ached for her.

Alice gazed out the window. Polly knew it was because she was wiping her eyes. Then she turned back to Polly and said, "So, Goldilocks . . ."

"I wish you'd stop calling me that," said Polly. "I have a bob now."

"I'll call you whatever I choose," said Alice. "So, how did you end up liking St. Winnie's?"

"I hate it," said Polly.

"But don't you like art?"

"I love art."

"Then that makes it all worthwhile, right?"

All of Polly's indecision rushed back. "Oh, Alice . . . I don't know what to do!" She blurted out the whole story—how Miss Guppy had promised her that if she didn't like boarding school, she would help her persuade Noni not to make her come back. She repeated to Alice all the pros and cons she had gone over so many times.

Alice listened in silence. Then she leaned forward and gripped Polly's arm as tightly as in the days when she had bullied her. "You listen to me, Polly Brown. You would be absolutely nuts not to come back! You'd be sacrificing your whole career. You have to get your priorities straight. Not liking school and missing the island *aren't important*!"

"Could you let go of my arm?" gasped Polly. "You're hurting me!"

Alice let go, but her voice was just as forceful as her grip. "Do you want to be an artist? More than anything in the world?"

Polly nodded.

"I don't believe you," Alice said coldly.

"What do you mean?"

"If that was true, you wouldn't even *consider* leaving. You'd know that you have to put up with things you don't like about the present because of what you hope for in the future. But you don't seem to know that, so I guess you don't want to be an artist." She shrugged. "Too bad. You would have been a good one. All that wasted talent for nothing."

"Shut up, Alice! I *will* be an artist!" snapped Polly.

"Well, then?"

Polly was stunned. Then she almost felt sick again as relief flooded over her. Her wish had come true. Someone had told her what to do. It was what Polly, deep down, wanted to do, as well.

She grinned. "Oh, Alice, you're right! It's so simple. I want to be an artist, so my only choice is to come back. Thanks so much for helping me decide."

"Whew! I was beginning to think I'd have to pinch you." Alice laughed. "Wait and see, Goldilocks—one day, you and I are going to be famous!"

As soon as Polly was released from the infirmary, she went straight to Miss Guppy's study. She hated to give the Guppy the satisfaction of knowing that she had decided to stay, but she might as well get it over with.

"Yes?" barked the familiar voice when Polly knocked. "Oh, it's you, Polly. What do you want? I can only spare you a few moments."

"I've come to talk about our bargain," said Polly.

"What bargain?"

Polly's voice shook. "The bargain we made last summer, before I came here. I promised to try St. Winifred's for a year, and *you* promised that if I didn't like it, you would help me persuade my grandmother to let me stay home. Don't you remember?"

Miss Guppy swung around from her desk. "Sit down, you silly child, and kindly do not speak to me in that tone of voice. Yes, I remember us discussing something like that. Did you actually think I meant it? I only said it to get you to St. Winifred's. Now that you're here, I'm certainly not going to let you leave. You've been a real disappointment this year, young lady, but perhaps next year you will improve. As for persuading your grandmother to let you stay home, I would never do such a thing."

"But you *promised*! We shook hands on it!"

"We may have done, but I certainly don't remember making any promises."

Polly stared at the Guppy's horsey face, trying to remember if she had actually used the word "promise." Maybe she hadn't; maybe Polly had just imagined it.

She dug her fingers into her palms so she wouldn't scream. "But you said *I* could decide!"

"Polly, I've just told you—I said that so you would try the school. I didn't mean it."

"Then you lied," said Polly.

"How dare you!" The Guppy looked as though she wanted to slap Polly. Then she took a deep breath and seemed to force herself to smile. "Let's both calm down. There's nothing more to discuss. You are coming back to St. Winifred's, as your grandmother and father would both want. We know what's best for you. I am aware that you dislike it here, but Miss Falconer says you're thriving at art. How could you miss that? You're only thirteen, Polly. You're much too young to think you can make such an important decision on your own."

Polly forced her trembling legs to stand. She had intended to tell Miss Guppy she would stay. Everything had appeared so simple when she'd talked to Alice, but Polly had forgotten how this dreadful woman infuriated her. But how could she endure her for another four years?

"I'm not too young," she said firmly. "I'm almost *fourteen*. And I'm not coming back. You can't make me!"

"Don't be ridiculous, child. Perhaps *I* can't make you, but your grandmother certainly can."

"She won't! I'll tell her how unfair you and some of the teachers are, how awful the food is. She loves me! She won't make me go to a school where I'm so unhappy."

For the first time Miss Guppy looked uncertain. Then she peered down her long nose and said proudly, "Your grandmother believes what I do—that girls should have a good education. That's why she sent you here, and that's why I am certain she won't let you leave. And I don't believe you're *that* unhappy here, Polly. You like your art classes, don't you? How can you consider giving those up?"

How could she? . . . Polly almost relented then. But Miss Guppy had lied to her! Her anger flared even more.

"I don't care!" she said. "I'm not coming back!"

Miss Guppy sounded tired. "Of course you are, Polly. I don't want to hear any more about it. You're acting like a foolish little girl, and I think you should leave." She turned back to her desk and Polly stumbled out.

When she entered her dorm, the others greeted her with joy. "Oh, Poll, you're better! We missed you!"

Polly blinked at their friendly faces. These were her *friends*. Three of them were, anyway. How could she choose never to see them again?

She pushed down her doubts and forced herself to speak. "I have something to tell you. I've decided I'm not coming back to St. Winifred's."

"You're *not*?"

For the rest of the evening, and long after lights out, they tried to persuade her to stay. But something hard had set in Polly. Miss Guppy had deceived her. Polly could not continue to be under the thumb of someone who lied to her, someone who dismissed what she said as if she were a naughty child. She had made her decision; she was not returning.

That Saturday was her last art class for the year. Miss Falconer had made a cake for Dottie and Katherine, who were graduating. She suggested that those girls who were returning keep a sketchbook of their summer. "Try to draw and paint in it every day. We'll spend the first class in September looking at one another's."

Polly had not been able to speak all afternoon. She had intended to take Miss Falconer aside and tell her she wasn't returning, but she couldn't bear to. *I'll write her a letter*, she decided.

"How quiet you've been today, little one!" said Miss Falconer as she kissed them each goodbye.

It was all Polly could do not to cry in her arms.

———

Polly *did* weep when she said goodbye to the rest of the Fearless Four. "I'll write to you," she promised Eleanor and Daisy.

Rhoda giggled nervously. "You know what, Polly? I think I'm actually going to miss you!"

Polly stared at her a second, then smiled. She would never *like* Rhoda, but in a funny way she would miss *her*, as well. At least she was going to see Eleanor again. She was to spend a week on the island later in the month.

And at least Polly wasn't going home immediately. She had a week to put off telling Noni her decision. She hadn't told Alice, either. And what about Daddy and Maud? *I won't tell any of them until after I've told Noni,* she thought.

Everyone would be so disappointed. *I don't care!* thought Polly. She stood in the hall with the other boarders, waiting for Mrs. Blake to drive her downtown. Miss Guppy was going around to all the girls, shaking their hands.

"Goodbye, Polly," she said. "Please give my best to Maud. I will see you in September," she added firmly.

Polly wanted to shout, *No, you won't!* Instead, she slipped her hand out of the Guppy's grip and put it in her pocket.

At the harbour, Polly gave Mrs. Blake an especially hard hug. She would never see her—or Johnny—again.

PART THREE

NOW EVERYTHING HAD CHANGED

Chapter Fifteen

Rescuing Danny

Now everything had changed. As soon as she sat down on the steamer, Polly pushed her decision and all its consequences deep inside her. School seemed a hundred years away. All she could think about was Maud.

Noni's friends met her in Vancouver, took her out for lunch, and delivered her to the train station. Jim grinned at her when she boarded the train. "It's my favourite young lady again!" Polly had a hard time smiling back. For the whole long trip to Kelowna the train chanted, *Maud is having a BABY—Maud is having a BABY.*

The next morning, when Daddy threw his arms around her and lifted her into the air, Polly had to force down Maud's secret as if she were shutting a wild animal into a cage. Her own secret was trivial by comparison. She sat in the kitchen with Daddy and Esther, chattering blithely about school as if she were looking forward to going back.

Maud had said she would stop writing after Polly finished the term. "I can't risk sending letters to Kelowna. What if Daddy or Esther noticed the postmark and wondered why you were getting mail from Vancouver? You'll just have to do without hearing from me until the baby is born."

How could Polly not hear from Maud for five whole weeks? Every minute, she wondered what Maud was doing and how she was feeling. Polly reread all her letters. Practical and brave as always, Maud seemed quite resigned to living at the home. She'd started a bridge club, and she'd befriended the youngest girl there, who was only fifteen. "Evie is so scared and lonely that I spend as much time with her as I can."

Polly was jealous of Evie. And how could a girl who was only a bit older than she was be having a baby? Maud described how the girls sat around and compared the size of their bellies. She told Polly they were allowed to go out shopping in pairs, borrowing some of the wedding rings the home supplied so people wouldn't know they were unmarried.

In her last letter, Maud had written that she was getting so large she bumped into things. Now she must be even larger! She never said she was frightened of the birth, but surely she must be.

And then she would give away her baby . . . give away *Danny*. How would that happen? Maud was to have the baby in a hospital in Vancouver. Would his new family be there waiting for him? Surely Maud would change her mind. Surely she would come back to the island in August with Danny, and everyone would accept him, and there would be a happy ending to her ordeal.

How stupid I am to believe that's possible! thought Polly. Yet she couldn't help wishing it.

Kelowna was summery and warm. The green hills were turning brown, and there was a tang of sagebrush in the air. Polly swam in the cool lake every day, and joined the crowd on the beach or on the wharf. Too shy to talk to anyone, she watched boys, and a few girls, launch themselves off the huge diving board. She didn't have the nerve to try it. *Maud* would . . .

Daddy and Esther were working just as hard as they had in March. Polly helped Esther as much as she could. While she scrubbed, and dusted, and washed dishes, she imagined Maud doing the same things.

Esther's younger brother, Ben, and his wife, Rachel, were coming from Vancouver for the August wedding and staying on for a week. "I haven't seen them for years," Esther told Polly. "They have a five-year-old son named David, whom I've never met. Ben and Rachel are so eager to meet Daniel!"

"I'm eager to meet them, as well," said Daddy, hugging her.

Esther was wearing an engagement ring with a small diamond in it. Daddy said it had belonged to Polly's mother. Polly was happy for them, but she couldn't get her mind off Maud.

"Is anything wrong, Doodle?" Daddy kept asking her. "You seem worried about something."

"Nothing's wrong," Polly answered.

But each time he asked, she was more tempted to tell him.

———

Polly was supposed to go home on July 3. On the morning before, she sat at lunch, trying to eat her stew. But her stomach lurched, and she put down her spoon when she noticed Mr. McMillan wipe his own stew off his drooping moustache. After he and the other boarders had left, Daddy and Esther were able to sit down.

"Your last day, Doodle," said Daddy. "We're certainly going to miss you."

"At least you'll be back with us in August," said Esther.

Polly stared at them, her eyes bleary and dry. For most of the night, she had tossed with anxiety. Should she tell Daddy? It wasn't right that he didn't know he was going to be a grandfather. It wasn't right that Maud was living with strangers and had to go through this by herself. Most of all, it wasn't right that Danny would live with another family. He belonged with *them*!

Maud had said that Daddy wouldn't understand . . . but he *loved* Maud. Surely he would accept what had happened. Daddy would make everything all right.

All the same, Polly was terrified of telling him.

"I'm going to take this afternoon off and spend it with you," Daddy told her. "What would you like to do?"

"Let's go for a walk," said Polly.

In a few minutes, she and Daddy were strolling along the lake. Polly squinted at its glistening blueness, dotted with boats and swimmers. She hadn't made one sketch of it all week; she was too worried to draw.

Daddy kept pretending he had spotted Ogopogo. "There he is!" he cried. "Oops, that's just someone's fat belly!"

Polly couldn't laugh. She kicked along a pebble, wishing Daddy would stop joking as if she were still a little girl.

They approached the huge ponderosa pine where Maud and Polly had had their long conversation. When Polly looked at the tree, all the shock of that day rushed back. "Oh!" she gasped, covering her mouth.

"Polly, my darling, what on earth is the matter?"

Polly broke into sobs and collapsed under the tree. Daddy crouched beside her and took her in his arms.

"Oh, D-Daddy . . ." Polly choked. "Oh, Daddy, Maud's going to have a *baby*!"

As Polly spilled out the whole story, she watched Daddy for his reaction. He listened with deep concern and growing indignation. "What I would do to that young Robert if I could get hold of him!" he muttered. "Imagine him abandoning our Maud!"

After Polly finished, he gently wiped her eyes with his handkerchief. "Thank you for telling me, Doodle. This is such shocking news it's going to take me a while to absorb it. Thank goodness your grandmother doesn't know!" Then he led her by the hand back to the boarding house. "We have a lot of things to do," he told her.

"What things?" asked Polly. She was so relieved to have unburdened her secret that she could hardly walk, and had to lean against him for support.

"Let me think, Doodle, and then I'll tell you. First I have to consult with Esther."

"Will she be upset with Maud?"

"Not my Esther! She'll be completely supportive—you'll see."

Daddy and Esther shut themselves in a room and talked for an hour, while Polly waited in agony. Then they all sat around the kitchen table for a conference.

Daddy was right about Esther. She kissed Polly and said, "Oh, my dear child, what a secret for you to have for so long. And poor Maud, going through this completely by herself!"

Polly's heart lifted when she heard Daddy's words. "We have to bring her here. I won't let her have a child on her own."

"She can live with us and have the baby at home," said Esther.

"But what will everyone think?" asked Polly.

"Your father and I are already outsiders," said Esther. "What do *we* care what anyone thinks?"

"All that's important is Maud's welfare and happiness," said Daddy.

"But what about Danny?" Polly asked.

"Who?"

"The baby! It's a boy, and she was going to name him 'Danny.' Except she doesn't want to keep him. She wants to give him away!" Polly started weeping again.

"Hush, Polly." Esther patted her shoulder. "It's up to Maud to decide what to do about her baby. Perhaps that would be the best—to put him up for adoption. It would be very difficult for her to raise a child on her own."

"But couldn't *you* take care of him? Couldn't he live *here*?"

"Hold your horses, Doodle!" laughed Daddy. "Let's just take this one step at a time. Esther's right. *Maud* has to decide what to do. However, if she decided to keep the baby, we'd be very happy to bring it up."

"Not *it*! Danny! He's named after *you*!"

Daddy smiled. "I'm very flattered, Polly, but it may not be a boy, you know."

"It is," said Polly firmly. "Maud's roommate did a test." Then she realized what Daddy had just said. "You and Esther would look after him?"

Esther smiled. "We've just discussed that possibility. I've always wanted a child, but I'm too old to have my own. I would welcome a child of Maud's."

"Would you adopt him?" Polly asked.

"Maybe . . . we talked about that, as well," said Daddy. "We're going to get married right away, so we can be eligible as adoptive parents. But don't get your hopes up, Polly. We don't know what Maud will decide."

"She'll decide to give him to you! Of *course* she will!" Polly clapped her hands as if she were little. The happy ending she had imagined was going to take place after all.

Daddy looked worried. "She may . . . but we'll deal with all that later. Right now we have to concentrate on getting Maudie here. Here's what I suggest, Doodle. Since you were planning to go back tomorrow anyway, you and I will leave for Vancouver this evening. The train arrives in the city at nine in the morning. We'll have all day to track down Maud, and then I can bring her back tomorrow night."

"I'll phone Ben and Rachel and they can start trying to find the home," said Esther.

Daddy grinned. "We'll be detectives! Go and pack, Doodle. Then we'll rescue Maud."

And Danny! thought Polly as she ran up the stairs.

———

During the long train ride, Daddy wouldn't talk about Maud. He encouraged Polly to read her book while he stared out the window, deep in thought. Polly had changed her berth for two seats, paying the difference with some of the money Noni had given her. She fell asleep with her head in Daddy's lap.

She woke up rumpled and thirsty as the train pulled into Vancouver. They had slept too long to have time for breakfast. Polly held Daddy's hand as they walked into the station.

They spotted a plump man holding a sign saying "Daniel Brown." Daddy waved and the man hurried up to them, accompanied by a dark-haired woman and a little boy.

It was Esther's brother and sister-in-law. "Hello there, Polly!" said the man. "I'm Ben Meyer . . . but I suppose you should call me 'Uncle Ben,' since that's what I'll soon be. This is your Aunt Rachel, and this scamp is David."

"How kind of you to come," said Daddy. "Hello there, young David. You can call *me* 'Uncle Daniel.'"

They went to the station restaurant for breakfast. Daddy took a long drink of coffee. "That's better. I didn't sleep much."

With three grown-ups in charge, Polly was suddenly relaxed and ravenous. She gobbled up scrambled eggs on toast while she listened to the grown-ups chatter. At first their attention was on David, who quizzed Daddy about the train.

"He wants to be a conductor when he grows up," Aunt Rachel said with a smile.

"Uncle Daniel, exactly how big are the engine's wheels, do you think?" asked David.

"Hush now, son. Eat your toast. It's the grown-ups' turn to talk," said Uncle Ben. "We have news for you," he told Daddy. "Rachel has already discovered where the home is!"

"It's in an area of Vancouver called Kitsilano," said Aunt Rachel.

"That's terrific. How did you find out?" asked Daddy.

"I phoned the Salvation Army headquarters. I told them I had a daughter who was in trouble and needed to go to a home—and they gave me the address."

"We'll go straight there as soon as you've finished eating, Polly," said Daddy. He smiled at his future in-laws. "I can't tell you how grateful we are for your help."

"It's nothing, Daniel," said Uncle Ben. "After all, you're family now. So is Maud." He chucked Polly under the chin. "I hope to see this lovely young lady again soon."

"You'll see her when you visit in August," said Daddy. "And then you can meet Maud, as well."

And Danny, added Polly fiercely to herself.

———

Kitsilano was a beautiful area of Vancouver, close to the beach. Its leafy streets were lined with tall wooden houses. Daddy and Polly got off the bus and walked until they reached the address Aunt Rachel had written down.

"Here we are," said Daddy. They stared at a tall, shabby brown house set well back from the street. Overgrown shrubs crowded the front yard, and all the curtains were drawn.

Polly shivered; it looked like a haunted house in a movie. Maud was somewhere in there!

"You wait out here, Doodle, and I'll go in and get her," said Daddy.

"No! I have to come with you."

Daddy sighed. "All right." They walked up the wide stairs and Daddy knocked on the door.

A woman in a nurse's uniform opened it. "Yes?" she said.

"We're here to fetch Maud Brown," said Daddy firmly.

"And who are you?"

"I'm her father, and this is her sister. We're taking her home."

The woman shut the door and came out onto the porch. "I don't think that's a good idea," she said. "Maud is in the best possible place she could be in her condition—away from prying eyes, and somewhere she can feel safe. I'll allow you to visit with her, but please don't try to persuade her to leave."

"You'll *allow* me to visit with her?" Daddy was furious. "Maud is my daughter! Please get her at once, and if she wants to leave with us, she will!"

"Very well," said the woman coldly. She ushered them into a room at the back of the hall and told them to wait.

The room was bare and chilly, with uncarpeted linoleum on the floor, and beige walls. The house smelled stale and was strangely quiet. Where were all the girls?

Polly got up and looked out the window. A tall hedge enclosed the yard. Eight girls with big bellies were lounging on the grass on chairs and blankets. Some of the girls were reading, some were knitting, and some were chatting. Where was Maud?

Then she appeared at the door. "It *is* you," she said quietly. "Captain Osler said it was, but I couldn't believe her. Oh, Polly . . . why did you tell?"

She just stood there, looking her most Maudish: fierce and proud. Polly hadn't expected this. She'd thought Maud would throw herself into their arms and be grateful for being rescued. But she was so aloof they didn't dare touch her.

"Come and sit down, Maudie," said Daddy gently.

Maud waddled into the room and lowered herself into a chair. Polly couldn't stop staring. Maud was *huge*! Her belly and her belly button stuck way out, like a pumpkin with a stalk. *Danny's in there,* thought Polly.

"Don't blame Polly," said Daddy. "It was right that she told me. You shouldn't suffer through this alone, my darling. You should have told me. I'm not angry at you. I'm sorry you got yourself into this predicament, but these things happen. And I'm very sorry that Robert has let you down. I'm glad you're not with him anymore, though—he doesn't deserve you." He gazed at Maud, his eyes welling with tears. "Darling Maud . . . won't you come home to Kelowna and have your baby there? Esther and I will be happy to take care of you."

Maud shook her head, her brown eyes so full of sadness that Polly longed to hug her. "No, Daddy. I would just embarrass you. What would your boarders say? And your neighbours? They'd all find out your daughter is having an illegitimate child," she added bitterly.

"I couldn't care less what anyone says," said Daddy fiercely. "Neither could Esther! She and I have discussed this thoroughly, Maud. We want you with us."

Maud's face softened. "Really?" she whispered. "You're not angry?"

Daddy got up and took her in his arms. "Oh, Boss, of course I'm not angry! Of course we want you! And I understand what you're going through, believe me."

Maud released herself and wiped her eyes. "What do you mean?"

"I'll tell you later," said Daddy. "Now, why don't you get your things and we can escape from this joint."

Maud stood. Her mouth smiled, but her eyes remained sad. She kissed Polly and said, "All right. I'll come home with you. I have to say goodbye to the other girls, though, so I might be a while."

"Take your time," said Daddy. "And be careful on the stairs!" he called as Maud started up them.

Half an hour later, the three of them stood at the front door.

"Goodbye, Captain Osler," said Maud. "Thank you for everything."

"Goodbye, Maud. I still think you're making a mistake, but of course I can't stop you. Could you mail back your maternity clothes when you're finished with them? And thank you for cheering up the girls so much while you were here."

"Please keep an eye on Evie," said Maud. "Can you give me her address so I can write to her?"

"You know I can't," said the woman. "Everyone is anonymous here. You'll miss that, Maud. As soon as you step out that door, you'll become a pariah."

But Maud was already down the steps, Polly and Daddy supporting her on each side.

People stared at them as they slowly made their way along the street. Daddy was carrying his small bag and Maud's larger one, while Polly carried her own suitcase and Maud's coat. Maud just carried the baby inside her.

"We have about four hours before we take Polly to the harbour," said Daddy. "Let's have lunch in that restaurant across the street, and then we can sit on the beach until it's time to go."

In the restaurant, a woman peered deliberately at Maud's left hand, then glared at her.

Maud met her eyes until she looked away. "Old bat!" said Maud. "I should have taken one of the rings the home has."

"I thought of that," said Daddy. He put his hand in his pocket and handed Maud a thin gold band. "It was your mother's," he said quietly. "Esther will wear it later, but you can borrow it for now."

"Oh, Daddy . . ." Maud's eyes brimmed as she slipped on the ring. "What would Mother think of me like this!"

"She would be in complete sympathy," said Daddy. He examined the menu. "Order your meal, girls. Then I have a story to tell you."

"I'm going to buy lunch," Polly told them. "Noni sent me some money to spend and I've hardly used it."

At first Daddy protested, then he smiled and said he'd be honoured if Polly treated them to lunch. Polly was relieved. Daddy would have to pay for both him and Maud to go back to Kelowna.

She ordered a roast-beef sandwich. Maud dug into half a chicken and vegetables. "Don't laugh," she told them. "After all, I'm eating for two. The trouble is, I get so hungry and then I get heartburn."

Daddy put down his fork. "Listen carefully, Maud and Polly. I want to talk to you about your mother."

He ran his hand over his face. "You know that Una and I got married very young. She was seventeen and I was eighteen. Younger than you, Maud. My mother wanted us to wait until we were older, but we *couldn't* wait. Can you guess why?"

"Oh!" said Maud. She stopped eating. "Daddy, are you saying that my mother . . . I can't believe it!"

"It's true." Daddy smiled. "Your mother was expecting a baby."

"I don't understand," said Polly. "What baby?"

Maud crowed with nervous laughter. "*Me*, of course!"

"*You?*"

"Yes, Polly," said Daddy. "We were careless—as you were, Maud. But we were luckier than you, because we loved each other deeply and planned to get married anyway one day. So when Una found out she was pregnant, we had the wedding as soon as possible so people wouldn't talk."

"Did Noni know?" asked Polly.

"She knew," said Daddy grimly. "She didn't want Una to marry me at all. As I've told you before, she and Rand and Jean didn't approve of me. But now they had to allow it, although they weren't at all happy about it. The day before the wedding, your grandmother said such terrible things to Una that she never spoke to her mother again."

So that was it, thought Polly. That was the quarrel the family sometimes hinted at. That was why Aunt Jean had once said she had never trusted Daddy after "what he did to our Una."

"So you see, Maudie," said Daddy, "I completely understand the predicament you're in. I don't want you to feel disgraced as your mother and I did. Even at our wedding people gave us strange looks—

I'm sure they guessed why we were marrying in such a hurry. I refuse to let you be a 'pariah,' as that awful woman called you."

"They were always saying that," said Maud. "They were nice enough, but they made us feel so ashamed."

"Don't feel ashamed! You and Robert made a mistake, just as Una and I did. But it's not a crime. I'm so glad we got you out of that place."

"So am I," said Maud. She wiped her eyes. "Thanks for telling me this, Daddy. It makes me feel better to know Mother was in the same situation."

Now what? wondered Polly. When would Daddy and Maud start talking about what would happen to Danny? She only had a few hours to find out before she had to leave them and go back to the island.

Instead, Maud changed the subject. "How was your last term, Poll? Are you looking forward to going back?"

Polly nodded quickly, avoiding her sister's pointed expression. This was certainly not the right time to tell Maud she wasn't returning. She told them about meeting Emily Carr, making them laugh when she described Woo clutching Jane's leg.

"What a lucky girl you are to meet such a famous artist!" said Daddy. "Maybe you'll see her again."

"Maybe," said Polly. Her eyes prickled; she would *never* meet Miss Carr again, and it was her own fault.

Daddy looked out the window. "Shall we go across the street and sit on that beach?"

Polly proudly paid the bill, then they found a spot on the sand. They leaned back against some logs, gazing at the dark forest across the bay and the huge mountains that stood like cut-outs against the sky. Even though it was cloudy, a few people were sitting on towels in their bathing suits, and some children were wading.

A group of laughing young people walked close to them, and Maud ducked her head. "I'm afraid I'm going to meet someone from U.B.C.," she explained.

"What a beautiful city this is," said Daddy. "You're lucky to be living here, Maud. Are you still planning to take law?"

That was exactly the right thing to say. Maud's eyes lost their sadness while she eagerly told Daddy what courses she was going to take next year. Daddy asked about her sorority, and laughed when she sang a funny Delta Gamma song.

"You sound very happy there," he said. "I hope that when all this is over, you can go back to being carefree again."

Now they'll talk about Danny, thought Polly.

But Daddy went on to warn Polly not to say anything to Noni. "I don't imagine your grandmother will be any more tolerant than she was with Una and me, and I don't want her love for Maud to be altered in any way."

"Of course I won't tell Noni," said Polly. "I've kept it a secret all this time and I still will. But . . ."

"What?" Daddy asked.

"Won't Noni *ever* be allowed to know?"

"Never!" said Maud firmly.

So if Maud keeps Danny, Noni won't know he exists, thought Polly. That seemed unbearably sad.

She leaned against the log and breathed in its tarry smell. Gulls quarrelled, and small boats putted by. If she closed her eyes, she could almost be on the island, except for the traffic going by on the street behind the beach.

"This is all so . . . odd," said Maud. "Here we are, the three of us again, the way we used to be. It's exactly the same, yet it's completely different." Then she sat up abruptly and rubbed her stomach.

"What wrong?" said Daddy. "Are you all right?"

Maud smiled. "I'm fine. He's just kicking, that's all. He does that so much now—I think he's going to be a football player!"

Daddy looked worried. "I hope you're going to make it through the train journey, Maud!"

"I will," said Maud. "Captain Osler told me he hasn't come down yet, so he's not ready to be born."

Polly stared at Maud's tummy. "Do you want to feel, Poll?" Maud asked. She lifted up her smock and, once again, held Polly's hand to her hard belly. This time Polly felt a strong kick, as if the baby was trying to escape.

"Oh, Maud . . . *Danny's* in there!"

Maud frowned. "Don't call him that, Polly. They told us at the home we shouldn't give our babies names."

"But Maud . . . what are you going to *do* with him?"

"I don't want to upset Maud with worrying about that right now, Polly," said Daddy. "She and I and Esther can discuss it when we get to Kelowna."

Polly didn't want to upset Maud, either, but she was too desperate to stop. "We need to talk about it *now*!" she told them. "I won't be there later. *Please* tell me, Maud—are you going to keep him? Daddy and Esther can take care of him. They even said they would adopt him."

"What do you mean?" Maud glowered at them. "Why are you making all these arrangements behind my back?"

Daddy frowned at Polly. "I wish you hadn't opened this up, Doodle, but since you have, we may as well continue. Polly means exactly what she said, Maudie. If you decide to keep the baby, Esther and I will pretend he's ours. We'll look after him while you're at U.B.C., and you can be with him in the holidays. We could even officially adopt him. We'd also totally accept it if you wanted to put the baby up for adoption by someone else. Please don't be angry, Boss. We're just trying to do what's best for you, but of course it's your decision, not ours."

Maud sighed. "I'm not angry. It's kind of you to offer to take the baby. But I couldn't bear that! Don't you understand? I want to be *free*, as I was before. If you had the baby, I'd see him every time I came home. He'd always *be* there."

"He'd be real," said Daddy gently. "The baby *is* real, Maud. You'll realize that the moment he's born. But you don't have to keep him, and we don't, either. Babies should be *wanted*. Una and I wanted you, so it was right that we kept you. But you shouldn't keep your baby if you don't want it. I'm sure there are many fine couples who are longing for a child and will give it a good home."

"That's exactly what I'm going to do," said Maud firmly. "I'm glad you've taken me away from that dreary place. I'm glad you'll be with me when he's born. But nothing else has changed. I'll give the baby up for adoption, and then everything will be the same as it was before."

"If that's your decision, Maud, then we'll fully support it," said Daddy. "Right, Polly?"

No! cried Polly inside. But all she could do was nod.

For the rest of the afternoon she could hardly speak she was so afraid of breaking down. They had rescued Maud . . . but they hadn't rescued Danny.

CHAPTER SIXTEEN

Waiting

"WHAT IS WRONG WITH HER?" ASKED AUNT JEAN. "SHE'S NOT our Polly anymore!"

"She's certainly troubled by something," said Uncle Rand.

"I've asked and asked, but she won't tell me anything," said Noni.

Polly had been reading in bed when she heard her name, and had crept to the head of the stairs. Tonight, as on every night since she'd come home, she had excused herself early, given each of her family an obligatory kiss, taken out Tarka, visited the privy, then fled to her room.

"Girls can be difficult at her age," said Aunt Jean. "Do you remember how trying Una was at thirteen?"

"Una was *always* difficult," said Noni. "Polly has never been like her. But now she's so sulky and unresponsive I don't know what to do with her."

"Would you like me to speak to her?" asked Uncle Rand. "Tomorrow I'm starting to prepare Polly and Biddy for confirmation. I could ask her if anything's wrong."

"Thank you, Rand. Perhaps that would help."

Why can't they leave me alone? thought Polly angrily as she got back into bed. She used to enjoy peaceful evenings with the adults. Now she couldn't bear to be with them. Their warm concern made her want to blurt out everything: mostly about Maud, of course, but also about her own decision not to go back to school.

Her two secrets weighed her down so much that she felt like a puppet: going through the motions of each day, but feeling mechanical and unreal.

The next morning, Uncle Rand spent half an hour introducing the catechism to Polly and Biddy. After Biddy left, he asked Polly to stay. She waited for him to work up the nerve to speak, wishing she could escape, as well.

At least the familiar space was comforting. It was littered with Uncle Rand smiled gently at her. Polly had once spent hours in here while he tutored her in arithmetic.

"How's your math going?" he asked.

Polly shrugged. "Not too bad. I got a C+."

Uncle Rand smiled gently at her. "That's a good mark for someone who doesn't like arithmetic. Are you enjoying the rest of your subjects?"

"They're okay. I like literature and piano, and especially art."

"You have an excellent teacher, am I correct? What's her name? Miss Hawk?"

Polly had to smile; she knew he'd said it on purpose. "Miss Falconer!" Then she squirmed, remembering she'd never take special art again.

Uncle Rand examined her kindly. "Polly, dear, you seem so morose these days. Is something the matter? Your grandmother and your aunt are very worried about you."

"I'm fine!" said Polly quickly. "None of you need to worry about me at all."

"You don't *seem* fine. You've lost your sparkle, and you're almost as quiet as when you first came to the island. If there *is* something wrong, you can always pray about it, my dear. You can ask God for help and he will send it. Why don't you go and sit in the church and try that?"

"All right," said Polly, because she could never bear to disappoint Uncle Rand.

She trudged over to the little church and slid into one of its hard pews. As usual, it was freezing in here. Polly clutched her bare arms and shivered, staring into the familiar space of wood and glass.

Why should she have to sit in church when it wasn't Sunday? She didn't especially want to be confirmed, either; memorizing the catechism was as boring as Scripture lessons in school. She didn't want to do *anything*—except to be unburdened of her secrets.

Since she was in here, however, she might as well try to pray. "*Please*, God, make Maud keep Danny!" she whispered. "And please make me brave enough to tell Noni I'm not going back to school."

Polly waited, gazing out her favourite window, the clear glass one that framed an arbutus tree. The church smelled like cedar and wax. Its arched wooden interior had always reminded Polly of the inside of a ship. Once, she had told Uncle Rand that, and he had turned it into a sermon: how the church was a boat ploughing through rough seas towards the harbour.

How proud Polly had been, listening to him use her idea for a sermon. She'd been about eleven then, so lighthearted and secure.

That was before Daddy came back, before she went away to school . . . and before Maud's momentous news.

She didn't feel any answer to her prayers. Why should there be? Why would God be interested in *her* problems? He probably had far more important matters to deal with.

———

Daddy had written Polly that he and Esther had got married right away. "Our only witness was Maud," he said. "How I wish you could have been there!" He told Polly that Maud had been fine on the train journey and seemed glad to be in Kelowna. "Esther is now wearing your mother's ring," he wrote. "We bought Maud a cheap one, so she can go out with us without people gossiping. We've told the boarders that her husband is studying overseas and that Maud will join him after the birth. I'm sure they don't believe that, since they saw her here before without a ring, but they seem to have decided not to ask questions."

Polly wept with frustration when she read Daddy's letter. She'd been left out of his wedding and she was going to be excluded from Danny's birth. It was as if she didn't matter.

"What's wrong with you, Polly?" asked Biddy. "You act as if you're not really here."

They were walking Tarka and Bramble to the lighthouse. "Nothing's wrong," said Polly, trying to pay attention. As usual, Biddy was going on and on about George, wondering if he liked her.

Polly hated to admit it, but Biddy was beginning to bore her. And now she was stuck with her for years. She had told Biddy her decision, swearing her to secrecy.

Biddy was thrilled, of course. "Oh, Polly, I don't know what I would have done with just Dorothy as a friend! We'll be exactly the way we were before."

But nothing could be the way it was before. Now Polly felt much older than Biddy. She imagined how shocked her friend would be if she knew about Maud.

Biddy picked up a stick to throw to the dogs. "Have you told your grandmother yet that you're not going back?" she asked.

"Not yet," said Polly.

"But you have to tell her!"

Polly grimaced. "She'll be so upset."

"She'll get over it. She's always been nice to you. Tell her tomorrow!"

"All right."

Tomorrow came, and Polly took Noni's breakfast up to her as usual. "Won't you stay and chat?" Noni asked as Polly hovered at the door.

"I have to walk Tarka," said Polly.

She just couldn't tell her. Every time she imagined the conversation, she was so overcome with dread that she felt sick.

———

That afternoon Polly ran into Chester at the store. They walked on the wharf and sat on the end, dangling their legs.

Polly tried not to stare at Chester too obviously. He seemed more like a man than a boy, with his broad shoulders and hint of stubble on his face. His brown hair flopped on his tanned forehead, and his hands were so strong-looking. Polly longed to stroke them.

Chester was telling her about a huge salmon he'd caught. Then he hesitated. "Polly . . . do you remember when we saw the whales last summer?"

"Of course!"

"Well, you said then that you were only going to St. Winifred's for a year. Is that still true?"

Polly nodded. "I'm not going back. I can't stand Miss Guppy—or anything else about the school. It's like a prison."

Chester laughed. "Mine is, too, but the other fellows and I have a good time. Isn't there anything you *like* about St. Winnie's? Don't you have friends there?"

"Yes," admitted Polly. "I have two friends, and I love my art classes. But I'm not going back."

"Your grandmother must be really upset. How did you talk her into it?"

"I haven't told her yet," said Polly, "but I'm planning to very soon."

"I *wish* you'd go back, Polly. Then when you're older and I'm at Victoria College, maybe we could go to a dance. Do you think the Gorgon would let you?"

Polly giggled. "'The Guppy'—not 'the Gorgon'! She might. Millicent, one of the prefects, was allowed to go to a dance after she got permission from her parents." Polly sighed. "But I won't be there, Chester. I don't want to talk about it anymore, okay? And don't tell anyone I'm not going back. I don't want my grandmother to know yet."

Chester agreed, but he looked so disappointed that Polly mumbled a goodbye and left.

Gregor and Sadie arrived for a week's visit. Polly decided not to tell Noni her decision until after they left.

Polly and Sadie embarked on a project of cleaning out Aunt Jean's pantry. They removed all the food and scrubbed down each shelf. Sadie was as jolly as ever; her constant cheerfulness lightened Polly's mood.

The only problem was, she kept talking about Maud. "How I miss her! We asked her to come and stay with us, but she said she was going to take this course in Oregon. I suppose she and Ann are better friends than she and I are now," she added wistfully.

Gregor had finished his curacy, and the parish liked him so much they had given him a job as an associate rector. Aunt Jean was over the moon. "Just imagine—he has a full-time job when work is so scarce!" she crowed to anyone on the island who would listen.

Sadie loved being a rector's wife. "It's just like a novel, kiddo," she said. "The ladies often come to me with their woes, and you wouldn't believe their stories. And the feuds! I'm the head of the altar guild, and I have to be so careful about whom I let polish the important silver. At first they wouldn't listen to me at all because I'm so young, but now I think I amuse them."

Aunt Jean cooked a special dinner for them on their last night. At the end of it, Gregor cleared his throat. "Listen, everyone. Sadie and I have something to tell you. We—she—" Then, to everyone's astonishment, he began to weep.

"What a silly boy!" Sadie put her arm around his shoulder. "I'll tell them," she said calmly. "We're going to have a baby."

"Oh, my goodness!" Aunt Jean's chair fell backwards as she ran over to Gregor and Sadie and showered them with kisses. "Oh, chickies, I can't believe it!"

"What wonderful news, my dears," said Uncle Rand, his voice breaking.

"Congratulations," said Noni. "I'm so happy for you both."

At first Polly couldn't speak. After everyone had settled down, she looked at Gregor and Sadie and whispered, "That's swell."

Then she sat silently as excited questions and answers buzzed around her. When was the baby due? December. How did Sadie feel? Fine now, although she'd been sick in the beginning. Where were they going to live? They'd found a tiny house to rent instead of the apartment they were in now.

"Just think, Rand—we'll be grandparents!" Aunt Jean said.

"And I'll be a great-aunt," said Noni.

"You'll be a *great* aunt," said Gregor fondly, "just as you've always been to me."

"What will *I* be?" asked Polly weakly. She had to say *something*.

"Let's see," said Aunt Jean. "Gregor is your first cousin once removed, so the baby will be your first cousin *twice* removed?"

"No, her *second* cousin," said Noni, "because she's the same generation."

"That's good," said Sadie. "We don't want our child to be at all removed from you, Polly. We hope you can visit us often, and become his or her good friend."

She smiled so warmly that Polly felt a bit better. At least there'd be one baby who was staying in the family.

But it wouldn't be the same as Danny. She wouldn't see their baby very often, and being a second cousin wasn't nearly as important as being an aunt.

What if Sadie knew that her best friend had a new life inside her, just as she did? If Maud decided to keep Danny, would the family be as excited about him as they were about Gregor and Sadie's baby?

Of course they wouldn't. They would be ashamed and embarrassed, just because Maud wasn't married. It was so unfair. "I'm going to bed," Polly told them, escaping from the happy gathering.

———

The next morning Noni asked Polly to stay after she'd brought up her breakfast.

"I need to clean the henhouse," muttered Polly.

"That can wait," said Noni.

"But you've been asking me to do it all week."

Noni chuckled. "You aren't exactly fond of cleaning the henhouse, Polly. You can do it later. Come and sit down."

Polly sighed. Noni was either going to ask her what was wrong, or ask why Maud was avoiding them.

But as Polly climbed onto the bed and leaned against a pillow, Noni said, "That was such welcome news last night. Gregor and Sadie will be excellent parents. Polly, hen . . ." Noni sounded embarrassed. "Do you know . . . are you aware of how a man and a woman create a baby?"

Polly blushed. "Someone at school told me. So did Maud."

"I hoped she had. That's all right, then. I just thought that, now that you're almost fourteen, you should know." Noni took a deep gulp of tea and put her cup on the table. "Polly . . ."

Noni's lips quivered, as if she were afraid of what words would emerge from them. Polly braced herself. Was Noni going to tell her at last about why she and Una had quarrelled? Would she be angry that Daddy had already told Polly?

Then Noni seemed to swallow what she was going to say. Instead, she sighed. "I'm so worried about Maud. Are you *sure* there's nothing she isn't telling us? Has she got some secret she's asked you not to tell, the way she did when you both pretended your father was dead? I know it's important to be loyal to your sister, but if something is wrong, it's more important to tell *me*. Then I could help."

Polly tried to still her breathing. Surely Noni couldn't have guessed!

"As far as I know, nothing's wrong," she said as steadily as she could. "She just wanted to take this course—that's all."

"Is there another young man in her life? Does Ann have an older brother?"

"I don't think so," said Polly, glad she could answer honestly for once.

"She's slipping away from us," said Noni. Then her voice became bitter. "Una did the same thing, but I never expected it of Maud. If she's chosen to spend so much time away from her family, then I suppose we don't mean much to her anymore."

Polly took her hand. "You mean *everything* to her. You'll see, Noni. Maud will be here in August and she'll be really happy to be back."

"Perhaps you're right. In her letters, Maud *does* say she misses us. Well, at least I still have you, hen. Are you *sure* there's nothing troubling you?" she asked, for what seemed like the trillionth time.

"I'm sure."

Noni kissed her. "I hope so. I count on you so much, my dear wee Polly. I couldn't bear it if you changed, as well."

———

All Aunt Jean could talk about was the baby. Her main concern was names. "I hope they'll decide on 'Jean' or 'Randolph,' of course. But if they don't want to use those as first names, they could choose 'Mairead' or 'Roderick' after our parents, Clara. 'Mairead Jean Stafford'—doesn't that sound grand? They could call her 'Maisie' for short. Oh, how I hope it's a girl! They're so much more fun to dress than boys."

"It's possible, Jean, that Gregor and Sadie will want to choose their own names, or use names from Sadie's family," said Noni dryly.

Aunt Jean ignored her. "I'm going to make a list of all the family names and send it to them."

She had already begun to knit a tiny pink sweater. "Here's some extra wool, Polly. Why don't you make some booties. Knitting will help you forget your worries."

Polly had to sit in the living room every night and struggle over the booties. She tried to pretend they were for Danny.

The next visitor was Eleanor. Polly was glad to see her, but having her there made her life even trickier. Eleanor had to be sworn to secrecy about Polly not going back to St. Winifred's.

"How I wish you would!" she said. "How did your grandmother react?"

"I haven't said anything yet," said Polly. "That's why *you* can't." Now she was putting off telling Noni until Eleanor left.

"Don't tell her! Oh, Poll, you're so wrong not to go back!"

She made Polly feel so guilty that Polly forbade her to talk about it. Eleanor's sorrow made a gulf between them.

Even worse was the antagonism between Eleanor and Biddy. The last time Eleanor had visited the island she had been nice to Biddy. This time, she was jealous that Biddy would have Polly all to herself.

"You'll forget all about me," she said one night.

"I won't!" said Polly.

"Yes, you will," said Eleanor, as if she were stating a scientific fact. "It's completely understandable. You and Biddy have been friends for much longer than you and I, and soon you'll be spending all your time together. But she's so boring, Poll! All she talks about is movie stars and her freckles and this George person."

"Eleanor's really smart, isn't she?" said Biddy to Polly when they were alone. "You must find me stupid compared with her."

Of course Polly couldn't say that she agreed. Everyone on the island that summer was reading a new novel called *Gone with the Wind*. Aunt Jean lent her copy to Polly after she and Noni had finished it. Polly and Eleanor decided to read it out loud together, alternating chapters. They were so engrossed in the story that they longed to spend all their time with it.

Biddy didn't want to hear them read, however. "It's too much like history," she complained, "and way too long." Polly and Eleanor began finding excuses not to be with Biddy so they could continue reading.

On some days Alice joined them for a swim or a bike ride. She and Eleanor chattered endlessly about school. "In the fall I'm going to recruit you two for the school play," she told them. "It's a musical, and I'm sure I'll be picked for the lead. Eleanor can help with the props, and you can paint some nifty scenery for it, Goldilocks."

Biddy looked smug. "Oh, but Polly—"

Polly poked her, and Biddy stifled a giggle. Luckily, Alice hadn't noticed.

On Eleanor's last night, she and Polly took Tarka for his bedtime walk. The nights were getting darker, and the moon glistened on the edges of the waves.

Polly wondered when she would see Eleanor again. "Could you come to the island for Thanksgiving?" she asked her.

"We always go to my grandparents' then," said Eleanor. "But I'd still like you to visit me after Christmas, Polly."

Christmas seemed years away! Polly blinked back tears. "Will you and Daisy and Rhoda be in the same dorm this fall?" she asked.

"No, we'll be in the east dorm. It's much larger and brighter than the junior dorm, and it's closer to the bathroom. It'll be swell not to be the youngest boarders anymore, don't you think?"

Polly shrugged. She didn't have a right to an opinion, since she wasn't going back. If she was, though, it would be nice to be in that big dorm near the bathroom. If she got there early enough, she could nab a bed close to the window . . .

But she *wasn't* going back. Miss Guppy had made that impossible.

They stopped to listen to an owl. "It's so peaceful here," said Eleanor. "I can see why you love it so much. But Poll . . ."

"*Please* don't say it, El," said Polly miserably. They began walking again.

"You've changed," Eleanor told her. "You're so detached, somehow. Is it because you're worrying about telling your grandmother?"

It's because my sister is having a baby! Polly wanted to scream. She'd already betrayed Maud by telling Daddy, however. She couldn't do it again by telling Eleanor.

Uncle Rand had given Polly and Biddy a holiday from confirmation classes while Eleanor was there. The day after she left, the classes resumed.

" 'To renounce the devil and all his works, the pomps and vanity of this wicked world, and all the sinful lusts of the flesh,' " recited Polly.

"Well done. Now, girls, tell me some ways in which the world is wicked."

"It's when people are cruel to one another, or dishonest or unfair," said Biddy. "Or when they fight, like in the war in Spain. And I just heard my dad and Captain Hay talking about another *big* war that Canada would have to be in," she added.

"There won't be one, though," said Polly. "Right?"

Uncle Rand sighed. "There might be, I'm afraid. We may have to go to war to stop Hitler. *There's* an example of wickedness."

He looked at their shocked faces. "Now, girls, I don't want you to worry about it—perhaps it won't happen. It's too sunny to stay inside—let's stop early today."

"Do you think there *will* be a war?" Polly asked Biddy as they walked out of the rectory.

"I'm sure there won't. Your uncle's right—there's no point in worrying when nobody knows," said Biddy.

Polly smiled at her friend. Biddy might be dull, but she was still as comfortable and reassuring as always.

———

Now that all the visitors were gone, Polly had no excuses left. Two days after Eleanor's departure, she marched into Noni's room, plunked down her tray, and blurted out her decision before she had time to procrastinate.

"You're not going back to school?" said Noni. "What on earth are you talking about, hen?"

Polly wearily repeated her words. "I hate it there," she ended. She flopped into a chair and steeled herself for Noni's anger.

But Noni was concerned, not angry. "So this is what you've been so gloomy about! I'm so sorry you feel like this, Polly. But you'd be giving everything up—especially your art! How could you not continue with that? You've told me so many times how much you love Miss Falconer's classes and how you want to be an artist when you grow up. And what about your friends? You and Eleanor are so close, and you seem to be fond of Daisy. Are you really saying you want to give up your art and your friends?"

"Yes," muttered Polly. "I'll miss them, but they're the only part of school I like. I can keep on with art on my own, and apply to go to art school later."

Noni's voice grew colder. "And how do you plan to carry on with the rest of your schooling?"

"Can't I share Biddy and Dorothy's governess?"

"You can if you want to receive a very inadequate education. From what Biddy's mother has told me, Miss Peate is a poor teacher."

Noni sat up straighter in bed. "Now, listen to me, Polly. I'm sorry you and Miss Guppy don't get along. I don't care for her myself. But you'll simply have to put up with her and with the rest of the school. I won't let you give up such a good education. Think of how well Maud is doing at university. That's because she received such an excellent foundation at St. Winifred's. I want you to have the same before you go to art school. I wish *I'd* had the opportunities you two have had, but my parents didn't believe in girls being educated."

This is about what I want, not you! Polly wanted to yell.

"Most important," finished Noni briskly, "I won't allow you to give up your art. So there it is, Polly. You're going back to school whether you want to or not." Then she smiled. "You've had a difficult first year—that's all. Next year will be better, I promise. Try to enjoy the rest of the summer, and try to enjoy what you *do* like at school."

"No!" said Polly. "I'm not going back!"

Spots of colour appeared in Noni's cheeks. "Polly, don't be ridiculous. You are, and that's that!"

Polly stood up. "You can't make me!"

They stared at each other. Noni appeared to be calming herself. Then she said quietly, "No, I can't make you. But if you don't go back, you'll be ruining your future. I think we're both too riled up to speak about this further. Here's what I suggest. I want you to think about your decision very seriously for the rest of the summer. By August I'm sure you will have come to your senses, and will decide to go back. Until then we won't speak about it, all right? I'm not going to say anything to Jean and Rand, and I hope you won't, either."

"All right . . . but waiting won't make any difference. I'm not changing my mind!"

"Then you're a very foolish little girl," said Noni, sounding exactly like Miss Guppy. "I'm disappointed in you, Polly. Go away now, and leave me alone."

Polly flew to her room, slammed the door, and sobbed into her pillow. She had finally done it. She'd told Noni her decision, but instead of feeling relieved, she felt even more miserable than before.

I'm disappointed in you . . . although Noni didn't repeat those words, Polly could feel them every time they were together. Now Noni was as wooden with Polly as Polly had been with her.

She'll come round, thought Polly. But what if she didn't? How was she going to live all the time with her grandmother when there was such a gulf between them?

Polly went through the last week of July in a fog. She spent most of her time on the beach with Tarka, attempting to draw. But even that comfort was gone. She hated the marks her pencil made on the paper. They seemed such a waste when Miss Falconer would never see them. Most of the time Polly just stared at the sea.

As the end of the month grew closer, Polly forgot her own worries and concentrated on Maud. How was she feeling? How would she know when the baby was coming? Polly spent the last days of July inside, so that she wouldn't miss Maud's phone call.

After breakfast on July 30, she was moping on the window seat, trying to read. Tarka was snoring at her feet and Noni was visiting a neighbour. When the telephone rang, Polly ran so fast that she skidded in the hall.

"Hello?" she said, her heart pounding.

"Hi, Doodle!"

"Oh, Maud . . ." Polly steadied her voice. "Did Danny come?"

Maud was triumphant. "Oh, Polly! It's not Danny. It's *Una*! She arrived last night and she's going to *stay*! I'll be home in about ten days and tell you all about her, all right? Oh, Poll, I'm so *happy*! I love you so much. I'm going to hang up now."

Polly was shaking so much she could hardly put down the receiver. If only Maud could have said more! But there was always the danger that someone would be listening.

She tried to take in Maud's words. *Una* . . . the baby was a girl! Polly had a few seconds' regret for Danny.

Then she began laughing and crying at the same time. She had a *niece*. She was named Una, after Polly and Maud's mother. And if she was "going to stay," that meant Maud was keeping her!

Tarka had followed her into the hall. Polly picked him up and whirled him around. "Oh, Tarka!" she cried, tears on her cheeks. "I'm an aunt—I'm an aunt!"

Then she stopped dancing and froze. Noni was standing in the doorway.

CHAPTER SEVENTEEN

P♥LLY aND N♥NI

"WHAT DID YOU SAY?"

"Oh, Noni . . ."

Noni gripped Polly by the arm and pulled her into the living room. She sat down, breathing heavily.

Polly sat opposite, gazing at her grandmother in terror. "Are you all right?"

"I'll be all right when I hear the truth! Just tell me, Polly. Tell me at once."

Noni's voice had never sounded so icy.

"Maud . . . Maud had a baby," croaked Polly. "It's a girl."

"I knew it! I knew it all along. I just couldn't let myself believe it. You should have told me, Polly."

"Noni, I couldn't! Maud made me promise not to tell *anyone*!"

"That doesn't matter. You should have told me anyway. Who is the father?"

"Robert," whispered Polly.

"And where is Maud right now? Is she with Robert? Are they married?"

"No. Robert didn't want to have anything to do with the baby," said Polly. "Maud's living with Daddy and Esther in Kelowna."

"So *they* knew. Has she been with them all this time when she said she was in Portland?"

Polly choked out the story. "After university ended, she went to a place in Vancouver that takes care of girls who are in trouble. But Daddy and I found out where it was and rescued her. Then she went back to Kelowna with him."

"So she told your father, but she didn't inform me," said Noni bitterly.

"*I* told him," said Polly. "Someone had to know."

"You should have told me, as well."

"I *couldn't*! Maud was too afraid of how you would react."

Noni's face was growing redder and redder. Polly ran to the kitchen and came back with a glass of water.

Noni took it without a word. She gulped some water and sat in silence for a few moments. To Polly's relief, her breathing calmed down and her face became less red.

"*Here* is my reaction, Polly, and you can tell it to Maud. She is a disgrace to the family, just as her mother was." Noni paused, then continued in a strained voice. "I've never told you this, Polly, but Una was pregnant with Maud when she got married."

"I know that," said Polly bluntly. "Daddy told us. And he told us that you and my mother had a terrible argument about it and that's why you lost contact with her."

Noni looked as if Polly had struck her. "You are correct," she said stiffly. "We did argue, and perhaps I was too harsh, but I had good reason to be angry. Una and Daniel broke the rules . . . just as Maud and Robert have done. It's *wrong* to have relations with a man before you are married. But at least your parents *did* get married. What about Maud? What does she plan to do with this baby?"

"I think she's going to keep it," muttered Polly.

Noni exploded. "She's going to *keep* it? That is a terrible mistake. She's ruined her life! She'll never be able to go back to university and take care of a baby. And what would people say? It was bad enough at Una and Daniel's wedding. Everyone on the island knew why they were getting married so quickly. No one ever said anything directly, but I had to live with the insinuations."

Noni shuddered. "The child is *illegitimate.* It's not fair to raise a child with such a stigma. It would live with that shame all its life."

"Not 'it'—*she!*" cried Polly.

Noni didn't seem to hear. She steadied her breathing, then said firmly, "Maud must put the baby up for adoption."

Polly hesitated. "Maud *was* going to give her away, but I don't think she is now. But Noni, maybe Daddy and Esther will adopt her and pretend the baby is theirs!"

"That would *not* be a solution. Maud would still have the baby in her life . . . so it would be in ours, as well. She should give it away immediately."

"She's going to *stay!*" Maud had said on the phone. Polly knew in her heart that her sister's joyful words were true. "Maud's not going to give her up," she told Noni.

Noni's expression turned to flint. "Then I won't have anything more to do with her."

"What do you mean?" whispered Polly.

"I mean exactly what I said. Maud is no longer my granddaughter. Your father and that woman can take care of her and her illegitimate child, instead."

"*Please,* Noni," begged Polly. "You can't do that! You *love* Maud. She loves *you.*"

"If she loved me, she wouldn't have done this to me," said Noni. "Tell her what I've just told you—that I never want to see her again."

"No!" Polly stood up. "You can't mean that! You just said you were too harsh with my mother. Now you're being the same with Maud!"

A flicker of doubt came into Noni's eyes, but she drew herself upright and said, "Perhaps I am, but Maud has left me no choice. She has done something very wrong, and she's continuing that wrong by keeping her child. I cannot condone it."

Polly was shaking so much she had to hold on to a chair for support. "You're the one who is wrong, Noni!" She tried not to cry, but her words were slurred. "You lost Una and now you're losing Maud. And you're going to lose me, as well. If you don't want Maud, I don't want *you*! I'm going to go and live with Daddy."

Noni pressed her hand to her heart. "No, Polly!" Her voice softened for the first time. "You're too young to understand what a shameful thing Maud has done . . . but it has nothing to do with you and me. Surely you know I feel the same about you as I always have. We'll just carry on as we did before."

"Not unless you accept Maud and her baby," shot back Polly.

"I'm sorry, hen . . . I can't do that."

"Then I'm going to live with Daddy!"

Noni's face blazed with anger again. "Don't be ridiculous, Polly. You are *not* going to live with your father, just as you are not going to leave school. I am your legal guardian, so you have no choice. I don't want to hear any more of this nonsense. Now, listen carefully. You mustn't breathe a word about what has happened—do you understand? We can't risk anyone knowing, not even Jean and Rand. Thank goodness they aren't here."

Polly wished they were. Maybe they would take Maud's side. But they were visiting friends on Walker Island for a week. Mrs. Hooper might also sympathize, but she was away, as well.

It was just Polly and Noni, two people who had once loved each other but now seemed like strangers. "Please leave me now," said Noni. "I need to be by myself and digest this dreadful news."

Polly ran upstairs, sobbing all the way. As soon as she got into her room, however, her tears halted. There was no time to cry; she had to make a plan.

Two hours later, Polly crept down the stairs, carrying her rucksack. She had heard Noni go into her own room, then a few minutes ago she had heard her leave it. She found her grandmother in the kitchen, slicing bread and chicken. Tarka was at her feet, waiting for something to drop.

"Noni?" she asked carefully.

"Yes?" said Noni, not turning around.

"Tarka and I going to sleep in the cabin tonight," said Polly. "Is that all right?"

Now Noni looked at her, but her expression was so cold that Polly almost shivered.

"Very well. When will you be back?"

"I'll have breakfast there and come home for lunch," said Polly.

"Take whatever food you need from the pantry, then. Would you like me to make you a sandwich?"

"I'll make it," said Polly.

"Very well," repeated Noni. She finished making her own sandwich and carried it into the living room.

Polly let out her breath. So far, this was working even better than she had hoped. She made herself two huge chicken sandwiches. Then she ransacked the pantry, filling it with as much food as she could stuff into her rucksack. She left room for Tarka's food, his dish, his leash, and a bottle of water.

Polly tested the rucksack. It was heavy, but she could manage it. Then she rummaged in the broom closet. At the very back she found Tarka's wicker travelling crate. He had used it only once, when he'd had to go to the vet in Sidney to have a thorn removed from his paw. The crate was very old; it had once belonged to Noni's Scottie. Polly inspected it anxiously, but it still seemed sturdy.

Now for the tricky part: getting the crate out to the cabin without Noni seeing her. Polly went into the living room. Noni was sitting in a chair, reading a book and eating her sandwich. Tarka sat hopefully at her feet.

Polly held out a bit of meat. Tarka looked from one to the other, then decided to go to Polly.

"Goodbye," said Polly tightly.

"Goodbye, Polly. I'll see you tomorrow," said Noni, her eyes on her book.

Oh, goodbye, goodbye! cried Polly's heart.

But there was no time to listen to it. She hurried back to the kitchen, with Tarka trotting after her. After hoisting the rucksack on her back and picking up the crate, Polly escaped out the back door and headed for the cabin.

––––––––––

Dear Noni,

You said I didn't have a choice, but I do. I'm going to live with Daddy and Esther, and you can't stop me. Tarka is with me.

I'll phone you when I get to Kelowna so you know I'm all right.
After that, I don't want to speak to you unless you change your
mind. If you are disowning Maud, then I'm disowning you!

Polly
PS. The baby's name is Una.

Polly pressed the pencil so hard she almost broke it. She placed
the note on top of one of the stumps she used for a table, and put a rock
on top of it so it wouldn't blow away. Then she checked her watch.

The steamer for Vancouver didn't arrive for another hour, so
she would have to stay in the cabin until she heard its whistle. Someone on the wharf would ask where she was going, so the later she
went, the better.

She paced the cabin nervously and kept going through her lug-
gage. She'd only packed underwear so she'd have room for food. Noni
would have to send on her clothes later. Once again, she counted the
money in her small purse.

Noni had been giving Polly a generous allowance for years, aug-
menting it every Christmas and birthday. Polly had saved the money
she didn't need in the flowered china pig she kept on her chest of
drawers. When she emptied out the bills and coins onto her bed, she
was pleasantly surprised. She had plenty of money for the train, with
a lot left over.

The piggy bank had once belonged to Una. Polly couldn't
remember her mother. What would she think of her daughters now?
One had just had a baby who was named after her, and the other was
running away!

Polly knew that Una had been headstrong and spunky, much
more like Maud than like her. Now Polly had to be as brave as they

were. Running away was terrifying. Never in her life had she done something so daring. But she thought of what she had just written and took a deep breath. If Noni was going to reject Maud, Polly had no choice but to reject her.

Finally, she heard the steamer whistle. This was going to be the riskiest part. A crowd of people would be at the wharf, waiting for the mail. Someone might tell Noni they had just seen Polly board the boat. Noni would call the police and Polly would be brought back from Vancouver in disgrace.

I may as well try, anyway, thought Polly. *What have I got to lose?* She picked up the rucksack and the basket, called Tarka, and made her way to the wharf.

———

"Why, Polly, what are you doing all by yourself? Are you going to Vancouver?"

It was Mrs. Wynne, whose husband ran the store. "I'm going to Kelowna to visit my father," said Polly, forcing herself to sound confident.

"But where's your grandmother? Why isn't she here to see you off?"

"She's not feeling well," said Polly rapidly.

"Oh, isn't that too bad! Perhaps I'll stop by later with some of my soup."

Oh, no! "She's—she's not eating," said Polly. "Her stomach is really upset and all she wants to do is sleep. It would be better not to disturb her."

"The poor thing! I'll drop in tomorrow, then, and see how she is."

Polly's heart thudded; the first hurdle was over.

When the steamer came into view, she pushed a protesting Tarka into his crate. He whined until she gave him a bone.

The crate was much heavier with Tarka in it, but Mr. Cridge carried it up the gangplank for her. To Polly's relief, he and his wife were the only other passengers travelling to Vancouver. Polly didn't know them very well. After her short explanation of where she was going, they picked up their newspapers and left her alone.

She gazed at the wooded island as it slipped out of view, at the dusty roads and rocky shores she had walked and played on for so many years. When would she see them again? Surely Noni would change her mind and forgive Maud. She would be angry at Polly for running away, but then she would forgive her, as well . . . wouldn't she?

There was no room in her head for worrying. Polly let herself have one last glance at the white lighthouse, then turned her eyes towards Vancouver. The next few hours were going to require all the courage she could muster.

———

Polly slinked through the crowd at the harbour, half expecting a policeman to come up and grab her. But when she passed one, he ignored her. Mrs. Wynne hadn't told Noni yet, then. That meant Noni wouldn't find out until Polly was well on her way.

Polly had put Tarka on his leash to lighten her load. He wasn't used to being on one and pulled her this way and that. He was so thrilled to be out of the crate that he kept stopping and greeting people, as if they were there to welcome him to Vancouver.

"Hey, little lady, that's a handsome pooch," called out a slovenly man. "You're not a bad looker yourself! How about a kiss?"

Polly hurried away from him. She finally found a taxi stand and timidly asked a driver to drive her to the train station. Then she sat in the back seat, quivering with fear. What if this man was as scary as the other one?

But all he said was "Aren't you kind of young to be travelling by yourself, Miss?"

"I'm fourteen," lied Polly, her voice coming out in a squeak. Tarka hopped into the front seat, the man laughed, and she relaxed a bit.

When they reached the station, the driver told her the charge. Polly carefully counted out the exact amount and gave it to him.

"Hey, what about my tip?" he snarled.

Polly was so rattled she just held out more money on her palm and he took what he wanted.

At least she was familiar with the station. The man in the ticket booth told her where to wait for her train and a porter helped carry the crate full of Tarka aboard. Finally, she was in her seat.

"Well, well, if it isn't my favourite youngster!"

"Hi, Jim," said Polly with relief.

"So you've brought your little friend with you this time."

Polly introduced Tarka. Jim put his hand through the grating and Tarka whined while he licked Jim's fingers frantically.

"He hates being in there," said Polly.

Jim winked. "I'll tell you what, young lady. As long as he's on a leash, you can let him out."

"Oh, thank you!" Polly released Tarka and he perched happily on the seat, peering out the window. An older woman sat down in the opposite seat, but she didn't seem to mind that Tarka wasn't in his crate. She took out some cookies and offered one to Polly. Tarka pressed against her knee, looking mournful, until she laughed and gave him one, too.

The woman's name was Mrs. Miller. Polly answered the usual questions, then leaned back and closed her eyes so she wouldn't be quizzed any further.

Every time the train stopped, Polly dashed out and found a grassy spot for Tarka to relieve himself. Luckily, he had always been able to hold it for a long time. So many people on the train stopped to pat Tarka and so many asked "Travelling all by yourself?" that she had no time to think until she was in bed. After Jim had changed Polly's seat into a berth, Tarka hopped up beside her, scratched the blanket into a nest, and settled into it as if he were at home.

The train didn't rock Polly to sleep as she'd hoped it would. She lay on her back with the blind open, watching the stars speed by as if *they* were moving, not the train.

So much had happened in just one day. A new person had come into the world—a baby girl named Una. And now Polly had run away! How was that possible?

Again, Polly tried to convince herself that Noni would change her mind. She just wasn't used to the baby—that was all. Soon she would relent. She would write to Maud and tell her she had forgiven her. Polly would return to the island, and everything would be all right.

But would it? Noni's fierce words kept replaying in Polly's mind. They hurt just as much as they had the first time. How could her grandmother reject Maud? Didn't she love her anymore? Didn't she love Polly?

And was Noni right about Maud? Would she be an object of shame because she had decided to keep her baby?

Polly's head swirled with confusing and sleepy thoughts as the long night went on. She had never heard her sister sound as happy as she had on the phone; yet Maud had done something that was utterly against convention. Polly pondered the other happy people she knew: Miss Falconer, Miss Carr, Daddy and Esther. Miss Falconer was living with a man she wasn't married to. Miss Carr lived alone and was a brilliant and innovative artist. Daddy had chosen to join his life with Esther, whom people like Noni disapproved of. It seemed that the happiest people were the ones who didn't worry about keeping up appearances.

Like Maud. Polly didn't know if her sister was going to be open about being Una's mother or not, but whatever she chose to do, that was her business. "What will people think?" Noni had asked; but what did it *matter* what people thought, as long as Maud was happy?

There was so much to worry about that Polly had almost forgotten about Una. Her brand new niece! Tomorrow she would meet her. With that to comfort her, Polly finally slept.

CHAPTER EIGHTEEN

UNa

WHAT HAVE I DONE? POLLY THOUGHT THE NEXT MORNING. JIM had helped her change trains when they reached Kamloops. Now she stared out the window at Okanagan Lake, too anxious to really see it.

Mrs. Wynne might have called on Noni by now. What would Noni do when she found out Polly had gone to Vancouver on the steamer? She would phone Daddy immediately. So Daddy and Esther might already know Polly had run away! Would they send her right back? Would Noni insist on that?

Polly wanted to weep. She could no longer pretend to be as brave as her mother and Maud. What was the point, when you were still under the command of adults?

Finally, the train drew into Kelowna. Polly stepped out into hot, dry air, steeped in the fragrance of wild roses. There was no one to greet her . . . so maybe Noni *hadn't* phoned Daddy. People looked at her curiously. Polly put Tarka on the leash and tried to act dignified as she began the walk to the boarding house, loaded down with her rucksack and Tarka's travel crate.

Tarka tugged at the leash so much she let him go free. At first he darted onto people's lawns, then he panted beside her. Polly had to stop and fan her face with her hat. She hadn't been this hot since she lived in Winnipeg. A dim memory rose in her, of trying to fry an egg on the sidewalk with her best friend then, Audrey.

She hadn't thought of Audrey in years. She seemed so far away from Polly, just as Eleanor and Daisy and Biddy did.

I'm all alone, thought Polly. She wiped sweat from her brow and batted away mosquitoes as she walked more and more slowly. Daddy and Esther and Maud would be overjoyed to see her, of course, but how long would she be allowed to stay?

But now Una lived there, too! Polly quickened her steps. When she reached the shabby grey house, she hesitated a moment, then knocked softly.

Esther opened it. "Why, it's Polly! What a wonderful surprise!"

"Is that *Polly*?" Daddy rushed into the hall and swept her into his arms.

Tarka barked wildly, leaped at Daddy, and then politely licked Esther, whom he'd never met.

"So you've brought the terrible terrier," laughed Daddy. "Doodle, we're so happy to see you! But why didn't you tell us you were coming?"

Polly's heart lifted. Noni definitely hadn't phoned, so they didn't know she had run away.

"I wanted to surprise you," she said softly.

Daddy hugged her once again. "Well, I can't think of a better surprise. Maud will be thrilled—come and meet your niece!"

Esther explained that Maud had moved to one of the downstairs bedrooms when Daddy brought her back from Vancouver. "Mr. McMillan had to switch rooms with her, but he's glad to have a view."

Maud's new bedroom was off the living room. "She may be asleep," whispered Daddy. He opened the door.

Maud was in bed, but she wasn't asleep. She was leaning against two pillows, holding her baby. When she saw Polly, her face burst into a grin. "It's *you*! I *thought* I heard Tarka bark, but then I thought I must have been dreaming. Oh, Doodle, what a wonderful surprise. Look—here's Una!"

Polly went up to the bed. The baby was sound asleep. She had a smooth round forehead, a shock of dark hair, and a snubby nose. Her wide mouth was almost smiling, and her chin was pointed, just like Maud's.

"Oh!" breathed Polly. "Oh, *Maud*!"

Maud handed over the baby. "Here you are, Aunt Polly. Here's your niece!"

Polly shook her head. "What if I drop her?"

"You won't," Maud assured her. "Keep your arm under her neck . . . that's right."

What a light weight Una was! Polly couldn't stop staring at her. The baby stirred slightly and stuck her tongue out between her rosy lips. Polly bent and kissed her forehead. She smelled delicious, a mixture of vanilla and flannel.

Polly wanted to sit with Maud and Una forever, but she was worried that Noni would call. "I'd better phone Noni and tell her I've arrived," she told them.

She went out into the hall to the telephone, relieved the others were staying with Maud. "I just wanted to tell you I got to Kelowna safely," she said quickly as soon as Noni's gruff voice answered.

On the other end of the line there was a long pause. Finally, Noni spoke, in a strange, chilly tone. "Beryl Wynne just told me she had seen you on the wharf. I pretended I knew you were there, but can you imagine how shocked and embarrassed I felt? I can't believe you were on your own in the big city!"

"It was fine," said Polly, trying not to think of the scary man and the taxi driver.

"You could have been in real danger. Why did you do such a thing?"

"I told you in the note I left in the cabin. Didn't you read it?" asked Polly.

"No, I did not . . . so you'll have to tell me now," ordered her grandmother sternly.

Polly lowered her voice. "It's what I said yesterday. If you can't accept Maud's baby, then I can't live with you, so I'm going to live with Daddy and Esther."

"Does your father know this?"

"Not yet," admitted Polly.

Noni was silent. Then she said, "Kindly don't tell him yet. Polly, you have hurt me profoundly. If you would rather live with your father than with me, then perhaps I should let you. But I need to think about this for a while. Then I'll write and let you know what I've decided."

"But Noni—" Polly was about to say that if only Noni would change her mind about Maud, she would come back . . . but the line was dead.

Polly stood in the hall for a few moments, struggling with her tears. Then she went back to Una.

Now she was lying beside the bed in a high basket on wheels. Her open eyes were like dark-blue almonds. "They'll change colour later," said Maud, "and the doctor says her black hair will probably fall out and be replaced by lighter hair."

"Look at her little hands!" marvelled Polly, stroking one of them. "Her fingers are so long. Down, Tarka!" she commanded as Tarka jumped onto the bed and sniffed Una in her basket.

Maud had had her baby at home at ten o'clock the night before last. "The doctor said it was one of the easiest deliveries he had ever done," said Esther.

Everyone kept watching Una. Her tiny presence was a magnet that pulled in all their attention. "She's not even two days old, and already it feels like she's been with us forever," said Daddy. He bent over Una. "Hello there, little one. I'm your granddad." Then he chuckled. "Imagine being a grandfather so young! But I was a young father, so I suppose I should have expected it."

Una squeaked like a piglet. Maud lifted her out of her basket and started to feed her. Polly couldn't stop staring as the baby sucked vigorously at Maud's breast.

"She loves to eat," Maud said fondly. "Just like her mother."

Soon the baby closed her eyes. Maud placed her gently back in her basket.

"We mustn't tire you, Maud," said Esther. "Try to sleep."

Esther started to make lunch while Polly and Daddy took Tarka down to the lake. "I can't tell you how wonderful it is to have you with us, Doodle," he said, hugging her. "Now we're all together as we should be." Then he looked worried. "You haven't told your grandmother about the baby, have you?"

Polly bent her head over Tarka's stick. "Of course not!"

"I didn't think you would, Doodle, but I had to make sure. Maud hasn't decided what she's going to do yet."

"She hasn't?" Polly stopped walking. "But she's going to *keep* Una, isn't she?"

Daddy grinned. "She's going to keep her, all right! The Boss made that very clear as soon as Una was born. But she hasn't told us yet whether she wants us to officially adopt her, or whether we'll just pretend Una is ours. We'll talk about that when Maud's stronger."

He rubbed his face. "The trouble is, Polly, folks are going to put two and two together. They saw Maud around town when she was pregnant, so they'll guess that the baby is really hers. I suppose we could admit that and say Maud has gone to be with her husband and left Una with us. But how will we explain it when she comes home for the holidays, and when her husband never shows up to see the baby?" He sighed. "It's so tricky! I hope Maud will let us know soon what our story will be. We have to get it straight before people start gossiping."

Polly remembered her thoughts last night. "Does it matter if they do?" she asked.

Daddy looked even more worried. "It doesn't matter to Esther and me, but I don't want Maud and Una to be scorned."

At noon the three boarders greeted Polly briefly, then attacked their lunch. None of them said anything about there being a new baby in the house.

"You look exhausted, Polly," said Esther. "Why don't you have a nap?"

"I *am* tired," admitted Polly. "I didn't sleep very well on the train. But where is my room?"

"You'll have to go in with Maud," said Daddy. "Two beds are in there. I hope you don't mind, but we have no other space."

Polly didn't mind at all. She crept into Maud's room and into the other bed. Maud and Una were fast asleep; almost immediately, Polly's breathing joined theirs.

Polly woke up when she heard a soft snuffling noise. She opened her eyes and blinked. Where was she? She could feel Tarka at her feet, as usual.

Turning over, she grinned as she saw Maud sitting up in bed and feeding Una.

Maud grinned back. "So you're awake. You've been in such a deep sleep. Tarka pushed open the door and jumped on your bed and you didn't even notice him. You didn't hear Una cry, either."

Polly sat up in bed and yawned. "Does she cry very much?"

"Only when she's hungry, and it's not really crying—it's more like mewing. She's my good girl, aren't you?" Maud kissed Una's forehead and put her back in her basket. Maud stretched, then lumbered out of bed. "I'm going to the loo, Polly. I'll be right back."

Polly stared when she saw Maud's tummy. She was almost as large as if she still had a baby inside her!

When Maud returned, Polly was examining her niece all over again. The baby was sleeping on her back. Her face was serene. Did babies have dreams?

"It's so good to get out of bed," said Maud, after she got back in. "But the doctor said I have to stay here for eight more days!"

Polly returned to her own bed and settled against the pillows.

"Doodle, I have so much to tell you," said Maud.

So do I, thought Polly, but she didn't want to tell Maud anything at all. "Start at the beginning," she said.

For the next half-hour Polly learned much more about childbirth than she wanted to. "The doctor was really kind," said Maud. "When I told him my husband was away, he didn't charge as much." She looked guilty. "I used the money Noni sent me for the cooking course to pay for him. But one day I'll pay her back."

Polly didn't want to think about Noni. "Did it hurt?" she asked shyly.

Maud grimaced. "It hurt, all right! But it's a different kind of hurt, Doodle, because you know it will end. And as soon as I saw Una, I forgot all about the pain."

Una squeaked, and Maud lifted her out of her basket and nursed her again. "The doctor said I'm only supposed to feed her every four hours, but that's ridiculous. Una knows when she's hungry better than he does."

"Why are you still . . ." Polly began to ask.

"Why am I still so fat? Because you don't lose the weight for a while. I didn't know that. I'm worried about visiting the island. But I'll just tell everyone that I ate a lot in the cooking class."

Oh, no! Polly couldn't tell her yet that Noni knew about the baby, and that Maud wouldn't be welcome on the island.

"Are you sorry Una isn't a boy, Poll?" Maud asked her.

"Not at all! Does she have a middle name?"

"'Zofia,'" said Maud.

"How did you think of *that*?"

"It's Daddy's mother's name. Don't you remember Grannie?"

"I remember her," said Polly, "but I never knew what her name was. It's pretty."

"I was going to name her 'Una Clara' after Noni," said Maud, "but you're so close to Noni I thought I'd leave 'Clara' for *you*, in case you have a little girl one day."

That made Polly so sad she couldn't bear it. "Maud, what made you change your mind about giving away the baby?" she asked, to keep from crying.

"Una did," said Maud. "As soon as I saw her, I knew I could never give her up."

"Daddy said you haven't decided what you're going to do yet."

"I've decided everything," said Maud firmly. "I just haven't told them yet. I know Daddy and Esther want to adopt Una. I can't bear the idea of that, though. She's mine! So we'll *pretend* they adopted her. At least then she'll grow up with two parents, even though they aren't her real ones. People will suspect, of course, especially if they saw me when I was pregnant. And of course the boarders know the truth. But if they gossip about it, so what? I'll keep it a secret at university, and of *course* I won't tell anyone on the island." She sighed. "I can't bear the idea of leaving Una. I'm supposed to start bottle-feeding her soon, but I want her to at least get this first milk. The nurse who came to see me yesterday said it's not real milk yet—it's something called 'colostrum.' It's really good for her."

That evening, after the boarders had been fed, Polly and Esther and Daddy brought trays into Maud's room and ate supper with her.

"Tomorrow I'm going to get up and sit in a chair," said Maud.

"Now, Maud, you're supposed to stay in bed," said Esther.

"I feel perfectly fine. If I can't move around, I'm going to go nuts!"

She certainly seemed fine. Her face glowed with vigour and her eyes were clear and determined. "All right, Boss," sighed Daddy. "You probably know best."

"Of course I do." Maud put down her fork. "I want to tell you what I've decided about Una."

Daddy and Esther listened quietly. When Maud finished, they agreed that they wouldn't officially adopt Una but would be happy to act as her parents.

"I can't thank you enough," said Maud. Now she was close to tears. "If it wasn't for you, I'd never be able to keep her."

KIT PEARSON

"She's part of our family," said Daddy. "Of course we'll take care of her."

Esther looked nervous. "I'd better start learning how to change diapers!"

Maud smiled. "Don't worry—I'll teach you," she said.

As the three of them talked excitedly about Una, Polly wondered how they would manage. Daddy and Esther both had to work hard all day. When would they have time to take care of a baby?

Then she remembered . . . she would be here, too! They didn't know yet that she had run away from Noni, but she would tell them soon.

I can look after Una, thought Polly. She'd have to go to school, but as soon as she got home, she could take over from Esther.

Una was so tiny and delicate, however. Polly felt terrified at such a huge responsibility.

———

The next morning Mrs. Janders, the nurse, arrived to check on Maud and Una. She was a brisk older woman with a broad English accent.

First she dressed Una's belly button, then she weighed her on a scale as if she were a small roast. "Seven and a half pounds," she pronounced. "Any trouble feeding?"

Maud shook her head. "She sucks really well," she said proudly.

"Your real milk should be coming down any moment. If you're not going to breastfeed her, you should start her on a bottle tomorrow."

Maud sighed. "I hate to do that so soon. What if I wait until I go back to university?"

"But I thought you said you were leaving Baby on August 9."

"I am," said Maud. "I have to visit my grandmother."

"Why can't you take Baby with you?"

"Because my grandmother doesn't know about her," muttered Maud. "She doesn't approve of my—my husband, so I never told her we got married."

Mrs. Janders looked suspicious. Did she guess that Maud was lying? "Well, Missy, you've got yourself into a right pickle, haven't you? It seems to me it would be far better to tell the truth—but that's your business, not mine. If you're going to leave Baby, you're going to have to start her on evaporated milk. I'll come back tomorrow and show you how to mix it. In the meantime you can lay in supplies." She turned to Polly. "You can make yourself useful and get them for your sister. Baby bottles, extra teats, evaporated milk, and corn syrup. Can you remember all that?"

Polly gulped and nodded.

"But is canned milk good for Una?" asked Maud.

"Not as good as breast milk. That's nature's perfect food. I don't hold with this modern trend of bottle feeding, but don't worry—plenty of babies have thrived on it. Goodbye, Maud. I'll see you tomorrow."

Mrs. Janders breezed out.

"Oh, Poll," said Maud tearfully. "I don't *want* to stop breast-feeding Una. I want the best for her!" She bent over Una protectively, then raised her head. "Doodle, it's just not possible for me to come back with you. I know we planned that, but I didn't know I was going to keep Una. You're going to have to tell Noni I can't come. Say I'm sick or something—say anything!"

This would be the perfect moment for Polly to tell Maud that she wasn't going back, either . . . and that Noni didn't want Maud. But she couldn't bear to hurt her. "All right," she murmured.

Polly tried not to think about Noni, or about how she would tell Daddy and Esther that she was going to live with them. She existed in a bubble of time, a bubble that contained only Una.

She was an easy baby, either sleeping or eating, and simply giving a few squeals when she was hungry. If there were an exam in looking after babies, the way there was in history or geography, Polly would have received an A. She knew the three best ways to hold her: in the crook of her arm, against her shoulder, or on her knees with a careful hand behind her neck. She could always get a burp out of Una. She changed her diapers and she even helped Maud bathe her in the sink lined with a towel. Best of all was gazing at her perfect features while she rocked her to sleep.

One day I could have a baby! thought Polly. She didn't want to do it the way Maud had; she wanted a husband to share the baby with. It would be named Danny . . . or Clara. *Oh, Noni, Noni . . .* would she have forgiven Maud by then?

Polly told Maud about Sadie.

"I'm so happy for them," said Maud. Then she looked sad. "I guess I can never tell Sadie about Una. This isn't going to be easy, Poll. How can I keep such a big secret? I want to tell everyone in the whole world!"

Maud was holding Una against her shoulder while Polly tied her flannel nightie at the back. Then Polly carefully swaddled her in a blanket, the way Maud had taught her. "I don't understand why it's such a disgrace," said Polly. "It's so unfair—Una is just a baby!"

"She's an illegitimate baby," said Maud bitterly. "She'll bear that stigma all her life if people know. It's not her fault, but it's just the way it is."

Polly made several sketches of Una sleeping in her basket. They were the best she had ever done. If only she could show them to Miss Falconer! But she would never see Miss Falconer again.

"Why, Doodle, you're getting so good!" marvelled Daddy. "I'm thrilled you're receiving such excellent instruction."

Not anymore, thought Polly. *When am I going to tell them* that? When Maud praised Polly for her decision to go back to school, Polly couldn't look at her.

Sometimes Polly took a break from the baby and wandered through town. She had bought herself a few clothes and snuck them into the house before Maud could notice that she didn't have any from the island with her. She also bought Una the largest teddy bear she could find. "She's bigger than Una!" laughed Maud.

Each time Polly walked back to the boarding house, she passed the local high school. She gazed at its brick exterior and shuddered. What would it be like to go there? She would have to make new friends all over again.

Four days passed—enough time for a letter from Noni to reach Kelowna. Polly woke up on the fifth day with a sinking heart. Noni must be sticking to what she had said. She must not be able to bring herself to forgive Maud. That meant Polly had to stick to what *she* had said. She couldn't go back to Noni, and she couldn't go back to St. Winifred's. So she had to stay here.

She soothed herself by imagining how much she could help with Una after Maud had gone to Vancouver. But she'd never be able to take care of her as well as Maud did. It would be wonderful to have Daddy in her life again, and she was growing fonder of Esther every day. But how could she bear to be away from the island or from her friends at school? And what would she do about art?

Worst of all, how could she carry on without Noni?

"Are you all right, Poll?" asked Maud after breakfast. "You look as if you're drowning in your thoughts."

"I'm all right," lied Polly.

She had to tell them everything. That she wasn't going back to St. Winifred's *or* the island, that Noni had disowned Maud. She would do it tomorrow evening.

Polly tossed in bed that night, rehearsing what she would say. Daddy would be thrilled she was going to live with them, but Maud would be upset that she was leaving school. She would be even more hurt about what Noni had said. Polly would have to soften her grandmother's words as much as she could.

―――――――

"Aren't you feeling well, Polly?" Esther asked when Polly barely touched her porridge. Rain and wind were raging outside, but the weather wasn't as agitated as the storm inside her.

Daddy didn't have a bricklaying job that day. He stayed home and spent all morning fixing a broken stair. Polly helped him in between helping with Una, glad of so much to occupy her mind. In mid-morning they all gathered in the kitchen for cocoa and cookies. Maud now insisted on spending much of the day out of bed. She sat at the table drinking beer instead of cocoa; Mrs. Janders had told her it would increase her milk flow.

Then there was a knock at the kitchen door. "Who could that be in such weather?" said Esther.

Daddy got up to open the door. A thin, angular woman stood outside, dripping with rain.

"I've come to see Una," said Noni.

CHAPTER NINETEEN

NOTHING, bUT THE TRUTH

UNA WAS ASLEEP IN HER BASKET IN THE LIVING ROOM. WHEN Noni bent over and picked her up, her dark-blue eyes opened and stared into her great-grandmother's grey ones. Noni murmured, "Una. I have my Una back." Then the baby closed her eyes again as Noni collapsed in a chair and rocked her.

No one knew what to say or do. Maud watched Noni with shocked eyes, and Daddy looked defiant. But none of that mattered. All that mattered was an old woman gazing with love at a newborn baby; such strong, true love that it radiated like a fire.

Eventually, they moved. Daddy took Noni's wet coat. Maud draped a blanket around her, pulled off her soaking shoes, removed her stockings, and dried her feet. Esther made tea.

Noni ignored them. She only looked at the baby, crooning and murmuring to her.

Polly sat at the side of the room, holding back Tarka, who longed to rush over and greet Noni. "Leave her alone," Polly whispered to him. "She's busy." She got him a bone from the kitchen to keep him quiet.

Finally, Noni lifted her head from Una. She handed her to Maud, and reached for the cup of tea Esther had placed beside her. Her eyes were brimming as they searched the room.

They found Polly. Noni put down her cup. "Oh, hen," she said.

Polly flew across the room and into Noni's arms. "I'm deeply sorry," said Noni, hugging her so hard that Polly gasped. "Can you forgive me for what I said? I don't know what possessed me. After I found your note, I woke up and came to my senses. Then I did a lot of thinking, and then I knew I had to come here."

Maud was next. "Can you give your foolish grandmother a kiss, Maud?" she asked.

Maud approached her slowly, Una in her arms. *She's frightened!* Polly realized.

"How did you know about the baby?" Maud whispered.

"I overheard Polly telling Tarka she was an aunt."

When he heard his name, Tarka jumped into Noni's lap. "Get off, you rascal!" she laughed. Polly pulled him away, then curled on the carpet at Noni's feet, stroking them.

"Are you angry with me?" asked Maud.

"I was," said Noni, "but I'm not anymore. I'm just sorry you had to go through this for so long by yourself. You can tell me all about it later. I'm so glad you're all right, and that you have such a beautiful child."

Maud leaned down and kissed her. Noni kissed her and the baby back.

"Are you hungry, Mrs. Whitfield?" asked Esther shyly. She seemed totally in awe of Noni.

"I ate breakfast on the train, thank you," said Noni. She was looking at Daddy. "Daniel, I want to apologize to you, as well."

"There's nothing to apologize for, Clara," said Daddy stiffly. He was standing by the door with his arms folded.

"Yes, there is," said Noni. "I've had a lot of time for remorse in the last few days. I'm so very sorry for all the pain I caused you and Una."

"That's all over with now," said Daddy, "but I greatly appreciate your saying it." He smiled at her for the first time.

"Polly has told me that you and Esther might take care of the baby," said Noni. "Is this right?"

"Yes," said Esther. "We got married last month. Maud doesn't want us to officially adopt Una, but we'll pretend we have. If anyone wonders about it, that's their concern, not ours."

To Polly's relief, Noni smiled warmly at Esther. "That's very generous of you," she said. "Babies are a lot of work, and I'm sure you already have a lot to do. I do hope you will let me contribute to Una's upbringing."

Daddy said simply, "Thank you, Clara."

"What will Maud do?" asked Noni.

"She'll go back to U.B.C. in September," answered Daddy. "During the holidays she'll live with us and be with her child."

"That's the right thing for you to do, Maud," said Noni. "You are welcome on the island anytime, but of course you belong with Una when you're not at university."

Maud put Una in her basket and cleared her throat. "Listen, everyone. I have something to tell you. I'm not going back."

"You're not? But Maud, what about your education?" said Daddy.

"I'll go back in a few years," said Maud, "but I can't leave Una yet. She needs me right now. She needs my milk and she needs her real mother." She smiled at Esther. "It's not that you wouldn't have taken good care of her. But I would miss her too much!"

They absorbed this news in silence. "I think that's a wise decision, Maud," said Noni finally. "Those first few years are so important. I hope you'll return to university later, though."

"I will," said Maud firmly. "I still want to be a lawyer."

Noni smiled at her. "How I'll miss you, hen. I hope you'll allow me to visit you and Una often. And perhaps you can tear yourself away from her sometimes to come to the island."

"I'll come a lot," said Maud. "Una will, too," she added calmly.

"Oh, but . . ." Noni hesitated. "What will we tell people?"

Maud lifted up Una again. She nuzzled her fondly and said, "We'll tell them the truth! I'm not keeping her a secret. Una is my child. That's all there is to it."

"Maud, does that mean you're going to be open about her here, as well?" asked Daddy. "You don't want us to pretend she's ours?"

Maud had never been so Maudish. "No, I don't. I'm so tired of all the secrets in this family! I'm not going to tell any more lies, only the truth," she repeated.

Daddy gulped. "All right, Boss. If that's your decision, we'll support you—right, Esther?"

Esther nodded, but Noni looked worried. "Maud, I understand why you want to do that, but you simply can't! Especially on the island. You know what it's like. As soon as they see you with the baby, every person there will hear of it. People will shun you. And when Una gets older, they'll shun her, as well."

"I don't care how they treat *me*," said Maud. "It will be hard for Una . . . very hard. But I'll help her not to care, either. It won't be easy, but no one's life is easy. Una will have me to protect her. We'll have each other—that's the most important thing. Anyway, they won't shun us if *you* don't, Noni. Everyone on the island respects you. If you accept Una, then eventually they will, too." She smiled at Daddy and Esther. "And the two of you *already* accept her, so we can all stick together, no matter what people here say."

Noni shook her head. "Maud, you simply cannot do this! You don't know how nasty people can be. It's best to pretend your father and Esther are Una's parents. When you visit the island, you'll have to come without her."

"I'm sorry, Noni," said Maud. "But you either get both of us or neither of us. If you can't accept that, I don't even want you visiting us here."

They stared at each other. Then Noni took the baby and held her close. She gave a long sigh. "All right, Maud. You win. I can't *not* see Una, so you leave me no choice. We'll tell everyone the truth, and let the chips fall where they may." She gave a faltering smile at Daddy. "What a strong-minded daughter you have!"

Daddy grinned. "I wonder who she takes after . . ."

Noni reached down and stroked Polly's hair. "And what about you, my bonny wee Polly? Do you still want to live here? Or are you going to come back to the island?"

"Polly, were you thinking of living *here*?" Daddy said. His face was so lit up that Polly had to avert her eyes. "We would *adore* that, wouldn't we, Esther?"

"Of course we would!" said Esther, smiling warmly at Polly. "You already feel like a daughter to me."

"We would have suggested it before, but it wouldn't have been suitable when we weren't married," said Daddy. "But now we are. Oh, Doodle, would you stay with us when you're not at school?"

"I would accept it if you wanted to do that, Polly," said Noni. "I understand that you would want to be back with your father after all this time away from him. And of course you'd want to be with your sister and the baby. I hope you would visit me occasionally. But I haven't turned out to be a very good grandmother. Perhaps you've had enough of me."

"This is an awfully hard decision for Polly to make right now," protested Maud. "Let her think about it for a while."

"I don't have to think about it," said Polly, getting up from the floor.

She looked around at her family. She loved them all: Daddy, Maud, Noni, Esther, and Baby Una. Not to be with Una every moment, to miss her first smile or her first steps, would be especially hard.

But Polly knew whom she belonged to: the person who had sheltered her, and healed her, and loved her when she had been lost and afraid. The person in the room who needed her the most.

Polly kissed her grandmother. "I can *never* get enough of you."

Then she turned to the others. "I'm sorry, Daddy and Esther and Maud. It would be wonderful to live with you, but I belong with Noni."

Daddy opened his arms and Polly ran into them. "It's all right," he whispered. "I've always known that. I gave you up to your grandmother a long time ago. But you're still my Polly-Wolly-Doodle, right?"

"Right," choked Polly through her tears.

Esther stood up, wiping her own eyes. "I'm going to make up our room for you, Mrs. Whitfield. Daniel and I can sleep on cots in the living room."

"That's very kind of you, Esther," said Noni. "I must say—I need a nap. I think we all do!"

———

Noni told them she would stay until Monday. Then Maud and Una would be strong enough to go to the island with her and Polly. It amazed Polly how natural it was to have her here. She and Mr.

McMillan talked about places they knew in Scotland. When Noni wasn't cuddling Una, she weeded the entire front garden of the boarding house. Polly showed her around the town, and they went for walks along the shore.

"Do Aunt Jean and Uncle Rand know you're here?" Polly asked her.

"They do now. They were still away when I left, but I wrote them a note saying when I'd be back." She grimaced. "Won't they be shocked when they see Una! It's not going to be easy, hen." Then she smiled. "But we must try to have as much gumption as your sister has. Maud is right—no more secrets."

Polly could hardly believe that Noni was being so accepting. "What made you change your mind?" she asked shyly.

"It was your note, hen. After I read it, I burst into tears and I couldn't stop crying for hours. You were so right, Polly! I had lost Una through my own stubbornness, I was about to lose Maud, and now you had run away from me. But then you told me the baby's name. All my love for your mother flooded back and cancelled out those past sorrows. Then I simply had to see Una."

On another walk Noni lamented that Maud was only coming home for a visit, not for good. "Now that we're being open about Una, Maud may as well continue to live on the island."

"Oh, Noni, that would be wonderful! Have you asked her?"

"I asked her last night. She was glad that I did—that I wanted them both. But she said she belonged with your father and Esther now, that it wouldn't be fair to take their grandchild away from them. I suppose she's right . . . but how I wish that we didn't all have to be separated!" She sighed. "We'll just have to work it out so that we see one another as much as possible. Maud and Una can come to the island for long visits, and you can still spend part of your school holidays in Kelowna, as you've been doing."

She gave Polly a sharp look. Polly skipped a pebble across the water to keep from answering. Noni seemed to be assuming that Polly had decided to go back to St. Winifred's. In all the turmoil, Polly had almost forgotten that she wasn't.

That evening, after the boarders had left the supper table, Polly pushed back her plate. "I have something to tell you," she said.

"Surely there's nothing *left* to tell!" teased Daddy.

"There is," said Polly solemnly. "I've decided . . ."

Noni looked worried.

"Out with it, Poll!" laughed Maud.

"I—"

Then the truth rose up in Polly so fast she almost choked. "I was just wondering . . ." She grinned at Noni, then she turned to Maud. "When I go back to St. Winifred's . . . what should I say about Una? Do you want me to keep her a secret?"

"No, Polly! I don't want her to be a secret from *anyone*. Tell whoever you want." Maud paused. "Well, maybe not the Guppy. I wouldn't ask that of you—she'd have a conniption! *I'll* tell her. I'll write to her before you go back, and I'll say she's not to talk to you about it, all right?"

"Thanks," said Polly.

"Are you eager to get back to school?" Esther asked her.

Polly nodded slowly. "I'm looking forward to seeing my friends, and I'll be really glad to start special art again."

Beside her, Noni squeezed her hand. "What a brave lass!" she whispered as Esther and Maud cleared the table. "I'm so proud of you!"

Polly couldn't believe she had changed her mind. It was as if another self—a more grown-up, better self—had taken over. But maybe she hadn't really changed. Maybe she had just realized that the decision she had made in the infirmary after she had talked to Alice was the right one after all.

I'm going to be an artist! Polly thought gleefully. She *had* to go back to St. Winifred's, therefore, to learn how to become the best artist she could. Miss Guppy's unfairness had sidetracked her for a while, but now she was back on course. She would have to be really brave to stomach all the things about school she didn't like, but that didn't seem so hard anymore. Look how brave Maud was being.

And wait until she told her friends about Una!

———

Polly, Maud, Una, Noni, and Tarka stood on the deck of the steamer as it approached Kingfisher Island. Maud arranged Una's blanket partway over her face to protect her from the sun. Polly squinted as the familiar landscape came into focus: the lighthouse, the dark firs pointing their tips towards the bright sky, and Noni's white house. What a long time it had been since she had first seen the island— what a lot had happened since then!

But now there were no more secrets left. As the boat grew closer, Polly saw Aunt Jean and Uncle Rand waiting on the wharf. Aunt Jean's archrival, Mrs. Cunningham, was standing beside them.

"I see the hotel is still for sale," said Maud.

"Yes, it's such a shame that it's standing empty and neglected," said Noni. Then she gasped.

"What's wrong, Noni?" asked Polly.

"Nothing, hen." Noni chuckled. "I've just had an idea! A *grand* idea . . . but I'll tell you later."

Now the steamer stood at the wharf. Uncle Rand had his back to them, but Aunt Jean and Mrs. Cunningham spotted them at once. Aunt Jean waved. Then she put her hand to her mouth as she saw what Maud was holding. Mrs. Cunningham's own mouth dropped open, then she said something urgent to Aunt Jean.

"Oh, dear, look at their expressions!" said Noni. She put her arms around Polly and Maud and Una, drawing them close. "Are we ready?"

"Ready or not, here we come!" joked Maud, but her voice wobbled.

Polly gulped. First there was the island to face, then going back to St. Winifred's. She felt as new and vulnerable as her tiny niece. But Una was swathed in love . . . and so was she.

Polly squeezed Maud's hand and said firmly, "Ready for anything!"

Epilogue

Vancouver Province, "About Town," May 23, 1961

A distinguished company gathered on Saturday as the beloved Vancouver artist Miss Polly Brown (Mrs. Chester Simmons) was celebrated at a festive evening at the New Leaf Gallery. The occasion was the opening of her latest exhibit, *Memories of an Island*. Miss Brown's mixed-media paintings are set on Kingfisher Island, where she and her family spend the summers. Accompanying her at the opening were her husband, Dr. Chester Simmons, a professor of biology at U.B.C., and their lovely twelve-year-old daughter, Miss Clara Simmons. Included among the large crowd of family and friends were the artist's sister, Judge Maud Brown; Judge Brown's daughter, Una, with her husband, Dr. David Meyer, and their newborn son, Danny; the artist's father and stepmother, Mr. and Mrs. Daniel Brown, who are the proprietors of the Kingfisher Hotel; the artist's great-uncle and -aunt, the Reverend Mr. Randolph Stafford and Mrs. Randolph Stafford; the Reverend Canon Gregor Stafford, Mrs. Gregor Stafford, and their daughter, Miss Maisie Stafford; the well-known artist Miss Frieda Falconer, accompanied by the writer Mr. Frans de Jonge; Miss Hilda Guppy, retired headmistress of St. Winifred's School for Girls in Victoria; and the internationally famous opera singer Miss Alice Mackenzie, escorted by her father, Mr. Thomas Mackenzie. The exhibit is dedicated to the memory of the artist's maternal grandmother, Mrs. Gilbert Whitfield.

ACKNOWLEDGEMENTS

For their advice and inspiration I would like to thank Garry Anderson at the Canadian Museum of Rail Travel Archives in Cranbrook, B.C.; Deirdre Baker, Donna Baker, Stuart Brambley, Marie Campbell, Hadley Dyer, Christine Godfrey, Lally Grauer, Ernest Hanson, David Kilgour, Larry MacDonald, Lynne Missen, Katherine Newlands, Louise Oborne, Anne Pearson, Doug Rhodes, the late Winifred Scott, Ellie Stone, and Valerie Wyatt. Extra special thanks, as always, to my beloved partner, Katherine Farris.

Emily Carr's words are created partly from my imagination and partly from some lectures she gave in the 1930s. They are collected in *Fresh Seeing: Two Addresses by Emily Carr* (Toronto: Clarke, Irwin & Company Limited, 1972).